ELIJAH-CO

ELIJAH-CO

a novel by

DAN W. LUEDKE MD

Indigo River Publishing
3 West Garden Street, Ste. 718
Pensacola, FL 32502
www.indigoriverpublishing.com

ElijahCo | Dan W. Luedke, author
LCCN 2021910982 | ISBN 978-1-954676-10-7

This is a work of fiction. Names, characters, places, and incidents
are either the product of the author's imagination or are used fictitiously.
Any resemblance to actual events, locales, or persons, living or dead, is entirely coinci-
dental.

Cover and interior design by Emma Grace

Special discounts are available on quantity purchases by corporations, associations, and
others. For details, contact the publisher at the address above.
Orders by US trade bookstores and wholesalers: Please contact the publisher at the address above.

With Indigo River Publishing, you can always expect great books,
strong voices, and meaningful messages.
Most importantly, you'll always find . . . words worth reading.

Thank you:

My son, Dr. Matthew Luedke, and my son-in-law, Kurt Jacob, for helping me put the science in science fiction.

Mary Ward Menke (WordAbilities), for much more than just dotting my t's and crossing my eyes.

Dr. Susan Luedke, for being everything to me.

1

DR. LARS SORENSON stood in front of the window, staring at nothing in particular. He was waiting for an audience with the new med school dean. This one kept faculty waiting. A leaf caught his eye. A gust of wind tossed it in the air. The momentary exuberance was followed by a downdraft. Just as the leaf was about to join the anonymous pile on the ground, another gust of wind blew it high into the air and out of sight.

"Good morning, Lars. Thank you for coming here on such short notice." Dean Henry Mitchell raised his hand, giving Lars an annoying high five.

Mitchell looked like a dean. He was in his midfifties, six four, and two hundred pounds. His hair was graying at the temples and receding on top. He wore a nondescript shirt and tie but covered them with an impeccably white laboratory coat. His size and booming voice dominated the room. His eyes studied Lars, making him self-conscious.

Lars, a physical match for the dean, was twenty years younger and had a head full of blond hair. He was not the alpha male, however, and the dean easily stared him down.

"Thank you for seeing me, Henry. Congratulations on your new position."

"Thank you. Damned shame it came as it did. Jim Hanley was a fine man."

"You know, I'm still confused about the car accident. Why would a medical school dean ride in a car without a seat belt? I mean, Jim was probably the most fastidious man I've ever met. I don't see how he'd fail to put on his seat belt."

"Who knows? Can I get you a cup of coffee or water?"

Lars waved off the offer as the two men sat down. He sensed a growing impatience and got straight to the point. "I know you're busy trying to pull together the loose ends of Jim's administration, but I need to know. Have you reviewed the status of the oncology program, or should I say, the Terrence and Jewell Fletcher Cancer Center?"

Henry sighed and leaned forward. "Yes, I have, Lars."

Dread prickled Lars's neck as the dean continued. "We've run into a problem. I met with the Fletchers yesterday. Jim wasn't only a dean in search of funding, but a dear friend of theirs as well. The many millions of dollars they pledged for the cancer center were mostly due to their love of the man. His death has changed the whole dynamic. I can't go into detail—confidentiality issues and all—but the bottom line is that they've withdrawn their funding of the cancer center."

The news hit Lars in the gut, rendering him speechless.

The dean continued, "We can squeeze some seed money from my

Dean's Fund, but the rest you'll have to raise yourself."

Lars found his voice. "I don't believe it! I came here because of the money promised for a cancer center and Dean Hanley's pledge that I could develop it without interference. I could have gone to a dozen other places—

Henry interrupted: "Perhaps you'd be happier at one of those 'dozen different places' that want you—"

"I can only wish. I committed academic suicide coming here. There's no going back."

"Well, Lars, I'm sorry I can't honor a dead man's promise, but I will pledge the space for a cancer center and full autonomy if you can raise the money for it."

Lars felt anger welling up. He'd been blindsided. His thoughts wouldn't gel. He was losing it. He had to leave before he lashed out and destroyed any chance left for his cancer center and career. "I won't take up any more of your valuable time."

"You know my door's always open to you." Henry reached out to Lars, who turned and bolted before having to exchange another excruciating high five. A wry smile cracked the dean's lips, which went unnoticed.

Lars left the office on rubber legs and joined the stream of white coats and scrubs winding its way to University Hospital and its specialty clinics. Nothing in his life had prepared him for this devastation. He had always easily met the succession of academic challenges he faced. Each success brought another challenge, and at a more prestigious institution. His academic achievements were crowned by a faculty appointment at the finest cancer center in the world—at least according to US News and

World Report. Filled with book knowledge and hubris, he was lured to High Plains University by the siren song of money.

Lars veered away from the stream and entered the building housing his office. He felt his legs stiffen and his mind clear. He greeted the oncology division secretary as if his soul had not just been crushed. "Hi, Patty. Has Sally come in yet?"

"Morning, Dr. Lars. Yes, she's in the bullpen. Tell me, how is Mrs. Dr. Sorenson?"

"She's doing fine."

"It's such a shame she had a heart attack at her age; she's so young and pretty—"

"I said she's doing fine. Excuse me. I have to find Sally."

Unfazed by the curt response, Patty said, "Here's your snail mail, and you have a ton of emails to answer. Just another busy day in paradise."

Lars grabbed the mail and entered the bullpen, a large room divided into cubicles containing computers. House staff and fellows hung out there. The name was given to the room when medicine was male dominated. Everyone was off making rounds, except for Sally Ming-Davis, the division's nurse practitioner. She was the first friend Lars had made at High Plains. She was what Lars was not, a soft-spoken, petite, and aging Asian American. Maybe that's why they had quickly bonded—or maybe it was shared angst over sickly spouses. Whatever the reason, they had become soul mates.

She was focused on texting, and without looking up, asked, "How did it go with the—" Glancing at Lars, she interrupted herself. "You look like you've seen a ghost."

"More like the devil, Sal."

"Uh-oh, it didn't go so well."

"The worst. The Fletcher money was jerked, and Mitchell is canceling the cancer center—unless of course I come up with a zillion dollars."

"But why, Lars? Why would the dean allow the Fletchers to renege on their promise?"

"I was too stunned to ask. But I did come up with some ideas on the way here."

"I'm all ears."

"Well, before he died, Jim Hanley took me aside for some sage advice. He told me to watch my back, that opposition to the cancer center was growing among the faculty. He said some were jealous of me and resented that their pet projects were going unfunded. He even suggested that some of them wanted High Plains to remain in the academic shadows. Then he told me he could pit one group against the other to prevent a united opposition."

"I see where you're going with this. Dean Hanley's death permitted the opposition to come together."

"I'm thinking you're right, but I can't understand why Mitchell supported the opposition after Hanley died. What did he have to gain?"

Sally thought a moment. "Well, rumor has it he's doing brilliant research but isn't ready to report his findings. Maybe those opposing the cancer center also opposed Hanley's effort to incentivize high-level research publications. The continued absence of a publish-or-perish mentality at High Plains would serve Mitchell well."

"Okay, if I accept the premise that Mitchell was a part of the opposition, then why would Jim Hanley hire him in the first place? Why would he recruit the nemesis to the crowning achievement of his deanship?"

"Hmm, that's a tough question." Sally paused. "I vaguely remember Dot Pearce, the pulmonary NP, telling me she overheard Dean Hanley say that when Henry was ready to publish, it would be his ticket to Stockholm. Maybe Hanley was playing the long game."

"I'm not ready to drink that Kool-Aid, but for now it doesn't matter. Any way you look at it, I'm screwed."

"You mean we're screwed. Don't forget I signed on because of the cancer center promise as well."

"Sorry, Sal. I didn't mean to negate you."

"Apology accepted. Say, Lars, why don't you call the Fletchers? The three of you seem to get along well. They owe you an explanation . . . Incidentally, I saw the look Jewell gave you the last time they were here."

"What look?"

"You are so blind. She thinks you're hot! Not a zillion dollars hot, but hot enough for you to keep your foot in the door. Besides, what can it hurt to give her a call?"

"And say what? 'Hey, baby, where's the hundred mil?'"

"Oh, you'll think of something. Why don't you use the landline in your office in case the residents return? I'll stay here in the bullpen, but I'll be available for moral support."

Lars slowly walked into his office, composing as he went. He took a deep breath and dialed the number. Sally strained to hear at least one side of the conversation.

"Yes, good morning. This is Dr. Lars Sorenson. May I speak with Jewell Fletcher? . . . Okay. When will she be available? . . . You're not being very helpful . . . Look, I'm not trying to be difficult, but I have to speak with Mrs. Fletcher . . . Try a hundred million reasons why I need to talk with her . . . Damn! He hung up on me!"

Sally called out from the bullpen, "Well, that conversation went nowhere. Now that plan A is in the dumpster, we'll have to go with plan B."

"And what would that be?"

"I don't have a clue."

"I want my cancer center, Sally!" Lars whined. "There's got to be a way to get it."

"It's been less than an hour since you found out you lost it. Give yourself some time to think it through. Meanwhile, let's go through charts. We need to deal with some patient issues. They'll also keep you from wallowing in self-pity."

"Good idea," Lars said, walking into the bullpen and pulling up a chair so he could sit next to Sally. "Speaking of patient problems, how's Fred doing? He was having back pain while we were fly-fishing last weekend. He soldiered on, but it was obvious he was uncomfortable. He just grunted when I tried to help. I thought I'd ask you what's going on, thinking he'd confide in his wife, not play the macho role like he did with me."

"He told me about the pain but minimized it," Sally said. "He spent most of Monday in bed recuperating. That man would endure anything to be trout fishing with you. What he really needs is back surgery, but he's resisting it. After the hip replacement and pacemaker, he's drawn a line in the sand—no more surgery. He grumbled about feeling like a damned cyborg. I can't force him to get his back fixed; that has to be his decision. But in the meantime, he can continue working. Software engineers just need a brain and two hands."

Sally hesitated a moment and then continued, "I'm more worried about your Kate. I mean, you just don't have a heart attack if you're a healthy twenty-eight-year-old woman."

Lars sighed. "I'm afraid I haven't been completely honest with you, Sally," he said. "Kate's not an otherwise normal young woman. Before we even heard of High Plains University, she started having health issues. She complained of joint pains and was easily fatigued. Her arms and legs became thinner as she lost muscle mass. Those symptoms might be expected in an aging woman but not one as young as Kate. She saw an endocrinologist, and a bucket of drawn blood later, we still don't have answers. So, he sent tissue samples to a dozen different laboratories doing research on premature aging. We struck out with most of them. We're waiting for results from the rest."

Lars paused, trying to decide just how much he could say without betraying Kate. He decided Sally could be trusted. "Some time ago, I was looking at Kate's high school yearbook, and she looked a lot more mature than her classmates. I think this aging thing may have been going on for a long time. Who knows? Maybe she was born with it. It's just so frustrating! This unknown 'it' is causing this beautiful woman to grow old before her time, and I can't do a damned thing about it." Tears filled his eyes, but he held it together.

What Lars didn't say was that since her heart attack, Kate seemed to be showing signs of mental decline as well. She was forgetful and often irritable, and she slept much more than usual.

"I'm so sorry, Lars," Sally said. "I had no idea this was happening to her. She looks so . . . so normal."

"Cover-up clothing and makeup can hide a multitude of sins. Just ask any aging actress."

"Is there any possible way I can help?"

"You're doing it by listening to my pathetic whining."

"You're not—"

"I'm losing my wife . . . my dreams. My life is falling apart." Lars put his face in his hands and wept.

Sally gave him space to grieve. She offered no words of consolation. Even the kindest words and gentlest touch would have felt like sandpaper on sunburn.

Lars reached the depth of his mourning and slowly raised his head. "I desperately need something else in my head, or I'm afraid I'll lose it."

"How about we look at the chart of a new patient we're seeing this afternoon?" Sally said. "His name is Edward 'Call Me Eddie' Kolinsky. He's a fifty-six-year-old man with advanced lung cancer. He's had chemotherapy and radiation, but the cancer is progressing. His community oncologist has recommended hospice. He wants a second opinion."

"What kind of shape is Eddie in?"

"His performance status is good. By and large, he can take care of himself. He has some chest pain, which he rates as a two on a scale of one to ten. He has a good appetite and has maintained his weight."

"In other words, he's a good candidate for experimental therapy, if he wants to go that route."

Sally nodded. "Yeah, he appears to want more than hospice. That's why he's knocking on the door of academia."

"Well, we're certainly not the academic center he needs. We don't have the experimental therapy. Now, if we had the cancer center, we'd have the experimental drug to treat him. And if we had the experimental drug, we'd at least have the start of a cancer center. It's a closed loop unless you have the money to break into it. We'll have to refer him to MD Anderson or Sloan Kettering."

He threw Kolinsky's records on the desk in disgust. "Some distraction he turned out to be."

"Well, we tried." Sally glanced at her watch. "Oops! It's almost noon. Time for the weekly resident conference."

"Who's giving it?"

"Norma Latchfield. She's lecturing on chronic myeloid leukemia."

"I better go to that. We need some good PR with the Pathology Department. We'll need them on board when we figure out plan B."

"Glad to see you're emerging from the dark side." Sally patted Lars on the shoulder. "There will be a plan B. I can feel it."

"Is that women's intuition?"

"No, a Chinese proverb: 'There are many paths to the top of the mountain, but the view is always the same.'"

"Hmmm, I'll consult my belly button on that one."

Sally smiled. "You're being silly. Go to your conference, and I'll prep for clinic this afternoon."

The sign outside the lecture hall announced:

CHRONIC MYELOID LEUKEMIA:
THE MAVERICK STEM CELL
Presented by Norma Latchfield, MD, PhD

Distinguished Professor and Chairman of the Department of Pathology

High Plains University Medical School

Lars, who had developed a good working relationship with Norma, listened carefully to her lecture.

She started with the basics, as the audience varied in sophistication. "Some bone marrow cells, called stem cells, are capable of becoming any and all blood cells, including red cells, white cells, and megakaryocytes. Critical signals from the body provide instructions to the stem cells. For example, the body signals that a pint of red cells is needed. The stem cells comply, turning off production when the quota is met."

Dr. Latchfield then went on to describe chronic myeloid leukemia. "It's a hematologic stem cell disease produced by a gene mutation, called the Philadelphia chromosome because it was discovered in the City of Brotherly Love. This mutation causes the afflicted stem cell to stop listening to those body signals that say, 'Stop production.' This unregulated proliferation causes the leukemic stem cell to produce either too many or too few red blood cells, white blood cells, and platelets."

She went into detail about CML and how it affects the body, and touched on treatment. She concluded her lecture with "CML is essentially a mutated stem cell with three major attributes: it has an unlimited ability to replicate, the cells produced will function normally, and it's immortal.

"Thank you for listening. Now I'll open it up for questions and comments."

Unlimited growth potential and immortality piqued Lars's interest. Those attributes sounded like the mirror image of Kate's problem. The stem cells in her body had a severely truncated growth potential and were dying out, leaving her to waste away.

He needed to talk to Norma Latchfield alone.

He waited for the question-and-answer session to end before approaching the podium. "Dr. Latchfield, congratulations on an excellent presentation."

Norma turned to him and replied, "Lars, so good of you to attend, and thank you for the compliment."

"The thanks are all mine. I thought I understood CML, but you gave me a different perspective. I had never thought of CML as a cellular model for human immortality."

"Wow! That's a pretty big leap."

"Well, the CML mutation causes a single hematopoietic stem cell to become immortal and literally take over the bone marrow by relentless cell division. Some of the daughter cells of that mutant become functioning blood cells. Aren't functionality and immortality the key components to a cell—or a human being—living forever?"

"Hmmm . . . that's an interesting thought, but the leukemic stem cell lacks penetrability, stability, and regulation—all of which would be necessary for a multicellular organism to live forever."

"That's fascinating, Norma. Why don't we continue the conversation over lunch? Somewhere off-site. This conference food is suitable for the palates of omnivorous house staff and medical students only. I have an hour before clinic, and I'll buy."

Norma glanced at her watch. "I can fit lunch in as well, but only on the condition we go halfsies."

"Okay, if you insist."

The two sat down to soups, salads, and soft drinks at a neighborhood café. Lars sipped his iced tea and nodded to Norma. "I've avoided talking to you about this before. Have you ever wondered why Kate didn't apply for a staff position in your department?"

"Not really. She had her reasons."

"It sounds like you know—"

Norma didn't wait for him to finish. "Women in medicine are in the minority in High Plains, both in and out of the university. You can count on one hand the number of female pathologists, even after you amputate a couple digits. We've talked through her decision. She's not a political being, which is a requirement if you're going to be an academic pathologist. That being said, she's good, real good, and I'll take her in a second if she changes her mind."

Lars smiled. "Kate had another reason to avoid the university."

"And what was that?"

"These are her words: 'Lars and I work apart and sleep together. If we worked together, I'm afraid we'd be sleeping apart.'"

Norma nodded her head. "She's a wise woman. Maybe if Jack and I had followed her advice, we'd still be sleeping together." Both fell silent, with Norma reflecting on her failed marriage and Lars on failed health—

not his, but Kate's. He saw her disease as the thief it was, robbing her of strength and energy, slowing her down both physically and mentally. She was no longer nimble of body and mind. She had found work all right, but work that avoided the demands of Norma's department. She hid that truth from the world, but she couldn't hide it from Lars.

Norma cleared her throat. "Ah, but I digress. Let's talk cells. They may be complex, but they're a whole lot simpler than human relationships."

"Amen to that. Now, please expand on penetrability, stability, and . . . what was the third?"

"Regulation. But let's look at a model for human immortality from a broader perspective, starting with the primordial soup of a billion years ago. Let's imagine that out of the soup came life, but only in the form of single-cell organisms, trillions of them. None of the cells died. They just kept dividing and growing."

"So this was the real Garden of Eden."

"I never thought of it that way, but I guess it was," said Norma. "So far, our CML cell hangs in there as a model for our immortal human being. It has unlimited growth potential and never dies. But here come those big three problems: The CML mutation is limited to the hemato-poietic stem cell. The mutation doesn't penetrate other cells of the body. There are no mutations in muscle, fat, brain, and most importantly, none in the sperm, egg, or the embryo. So it can't be passed on. As soon as our primordial soup produces a multicellular creature, out goes our model. Furthermore, for the soup to produce that multicellular organism, it has to control the stem cell. That is, there must be regulation of growth to control the numbers and types of cells produced. Finally, I only touched on it in the lecture, but that mutated stem cell isn't stable. Over time, more mutations occur, which rob the CML cell of the ability to produce functional progeny. There will be no new red cells or platelets. The dividing stem cell will only produce useless blast cells.

"Eventually, every organism, every cell must grow old and die. Whatever causes that aging process is both ubiquitous and an extremely stable part of each and every cell. And oh, by the way, whatever causes aging must be flexible as well, because we all age at different rates. It can be tweaked by the content of each person's gene pool and the lifestyles we choose."

Lars scratched his chin. "So you are implying that immortality is not just a slip of the gene, so to speak, like we see in CML."

"Well, if it were a gene mutation, it must have occurred at the dawn of evolution and have unprecedented stability. I'm just not sure that's possible. I think every gene has the potential for mutation, and the mutated gene is more prone to further mutation than the one it replaces. After all, that's how we evolved from that single-cell organism in the primordial soup to you and I having lunch."

Lars glanced at his watch. "Whoops, I'm late for clinic. Sally will tan my hide."

"Say, you're adopting the High Plains jargon very nicely. Speaking of High Plains, how are things going with the new cancer center? The Pathology Department is all abuzz over the possibilities."

"Ah . . . there are issues, just like with any bureaucracy. But I think things will work out."

"So no major fallout with Dean Mitchell and the new administration?"

"Like I said, there are issues," said Lars brusquely. "Thank you for joining me for lunch, and for your tutorial. I do feel badly I can't go home to my workshop and turn out a few Frankensteins—"

"Well, maybe it's best you can't. I look forward to hearing more about the cancer center. Now, I'm off to the morgue. I promised the new residents I would proctor their first autopsies."

The two parted ways with Lars gloomier than ever.

2

KATHRYN (KATE) SORENSON wasn't having a good day either. She plopped down on the couch at home, determined to finish the novel she'd been reading. No such luck. She just couldn't concentrate. She sighed and put her iPad down.

Recuperating at home since her cardiac event a couple of weeks ago, she was doing well physically after emergency stents prevented any serious heart damage. Emotionally, however, she was a wreck. Her inability to focus for more than a few minutes and her occasional bouts of forgetfulness were taking their toll. How would she ever be able to return to work in just two weeks? Just a few days ago, she had overlooked her hair appointment, which was absolutely a downer first for her. "Oh my God, am I losing my mind?"

Bartholomeow, her ragdoll cat, nudged her for affection. She scratched him under the chin, and the cat began to purr his appreciation.

"You know, Bart, cats are supposed to be imperious, but you're such a cuddle bunny. I know it's normal to be depressed after an MI, but I feel like I'm in a hole and can't crawl out. I mean, come on, a heart attack at age twenty-eight! I look in the mirror and see gray hair and wrinkles. I ache in the morning like an old lady. Did I say 'like' an old lady? I am an old lady, and before my thirtieth birthday."

Bartholomeow headbutted Kate and rolled over on his back, desperate for a tummy tickle. She complied, and he resumed his purring.

"Cats grow old too, but you couldn't care less as long as you get food and loving. Lacking a sense of the future is a God-given gift to you. You know, it's ironic: when I was a teenager, it was cool to look mature. I was flattered when older guys hit on me. Now looking older is depressing. Feeling old just makes it worse. I want children and a career. I want to live with Lars until we're a hundred years old."

Kate sighed. "The heart attack woke me up to the reality of my future—no children, and my marriage and career will be truncated by my death."

Bart sensed her growing angst and jumped from the couch to a chair next to the window. He sat alone, staring at the birds outside. The cat's desertion jerked Kate from her melancholy. "You're right, Bart: nobody wants to be with a grumpy old lady. I better make the best of whatever—"

Her new philosophy was interrupted by her cell. "Hi, Sally. What's up?"

"I'm looking for Lars. I thought maybe he went home after clinic."

"No, he's not here. Have you tried his cell?"

"You're joking. He never answers his cell phone. It just goes to his voice mail, which is full this evening."

"Can I give him a message, other than to tell him to answer his cell?"

"Sure. Please tell him we got the new lung cancer patient an appointment at MD Anderson. The guy wanted to thank Lars for his help. I thought patient appreciation might cheer him up."

"Cheer him up? Is there something I don't know?" Kate asked.

"Didn't he talk with you after his meeting with Dean Mitchell?"

"When did he meet with him?"

"This morning."

"He called several times to check on me, but he didn't mention a meeting with the dean. Come on, Sally. What's going on?"

"I guess I might as well tell you. The cancer center project has been put on hold."

"What do you mean, 'put on hold'?"

"The Fletcher money's been withdrawn."

"What? Why would they do that?"

"The dean wasn't forthcoming, and when Lars tried to call Jewell for an explanation, he got nowhere," Sally explained.

"Oh, poor Lars! The cancer center was his dream. It's the glue that held him together during my heart thing."

"I'm so sorry, Kate. Lars told me all about your mystery illness. I would never have guessed—"

Kate was miffed at Lars's betrayal and cut her off. "Is there anything else I don't know about?"

Sally tried to smooth things over. "I'm sorry, Kate. I think Lars was just trying to protect you, maybe waiting for a better opportunity to tell you."

"God, men have such a convoluted sense of chivalry."

"You think?"

"Oh, Sally, so many bad things have happened, I've run out of tears. I guess I've let anger fill the void. Sorry for directing it at you."

"I can only imagine what you've been through. Maybe we could do coffee or lunch sometime soon. I've got broad shoulders and patient ears. You should try me."

"Thanks, Sally. That sounds good."

Kate put down the phone with a deep sigh. Bartholomeow sensed her angst dissipating and curled up next to her. "I'm okay, Bart. Remember our new philosophy: we're going to make the best of whatever comes our way. The best for Lars is for me to get out of this funk . . . Hmm . . . I've got an idea. If I substitute the letter c for the n in funk, I can really put a smile on his face." She giggled like a schoolgirl at her own joke.

Kate bathed and put on makeup. She put a big spritz of his favorite perfume behind her ears. She looked in her closet and found her one and only sexy outfit. Lars had bought it for her at Victoria's Secret one Valentine's Day. She joked that it was his gift to him from him. Unable to bring herself to wear it or to toss it out, she had let it drift to the back of her closet. She chilled wine and turned the heat up.

"Brrr! A girl could freeze to death in this thing. Bart, come over here and help me warm up."

The cat bounded over to her, and the two of them curled up and fell asleep on the couch.

A key rattling in the front door lock awakened Kate and the sleepy-headed cat. Lars came over to the couch. "Hi, honey . . . Whoa, love the getup! What's the occasion?"

It took a moment for her to regain her bearings and remember where she was. Then she gave him a coy smile. "Just waiting for you, sailor."

Lars responded eagerly with a guttural "Wait no longer, baby. The sailor has made port—hold it. Where is he?"

"What are you talking about?"

Lars couldn't suppress a grin. "Where's the other guy? I bought you that negligee years ago, and you never wore it for me, so there must be another man." Lars bent down and looked dramatically under the couch. As he stood back up, he slyly raised the hem of her negligee. "He must be somewhere."

Kate gave him a slap on the wrist. "Don't get ahead of yourself, sailor. I wore this to lure a strange man into my boudoir. You're the stranger, at least since my heart thing. I gotta keep my man interested. I don't want him wandering."

Lars's grin disappeared and he became serious. "Oh, Kate, I adore you. I'm not going anywhere. The cardiologist said not to overdo—"

Kate was determined to keep the mood light. "Cardiologist be damned! Besides, I'll just lie still. You can fantasize making love to a cadaver."

"That's so kinky."

"Well, you always wanted to add a little kink to our love life. Here's your chance."

Lars jettisoned his clothes and climbed onto the waiting Kate. The displaced Bartholomeow hissed his displeasure and jumped off the couch. Lars tore at the negligee in his lust for Kate's body. "Damn! I ripped it."

"Consider it a one-trick outfit . . . Oh my, you are an eager boy!"

"It won't be long."

"Don't hold back," she gasped. "I'm right here with you."

The lovers broke space-time barriers and, alas, the couch as they tumbled back to Earth.

"Wow!" Lars gasped. "You okay?"

"Never better," Kate said demurely.

"No chest pain?"

"None."

"No shortness of breath?"

"Well, there is that," she said with a grin. "You took my breath away. You were wonderful!"

Lars gave her a long, deep kiss. "It's your fault. You got me turned on with the cadaver kink."

"Pervert."

"Yup, and proud of it. Hey, now that the afterglow has been dimmed by the broken couch, I have to ask: Why sex tonight?"

"Do I need an excuse to seduce my husband?"

"Come on, Kate, I know there's more to it than that. Spill the beans."

"Oh, all right. Sally called looking for you, and, well, it all came out. I thought you needed a little cheering up. I don't do stand-up comedy, so lie-down comedy seemed to be the next best thing."

"It sure made the bad things go away, at least for the moment. Thank you."

"Hey, sailor, this wasn't charity sex."

He gave her a big hug and another soulful kiss.

"By the way, Lars Sorenson, why didn't you tell me you were having a meeting with the dean? And why hold back on the Fletcher debacle?"

"I just wanted to protect you."

"Protect me from what—reality? No secrets, Lars. If you don't tell me what's going on, I can only assume you're protecting me from something terrible. I can't handle that perpetual insecurity. Besides, I'll find out anyway. Witness my conversation with Sally. Promise me now—no more secrets."

Lars raised his right hand and said, "I promise. Anyway, back to our original topic—sex—weren't you cold in your nightie?"

"I'm still freezing. Now be a good boy and grab a blanket."

Lars got off the broken couch and retrieved her favorite comforter. Bart took the opportunity to snuggle up next to her and meowed to be petted.

Lars studied the broken couch. "Hmm, I think I'll bronze it and leave it here as a symbol of our love."

"Now you're really getting kinky."

"Hey, what's for dinner? I'm starving."

"You men are never satisfied. Go check the freezer. This short-order chef is still recovering from her heart attack."

"How long's that excuse going to last?"

"I'm gonna push it as far as it'll go."

"I'll order in. Does Uber do dishes?"

"Not a chance. Neither do I, but I can throw out paper plates."

"Just one more kiss? I want the afterglow to continue."

"Maybe after I tinkle."

"So much for afterglow."

"I don't want to add honeymoon cystitis to my list of ailments, particularly with my return to work next week. I feel challenged just getting out of bed in the morning." She paused a moment as Bart jumped on her lap. She gave him a hug and continued, "Bartholomeow and I have a new mantra."

"And what might that be?"

"We're going to make the best of whatever comes our way . . . I'm grateful we can still have sex together."

Lars sighed. "I'll order dinner and throw away the negligee."

"Welcome home, sailor."

3

LARS WALKED INTO the oncology office two weeks later, feeling like an addict desperate for a fix. His drug of choice, money, was in short supply. He had all but knocked down the Fletchers' door, without gaining access to them or the reason they had withdrawn their funding. He had hit on friends at the National Cancer Institute, along with every NGO that might provide funding. He'd struck out with all of them. In desperation, he had snuck over to the Sinclair station and bought a hundred lottery tickets. His return on investment was two dollars and a free lottery ticket, which also turned up a loser.

"Good morning, Patty."

"Morning, Dr. Lars."

"Ah . . . what did you do to your hair?"

"Whaddya mean?"

"Well, it's red, white, and down to your waist."

"Oh, that! I did it last week. You didn't even notice. The holidays are coming. Don't you think I look festive?"

"I'll go along with that description. . . . Anything going on I need to know about?"

"Oh, yeah, I almost forgot. Someone's in your office. Apparently, the two of you were friends in college."

"Oh yeah? What's his name?"

"It's a her. She said, 'Just tell him it's Jenna.' Oh, here's your snail mail, and you still have a ton of emails to answer."

Lars glanced at the mail. Avoiding the bullpen, he entered his office from the hall. As he opened the door, Patty called out, "BTW, Mrs. Dr. Sorenson says your voice mail box is full again and wants me to gently remind you to answer your phone. I vote with her on that."

"Hello, Lars," the attractive young woman said as she got up from the chair across from Lars's desk and greeted him with a smile. "It's been a long time. I hope you still remember me—Jenna McDaniel."

Lars almost dropped the mail. "My God, Jenna, I couldn't forget you in a million years." He hesitated. "I don't know whether to shake your hand, embrace you, or run like hell the other way."

"Friends hug friends," she said, wrapping her arms around him.

Her perfume brought back memories of sexual exploration and carefree college weekends. She was the first love of his life and still the same gorgeous woman who had made him a man. "It's very simple, Lars, honey," she had whispered. "You insert tab A into slot B. Before you do that, however, you have to make sure they're ready to be joined. Hey, no blushing; getting ready is the fun part."

He tentatively returned her hug. "Jenna, you haven't changed a bit."

"And you look positively haggard."

"Us cowboys call it fit and trim," Lars said. He motioned for Jenna to return to her seat, and he sat behind his desk.

"Whatever, Lars. I've heard through the grapevine that you're going through a difficult time."

"Oh really? Does this grapevine have a name?"

"George Snelding."

"Ah, yes, George, my old boss at Anderson. He put together a wonderful program there. I'm privileged to have been a part of it."

Lars looked down at the floor, and in a barely audible voice said, "I'll never forget sitting in his office trying to explain why I was leaving Mecca to come to this godforsaken place. I explained the money and the chance to build my own center and every other reason I could muster. He just shook his head and said, 'You realize, of course, you're committing academic suicide.' Those words keep haunting me."

"He holds no animosity. He's sympathetic; we've all lost funding at one time or another in our careers. Your loss of the Fletcher dollars is just larger than most. He did add that he would consider taking you back."

Lars shook his head. "That bridge is burned. I left for the opportunity to have my own cancer center while I'm young enough to enjoy it. I don't want to stand in the long line of succession to get his.

"I'm curious, Jenna: How do you know George?"

"My company, ElijahCo, does business with MD Anderson."

"I see." Lars nodded thoughtfully. "Enough about me, Jenna. Tell me about yourself. Are you still with Tina, uh, whatever-her-last-name?"

"Silverstein. And her name isn't Tina, it's Tammy." She shook her head. "No, she was experimenting sexually, and I was her laboratory. The relationship was doomed from the beginning. She ended up marrying some dick-headed lawyer from Boston. No, right now I'm in a stable relationship with Kendra, a grade school teacher. Both of us have been hurt before, so we're taking it slowly. Speaking of hurt . . . I know I left you—"

"We were young and, truth be told, had our own experiments. I turned out straight—"

"And I a lesbian."

"No hard feelings on my part, Jenna. I have both wonderful and painful memories, but hey, isn't that what growing up's all about?"

Jenna looked hurt. "How can you be so blasé about us? I really loved you. It's just that—"

"No, 'just that' isn't necessary, and no, I'm not blasé. I mourned the death of our relationship for years."

"Maybe sex between us died, but we could have remained best friends."

Lars frowned. "No, I couldn't be that person with you. Our relationship had once been complete. I couldn't handle being with you and never having you again. So I left the field."

Jenna sighed. "So you did."

Awkward silence was broken by Jenna. "Ahem . . . well, Lars, I'm not here just to renew an old acquaintance. After you and I split, I completed my PhD in molecular biology, and now I'm associate director for research at ElijahCo. We're a privately held pharmaceutical company."

She continued, "One area of our research interests is cancer treatment. We have a drug that's shown promise in animal tumor models. Phase 1 trials on human beings have been completed at Sloan Kettering. They've determined the dosing schedule and reported some exciting responses in far-advanced cancers. We're now ready to start Phase 2 trials."

"Whoa! Slow down, please," Lars said. "Words mean different things to different people. What I'm hearing is that you want to see how this new drug will perform against a wide variety of human cancers. What's the name of the drug, and what's it got to do with me?"

"First things first: the drug's scientific name is a jawbreaker, so we just call it EJ 75. We'll talk about the part we want you to play a bit later. Let's talk about the drug first."

Now she had Lars's interest.

"I've read about EJ 75," he said. "It's gotten some hype in the journals. Then again, lots of drugs look good initially, only to fizzle out when submitted to broad human trials. So what's the big deal about EJ 75?"

"Oh, this one won't fizzle out. Trust me. I understated the results from the Sloan Kettering trial. They're spectacular."

"How does it work?"

"Essentially, it activates the body's immune system through a series of molecular interactions. The result is that cancer cells are specifically targeted. We don't know yet how this is done or even if cancer cell death is directly related to the activated immune system. Most cancer drugs that fiddle with the immune system have some nasty side effects because they incite a more generalized inflammatory response. In essence, they attack normal cells as well as cancer cells. EJ 75 is like a smart bomb with its target cancer cells. Research is ongoing. I'll forward the few studies published so far."

"Sorry to be pushy, but again, what's this got to do with me?" Lars asked.

Jenna appeared amused. "You haven't changed, have you? You still gulp and don't savor."

"Okay, here it is," she continued. "ElijahCo wants you to conduct one of the Phase 2 trials here at High Plains."

A surprised Lars studied her for a moment. "Why me? And why High Plains for the pivotal trials of this red-hot drug?" He averted his eyes. "I've trapped myself in an obscure university in the middle of nowhere. Sloan Kettering should do the studies."

"Oh, Sloan Kettering will participate in the trials, and so will MD Anderson," Jenna said. "We need a number of centers involved in order to get rapid FDA approval for licensure. Adding High Plains isn't a problem."

"That's mighty generous, but what's in it for ElijahCo?"

"Here's where I have to ask you to sign a confidentiality agreement."

"What, you don't trust me?"

"Don't take it personally, Lars. ElijahCo demands a pledge of silence from everyone sharing our secrets." She paused dramatically. "The second area of our research interest is what we like to call 'death prevention.'"

Lars was taken aback. "What the hell does that mean?" he asked.

"Ever heard of the Gilgamesh Project?"

"Oh yeah," Lars said, wondering just where this discussion was headed. "A bunch of nutcases looking for the fountain of youth. Those folks read too much science fiction."

"Oh, that's harsh, Lars," Jenna replied. "Not all of us studying the aging process are nutcases. The National Institutes of Health has the National Institute on Aging. Baby boomers don't want to get old and die.

Come to think of it, our generation doesn't either, but most of us are too busy to worry about it."

"But apparently ElijahCo isn't."

"The Gilgamesh Project is built on an ancient myth of a ruler who sought and failed to attain immortality. Our company plans to succeed, and in that spirit is named ElijahCo after the only man to never die—"

Lars's face lit up. "Oh, yeah! The prophet Elijah went to heaven in a fiery chariot."

"Right."

"So ElijahCo is developing a chariot of fire?" he said, chuckling.

"That's cute, but no, we're not."

"Then what are you doing?"

Jenna sighed. "I'm getting to that. I'm trying to give you background to provide the premise for our project."

"Sorry. I didn't mean to jump the gun."

"There you go again with the gulping, but apology accepted."

"Please continue. I'll lean back in my chair and listen."

"ElijahCo has evidence of a molecule that controls the aging process. Deactivating this molecule may prevent further aging and the ills that it brings, like cancer, heart disease, and Alzheimer's dementia."

"So, in effect, you're trying to make all the cells of the body immortal."

"That's right. If cells don't age, they won't die."

Lars recalled Norma's lecture. "Chronic myeloid leukemia arises from a single immortal cell. It replicates relentlessly until it destroys the host. Have you considered the devastation if all of the body's cells become immortal?"

"Whoa, boy! Before we let our imaginations go wild, let's look at what we know about aging, and how we might alter the process. Bear in mind that ElijahCo is not a seventh-grade biology lab, so just cool your jets and hear me out. The alternative, of course, would be for you to send me packing."

"No, no, I don't want you to leave. I'll shut up."

"Well, hold on to your chair, because we're pretty sure the molecule responsible for aging is the prion protein."

He couldn't contain himself. "You've got to be kidding! The protein causing mad cow disease and other nasties that rot the brain?"

"Ah, but that's only one form of the prion protein, and a rare one at that. The prion protein is confusing. Fold it one way, and you get an apparently harmless form of the prion. Fold it the other way, and you get the disease-producing prion. We like to call the harmless form a membrane prion. This is the form that's responsible for aging. 'Rotting' is an inaccurate description of what the disease-producing form of the prion does. ElijahCo scientists prefer to characterize it as accelerating the aging process of brain cells, resulting in death. Our studies indicate the membrane prion ages each cell of the body at a much slower pace. That prion molecule is stable and ubiquitous, sitting unobtrusively in the cell membrane. They're smaller than a virus; they need to aggregate before you can see them with an electron microscope. The more you look for these membrane prions, the more you find them. Prions are even found in yeast cells."

"I'll grant you that prions may hang out in pretty much all cell membranes, but they don't seem to do a whole lot," Lars said. "They may even help keep cells alive longer."

"They appear to do that by inhibiting apoptosis, the alleged programmed cell death. Apoptosis brings rapid death. There's no logical reason membrane prions can't put the brakes on apoptosis and still cause the aging process. Aging is so agonizingly slow. The molecule that causes aging may appear at first blush to be inert or have other secondary effects. The membrane prion then becomes a good candidate."

"As you said, aging is such a slow process. How did ElijahCo discover that the prion is responsible?"

"Serendipity, Lars. Remember how Fleming discovered penicillin?"

"Yeah, he noticed bacteria didn't grow on a mold."

"Right. The mold was growing on a petri dish accidentally left out in the air overnight."

"So what's that got to do with aging?"

"Our research director was testing another drug, EJ 181, for anti-cancer activity in mice. This drug has similar properties to EJ 75; it activates the immune system. First, he injected two sets of mice with cancer cells. Then he treated one set with EJ 181. The others acted as controls and received no EJ 181. Two weeks later, both sets of mice were euthanized and autopsied. The research team compared the treated mice with the controls, looking for an anti-cancer effect of the drug—which, incidentally, they found."

"I still don't get what this has to do with prions and aging."

"I'm getting there, Lars. Be patient. Anyway, the lab tech responsible for caring for the mice didn't realize that two of the EJ 181–treated mice were never sacrificed, so she continued providing them with the same care she gave to the other mice on her watch. Over six months passed before the mistake was discovered. The two surviving mice were vigorous and healthy. They were sacrificed and autopsied. Tissue samples were taken and examined. One of the postdoctoral fellows was doing prion research. He noted the expected activation of the mouse immune system, and he noticed something totally unexpected: the membrane-bound prions had disappeared from every organ he examined."

"Did the immune system knock out the prions?"

"That's our theory, but who knows? We're very early in our studies of the drug's activity on the prion. While that work is ongoing, we want to move forward on our clinical trials.

"Oh, you might remember Fleming didn't know for some time how the mold was killing the bacteria. He just knew it was doing the job and went on from there."

"Wow! You've got my head spinning," Lars said. "Let's take a break."

"Okay. Then how about a cup of coffee?"

"Sure thing. I could use a cup myself." Lars slipped into the deserted bullpen, leaving his office door open. "If I remember correctly, you take it with skim milk and no sweetener."

"Very impressive!"

"Do you still drink strawberry daiquiris?"

"No, they're too sugary for me. I've taken to dry white wine. You still drink scotch?"

"Yup, and lately a little too much." He returned with the coffee. Good times with Jenna flooded his brain. He fought them off, trying to focus on prions and cancer trials. Then his thoughts turned to Kate, the love of his life, who was growing old before her time. What if prions were the cause of her aging disease? Could EJ 181 possibly be her salvation? He wouldn't let himself jump to conclusions just yet—too little data for the scientist in him.

"Did the two surviving mice show signs of aging in their autopsied organs?" he asked.

"None whatsoever. When prions are present, we have aging. When prions are absent, we have no aging. That's why we're thinking prions are the culprits responsible for growing old."

"That's pretty flimsy evidence on which to base an entire theory of aging."

"We've repeated the EJ 181 mouse drug trial with a much larger population of both drug-treated animals and controls. The results remain the same: no prions and no aging. EJ 181 looks like a very impressive anti-cancer drug as well."

Lars thought for a moment, then asked, "Do you think tumor cell kill and aging are separate or related functions of EJ 181?"

"I don't have a clue, but that's an intriguing question."

"My God, Jenna, there's so much you don't know about EJ 181! Are you sure you want to enter it into human trials?"

"We have additional data supporting our moving forward with clinical trials. I just can't tell you about them right now. Let me just say that ElijahCo does damned good science. We don't make hasty decisions."

"So how does High Plains University fit into this prion aging theory?"

"I'll be honest with you. I've already toured your facility and met with Dr. Latchfield. I think it suits our purposes well. We need to rush this drug through human trials before word gets out about what we're doing. So we need to do it in an obscure setting, not in the middle of Manhattan or the center of Houston, Texas. Can you imagine what would happen if EJ 181 hit the cable news cycle?"

Lars nodded. "There'd be worldwide repercussions."

"That's an understatement. Some would demand the right to live forever and sue ElijahCo to get it. Others would say it's unethical to even test the drug in humans. Conspiracy theorists would come out of the woodwork. The net result would be endless bickering and red tape—perhaps even a permanent postponement of human trials. We'd be opening Pandora's box."

"That's an interesting analogy and a pretty good one at that. So we keep the lid on the box, and this backwater institution becomes the cradle of immortality."

"Actually, it will be the cradle of amortality," Jenna said.

"Amortality, immortality. What's the difference?"

"Immortality brings the unconditional promise of living forever. Amortality, on the other hand, brings the promise of never aging and the hope of never dying. EJ 181 may prevent aging, but it can't guarantee you won't be hit by a truck or shot by a jealous lover."

"Amortality is the new evil you'll release on the world if ElijahCo opens Pandora's box with EJ 181," said Lars. "Those who possess amortality will build silos to prevent their accidental death—or, for that matter, their murder."

"We'll be doing our damnedest to keep our findings under wraps. If not . . . well, we can't control human behavior. People doing evil with their amortality isn't our responsibility. Should Robert Oppenheimer have been jailed for heading the Manhattan Project? Was he a war criminal because hundreds of thousands of innocent people were killed by atomic bombs? Do we blame him for the deaths at Chernobyl?"

"Maybe," Lars replied. "But we can debate that another time, perhaps over wine and scotch. Meanwhile, ElijahCo has a hell of a lot of work to do, plus a big dose of luck, before it can celebrate the conquest of aging. So far, you've only shown EJ 181 clears prions out of mouse membranes. What does ElijahCo propose going forward?"

"Well, we give you and the other centers EJ 75 and the funds necessary to carry out the Phase 2 and 3 cancer patient trials. We can easily get the necessary approvals of the university's scientific and human trials committees.

"Meanwhile, we quickly gin up your cancer center to accommodate human research trials. We quietly pass EJ 181 through the university committees as a purely anti-cancer drug. There shouldn't be a problem if we piggyback the 181 submission on the shoulders of EJ 75."

She went on to explain that the first humans to get the drug would be end-stage cancer patients. Frequent biopsies would be scheduled, ostensibly looking for anti-cancer effects, but the real purpose would be to see what the prions were doing.

"And how do you propose we study EJ 181's effect on aging?" Lars asked. He was excited about the cancer patient trials, but his interest in EJ 181 was far more personal.

"The answer to that question is on a need-to-know, and when-to-know, basis," Jenna said. "We'll supply you with the necessary information when you need it. I promise ElijahCo will provide the funding to get your cancer center up and running. We won't pull the rug out from under you."

Jenna paused and then added an ominous "Unless, of course, you violate the terms of our agreements."

Before Lars could respond, she moved on. "The Pathology Department will need to expand to accommodate a new laboratory. It's currently not equipped to process the tissue samples from the patients receiving EJ 181. Perhaps you can run interference if Dr. Latchfield objects."

"Wait a minute. I feel like I'm being steamrolled," Lars said. "I don't mind being spared the headaches of the planning process, but I want to make it clear I'm the principal investigator. I want to share in the decision-making process, and I want all the data to go through me. I'm responsible for all aspects of the trial and I'm custodian of the data. Results will need to be published regardless of outcome. I must be able to certify intellectual honesty."

Jenna nodded. "I understand your position, Lars. ElijahCo only wants control of the prion data, which is outside the scope of the trials. It also wants to work with you on the timing of data release. Remember what I said about the evils of releasing results prematurely. Cable news can be vicious."

"I don't mind input from your company. I'm just concerned about potential conflicts of interest if either drug is a bust. It would be unethical for me to polish shit."

"I'll share your concerns with top-level management. I don't think publishing negative data will be an issue. However, if we document a credible anti-aging effect of 181, then we may have a problem."

"Conflict over publishing positive results will be a scientific first. Then again, EJ 181 clinical trials will be unique."

"That's why ElijahCo needs a seat at the table."

Both were silent for a moment.

Jenna's beeping phone breached the silence. She picked it up and answered. "This is Jenna. Yes, we're almost finished here. Yes, I think it went very well. I'll meet you at the airport."

She put her phone down and looked at Lars.

"What can I say, Jenna, except thank you for the chance to build a cancer center at High Plains."

"This isn't charity, Lars. ElijahCo needs your talent as much as you need their money and study drugs. You present us with a unique opportunity to do groundbreaking research in a protected, competent environment."

"Then I believe we have a deal. I'll need to run this by the dean, of course. I don't think he'll object, considering his promise of space if I come up with the money. Besides, he owes me after the Fletcher fiasco."

Jenna hesitated, then spoke: "Uh, Lars, why don't you leave out the prions when you talk with the dean? I went out on a limb by sharing that information with you. We're testing two anti-cancer drugs. He doesn't need to know more—at least not at this time."

Lars stuck out his hand to shake on the deal. She brushed it aside with a reminder: "Friends hug friends, Lars."

The two walked to Jenna's waiting limo. "Whoops," she said. "I almost forgot to give you my business card. I added my personal cell number and email address. Send any routine information to my business email. Send anything pertaining to prions or an anti-aging effect of EJ 181 to my personal address or call me. You'll need a filter for such information. Oh, and remember to be discreet with your dean."

"Yeah, you said that. Why the secrecy with Henry?"

"Let's just say the fewer people who know about 181's potential, the less chance of opening that box. I'll send you and the dean copies of the contract with us. I'll try to keep it simple, but it has to pass muster with our legal department."

"Same on our end."

Standing outside the limo, they talked about the need to get High Plains University up to speed as a cancer research center. Jenna threw out a few numbers as they roughed out the terms of a preliminary budget. "It's going to be expensive," Lars said.

"ElijahCo is aware of that."

"And it's going to be difficult planning long distance. High Plains is far from Silicon Valley."

"You're right. So I plan to temporarily relocate here. I'll get a suite at one of the hotels downtown till space can be freed up at the university."

"You don't waste time, do you?"

"Industry has a faster clock than academia. You'll need to adjust to that. I gotta run," she said as she slid into the back of the limo.

On the walk back to his office, Lars tried to make sense of what had just taken place. On the surface, the opportunity to participate in patient trials with funding for a cancer center was a dream come true. But what excited him, what truly rocked his universe, was the vision of Kate as a young woman again, courtesy of EJ 181. The idea that the drug could possibly reverse Kate's premature aging was even better than a dream; if it were true, it was a miracle.

The first challenge would be figuring out if prions were indeed the cause of her aging. If they were, the next challenge would be getting EJ 181 to her without arousing suspicion.

Lars returned to his office, where he was accosted by Sally. "You look like the proverbial cat that swallowed the canary."

"We may yet test the wisdom of your philosopher."

"What're you talking about?"

"Is the view at the top of the mountain the same regardless of the path taken?"

"Hey, I'm supposed to be the inscrutable one."

"I think we have plan B for the cancer center. I just met with a private pharmaceutical company called ElijahCo. They're giving us two hot new drugs to test. What's more, they're giving us a jillion dollars to run proper studies."

"What? Why us?"

"There's an old cowboy proverb: 'Don't look a gift horse in the mouth.'" He glanced at his watch. "We're way late for clinic. I'll fill you in on the details later."

"Promise me you will; no fair keeping me in the dark."

"Of course I will," said Lars as they hurried off to clinic. Sally didn't notice the smile that crossed his lips as he thought, Well, not everything. Just as quickly, the smile faded with the reminder of Kate's relentless illness. He feared even thinking of hope with EJ 181, lest he doom it to failure. He forced himself to concentrate on the clinic patients.

Lars checked his email after clinic. "Looky here, Sally. I think Elijah-Co really loves us. Jenna already sent me a copy of the contract."

"Who's Jenna? Come on, Lars, no fair. I'm dying of curiosity."

"Oh, Jenna McDaniel is associate director for research for ElijahCo and is running point for them on the drug trials."

Lars scanned the contract for sensitive information. Finding none, he nodded to Sally. "I'll copy you on the contract, which will bring you up to speed. I think Henry will be able to sign off on it. I'll try to get an audience with his nibs and present it to him. He'll have a copy, but I doubt he'll take the time to read it."

"How are you going to find time for both projects and patients? You're already stretched thin."

"The contract calls for ElijahCo to provide clinical and research support. Get Patty to contact the university's accreditation department so we can expedite their appointments. Try to find workspace and temporary residence for them."

"Aye, aye, Captain. Shall I fire off a few torpedoes or hold fire?"

"Can't you give me a moment to celebrate the birth of my cancer center?"

"Sorry, but hubris does not become you. Remember, 'Pride cometh before a fall.'"

"That's not Chinese philosophy."

"We occasionally plagiarize," Sally said with a grin. "Joking aside, I'll get on it after clinic. You know I want the cancer center almost as much as you do."

Lars called for time with the dean and was surprised to get an appointment the next morning.

He called Kate. "Hi, honey. I have some really good news for a change. Do you remember me telling you about Jenna McDaniel?"

"You mean the bitch who broke your heart in college? I keep trying to forget."

"Ooh, that's harsh, but oh so true. Anyway, she appeared in my office today."

"What the hell was she doing there? Should I be jealous, or has her sexual orientation remained the same?"

"No, you shouldn't be jealous. And sex was not the purpose of her visit."

"I'm not sure I want to hear this, but then again, you've roused my curiosity. So tell me why she came to see you."

"Do you want the CliffsNotes version or the full story?"

"Please spare me the details."

"She's Dr. McDaniel now, as in PhD. She's associate director for research at a company called ElijahCo."

"I've never heard of it."

"It's certainly not a household name, and it appears they want to keep it that way. Anyway, they're a privately held pharmaceutical company working with two new anti-cancer drugs, one of which is red hot and ready for broad Phase 2 trials. The other is one I hadn't heard of before. It's ready for Phase 1 trials."

"Don't tell me Elijah-whatever wants you in on the trials?"

"Yup, they sure do. We'll be participating with other centers on the Phase 2 trial. The Phase 1 trial is all mine."

Kate's brow furrowed. "I don't want to sound skeptical, but beware of bitches bearing gifts."

"Oh, I have my concerns, believe me."

"Why High Plains University? I mean, there are so many big-name centers out there."

"Like I said, ElijahCo doesn't want to become a household word."

"Well then, I guess they picked the right place for their trials."

Lars was crestfallen. "Thanks a whole bunch for your vote of confidence."

"No, no, I have all the faith in the world in you. That company, whatchamacallit, couldn't have found a better person to conduct their trials. But I still wonder, why here?"

"I think George Snelding put the bug in Jenna's ear."

"I'm sure being old bed-buddies with Jenna didn't hurt either."

"You think I'm a gigolo?"

"Personal relations count in business. Every little thing helps."

"Thank you again . . ."

"Whoops! I mean every big thing helps."

"That's better."

"So when does this all begin?"

"Tomorrow morning I meet with the dean to get his blessing."

"Isn't that rushing it a bit?"

"I thought so too, but Jenna said industry has a faster clock than academia. Besides, High Plains red tape will slow things down to a crawl. If we don't have to wait on ElijahCo, it will help move things along."

"I do hope your dream will come true this time," Kate said, trying not to sound as concerned as she felt. "You're a talented man who has been denied too long. But I have to be honest: I'm just not comfortable with what's happening. That being said, I'll be by your side . . . as long as I'm able."

She paused a moment. "Oh, Lars, I was going to make you a nice dinner. I'd hoped I had been back to work long enough to build up some endurance. But I'm totally exhausted. If you don't mind, I'll order takeout and have it delivered. Pretend I'm your waitress. May I have your order, sir?"

"How about pastrami on rye?"

"You want pickles on the side?"

"Yup, and the coarse-ground mustard as well. Have them put it on the side, too, so the bread doesn't get soggy."

"Yes, sir. I love you, Mr. Director."

"Whoa! Don't curse me by speaking too soon."

"I know you, and you'll be a fine cancer center director."

Lars stayed late at the office going over his presentation to the dean. When he got home, Kate was in bed asleep. Bart was up on the table sniffing an unopened box of pizza to which Kate had attached a note. "Enjoy dinner. I'm too exhausted to join you."

The pastrami on rye was nowhere to be found.

Lars picked up the cat. "Jesus, Barb, we have a lot more to worry about than a meeting with the dean."

The next morning, Lars put the finishing touches on his presentation, took a deep breath, and walked into the dean's office. His reception was far different from last time. He was ushered straightaway into Henry's study. He endured the high five, but this time from a smiling, lighthearted man.

"Thank you for seeing me so quickly, Henry. It's my turn to bring news, and it's all good."

"Yes, it is, Lars, and I'm thrilled for you. Getting a research opportunity with ElijahCo is no small feat."

"So you got a copy of the contract and know about the clinical trials?"

"Of course. Teddy Everett is their CEO. He and I date back to graduate school. He called after the McDaniel girl reported on your meeting with her. It obviously went very well."

"You're friends with ElijahCo's CEO?"

"Yes, and we went over the terms of the contract. It's a win-win deal."

"I have some issues with data management—"

"We can work through details later, with an amendment if necessary. Meanwhile, let's get going. We're on industry time."

Lars noted that Henry and Jenna used the same figure of speech, but let it pass. "I'll need space—"

"Got you covered. I promised you that at the last meeting."

"What about the table of organization here at High Plains?"

"I don't see that as a problem. You will be project manager–cum–cancer center director when the time is ripe. You'll report directly to me."

"What about the Medicine Department? Won't Louis Chapman balk at that? He's my chairman."

"I'm sure he won't mind. I'll throw him a few dollars for his pet project. Besides, he doesn't do confrontation well, particularly with me."

"Dr. McDaniel asked me to run interference for her. She wants to develop laboratory facilities in conjunction with the Pathology Department. She needs Dr. Latchfield's cooperation. I may get pushback when I approach Norma."

"Let me handle Norma Latchfield. You handle the science; I'll handle the politics."

"I'll need admin support."

"I was thinking of Deborah Steiner, special projects director."

"What happened to Helen Briggs? She worked with me when we thought we had the Fletchers' support."

"She's gone. Didn't fit into our plans. I think you'll work well with Debbie. She's a bright gal with tons of experience. I'll assign her full-time to the project. She can also function as the university's liaison to ElijahCo. That will free you up to work on the scientific side of the street. Incidentally, I asked her to stop by your office this afternoon to get acquainted. She'll bring papers for you to sign as well. High Plains red tape is never far behind."

Lars was taken aback, awed by the dean's forward charge. Yet lurking behind the awe was a growing discomfort. Henry seemed to have more than twenty-four-hour knowledge of ElijahCo's offer. His planning was too thorough. Lars felt he was being washed away by a tsunami of events, many of them shrouded in mystery. Big Pharma was merging with academia, and he was the man in the middle.

Lars was at the computer, finishing clinic, when he heard a woman's voice behind him. "I finally found you, Dr. Sorenson. I'm Debbie with Special Planning. Dean Mitchell asked me to come by and introduce myself."

Lars turned to see a heavyset, well-groomed, fiftyish woman with a disingenuous smile. She extended her hand in greeting, and he shook it, grateful she hadn't adopted Henry's high five.

"Please call me Lars. I'm not a fan of formalities. Oh, and sitting next to me at computer number two is nurse practitioner Sally Ming-Davis."

Sally nodded and turned to Lars. "I can wrap up clinic."

"If it's okay with Dr. Sorenson—ah, Lars—you're welcome to join us," Debbie said briskly. "I have no secrets, just a lot of work for all of us."

Lars grunted an apparent yes as Debbie led the way to his office. Debbie was too bold for Sally. She had interrupted clinic and unabashedly entered space assigned to clinical personnel only. She showed little deference to the oncology division director and had the nerve to lead him to his own office.

Debbie set her briefcase down on Lars's desk and took out a folder with several sets of papers. She offered Lars a pen as she explained, "The first document is the contract from ElijahCo. It won approval from both finance and legal. I assume you've read it. If you have no questions, sign here as principal investigator."

Lars looked over the contract. "So by signing this document, it looks like I assume full responsibility for fulfilling the terms of the contract. I absolve ElijahCo and High Plains University of all liability. Is that correct?"

Debbie gave a full-toothed grin. "Yes, both institutions want your total commitment. Don't forget you'll receive full recognition for the success of the project. ElijahCo also permits you access to and joint control of all the data. You'll be first author of all publications resulting from research conducted under this contract. The only exceptions are publications related to the Phase 2 trials generated by EJ 75. Investigators at the larger participating institutions will most likely enroll more patients, making one of them entitled to lead authorship."

"EJ 181 is my study drug."

"You'll be lead author on all publications."

"Fair enough. I'll sign."

"The next documents are applications for High Plains Human Trials Committee approval," Debbie continued. "You'll need their blessing before you can start treating patients. Since they're straightforward Phase 1 and 2 trials of anti-cancer drugs, there should be no major issues. Clinical trials of EJ 181 require tissue biopsies, but that's not uncommon. You'll be required to appear before the committee to explain your trial design, together with the potential benefits and hazards of taking the medications. Again, I see no major impediments to passage. Just be charming and patient. Most committee members are lay people.

"Oh, yes: Dean Mitchell has called the committee into emergency session tomorrow afternoon. Each member was emailed a copy of the submitted trials, sans your signature. After you've signed, they will get the updated version."

"Don't the EJ 181 trials need scientific approval?" Lars asked.

"Yes, they do. Since those trials originate here, they must pass muster with the High Plains University Scientific Committee. Dean Mitchell, as chairman, is circulating the proposed trials. You'll need to sign those as well. No one will challenge them. You're the authority on cancer in this institution. Besides, they don't want to irk Henry since he could table any future studies a member might submit."

Lars complied and signed the documents.

Debbie excused herself with "If you have no further questions, I have to prepare for the meeting tomorrow. I hope you'll do so as well. See you at two tomorrow afternoon, and we can run through your presentation before the meeting at three." She shook hands with Lars and Sally, leaving the two with mouths wide open.

"If Debbie is any indication, I'm not sure I like your new friends. She's a real ballbuster," Sally said.

"I think I just signed my life away," said Lars.

"Yep, you sure did." Sally sighed. "I'll finish clinic while you rehearse your performance for tomorrow. You'll be debuting Dr. Sorenson, Principal Investigator," she said with a twinkle in her eye, leaving Lars alone with his thoughts.

Lars began watering the plants in his office, trying to avoid what he was dreading—a crisis of conscience.

Come on now, Lars, get with the program. ElijahCo is giving back your lost dream . . . and maybe Kate's life. Ah, but those gifts come at a high price—my integrity as a physician scientist and perhaps my mortal soul. My presentation tomorrow will be filled with half-truths. We're testing EJ 181 for its effects on human cancer; no mention of our search for the elixir of life. We're obtaining routine biopsies of treated patients; no mention of our search for prions. And perhaps the most deceptive of half-truths, we'll fully report all anti-cancer data generated by studies of 181, regardless of whether they're negative or positive. No mention that any evidence of amortality will be withheld lest we create chaos in the scientific and ethical communities. Dear God, does evil creep into the world on little half-truths?

Finished watering the plants and once again sitting behind his desk, he gave a silent scream. I'm not evil! I only want my life back! His face fell into his hands, and he cried like a baby until he could cry no more.

Lars awoke to a darkened office and glanced at his watch. "Christ! It's eight thirty!"

He drove home to find Kate asleep in her chair. He turned off the TV and awakened her with a kiss. "Hi, sleepyhead."

He saw a moment of confusion in her eyes before recognition. "Oh, it's you, Lars."

Her response frightened him, but he forced a grin. "Yes, indeed. Sorry I'm running so late. Have you had dinner?"

"I don't think so. I remember sitting down to wait for you, then . . ."

"You and your buddy Bart fell asleep. I'll get you a cup of tea and pour myself a scotch."

Kate remained curled up in the chair. Bart whined his disapproval on being disturbed.

Lars returned with her tea. "Here, honey. It's hot so be careful. I'll be in the kitchen putting something together for dinner."

Kate sipped her tea. "You're right. It's hot."

"What'd you say?" Lars called from the kitchen.

Kate raised her voice. "I said the tea is good."

Lars began talking loud enough for her to hear. "You and I've talked about no secrets. You may not like what you hear, but there's so much I have to say. I can't hide from reality or protect you anymore."

Full truths flowed from his lips, and he didn't stop till all was said. When he finished, he left the kitchen to join Kate—only to find she'd fallen asleep. He shook his head. "My God, Kate. I'm losing you. Half-truths and lies be damned! I can't turn back now. Too much is at stake."

The next day, Lars's performance was flawless. Both drugs were unanimously approved by the human trials committee.

4

PATIENT ACCRUAL TO both ElijahCo drug studies was brisk at High Plains University Medical Center. Despite additional help provided by industry, the medical oncologists worked feverishly to keep up with the growing patient load. Late one Thursday afternoon, Lars and Sally were on their computers, entering patient data.

Lars looked at Sally. "You doing okay, Sally?" he asked. "I worry we're working you too hard."

"I'm doing okay for now. Research trials are exciting, and that keeps the juices flowing."

"Is what's-his-name from ElijahCo shouldering some of the burden?"

"You mean Dr. Thorndike; I think his first name's Charles. Yeah, he's helping, but he's kind of bland. I mean, he's doing the job, and the house staff seem to like him okay, but he's not Mr. Personality. I read his CV, and his credentials are okay but nothing outstanding. He seems to be a vanilla doc doing a white-bread job."

"Remember the old mob saying," Lars said.

"I thought you quoted cowboy philosophers."

"I'm trying to expand my philosophical horizons."

"Okay, what's the old mob saying?"

"You don't hire a gun man to smile. You hire him to shoot straight."

"So as long as Dr. Thorndike does his job, I shouldn't expect him to be entertaining."

"You nailed it."

"Oh, hey, Lars, I have one more patient to see, and I want you to meet him in person. Remember Eddie Kolinsky?"

"The name is vaguely familiar."

"He has metastatic lung cancer. You pulled strings at MD Anderson to get him seen quickly so he could go on a therapeutic trial. He didn't want to go on hospice, and he wanted more therapy than we were capable of giving him."

"What's he doing back here?"

"Well, the study drug he received was EJ 75, and he's having a terrific response. Anderson agreed to his transferring back to us for maintenance therapy. We're much closer to his home."

"Hey, that's neat. I'd love to meet him."

They walked to the exam room, and Sally opened the door.

"Hi, Eddie," Sally said. "I want to introduce you to Dr. Sorenson."

"Hi, Doc. It's nice to meet you."

"It's my pleasure, Eddie. Do you feel as good as you look?"

"I sure do. I thank you for getting me hooked up with MD Anderson. They've been real nice to me, but they're so far away. They said I could get the same treatment here. You guys must have something going for you, playing in the same league with the big boys."

"I consider that a real compliment. I'm happy we can accommodate you. Sally and I will do our darnedest to keep your response going." He nodded to Sally and returned to his computer.

"Excuse me, Lars . . ."

"Debbie, what brings you to the trenches? I hope nothing bad's happening."

"No, no, on the contrary, things are going smoothly. I'm here to invite you to take a private tour of the renovated research center."

"We've been so busy with patients, I forgot all about the lab."

"Your personal guides will be Drs. Norma Latchfield and Jenna McDaniel."

"Wow, I'm impressed. I thought those two would be in the midst of a turf war. So they've actually finished the lab and are ready to go?"

"Ready to go and more. They've started analyzing tissue biopsies from patients on EJ 181. Apparently, the initial specimens did fine in the freezer."

"I'm flattered they granted me a private tour."

"Well, you're responsible for the research project. You're entitled to a few perks."

"When's the tour?"

"First thing tomorrow. I've asked Patty to move your start time in clinic. Meet the lady doctors at seven o'clock in the lab. As you recall, it's in the old CDC building. The main entrance is just off campus. You can also get there by going through the tunnel from the Pathology Department. Security will be expecting you."

*   *   *

The next morning, Lars entered the tunnel and walked toward the old CDC laboratory building. It was constructed in 1990 in response to the mad cow disease epidemic in the United Kingdom. American cattlemen were near panic over the devastation mad cow disease would cause if it reached American shores. Congress authorized money for a secure laboratory to study the disease and screen for its presence in American beef. What better place to build it than High Plains University, which sat unobtrusively in the midst of cattle country? The laboratory was built a short tunnel walk away from the resources of the university's Pathology Department, but far enough away to keep disease, and rumors of same, away from the public. The mad cow disease epidemic came under control shortly after the turn of the century. Congress and public alike lost interest in it. The CDC shuttered the laboratory and ceded the space to the university. For nearly a decade it remained a ghostly appendage of the Department of Pathology.

Lars walked briskly through the brightly lit tunnel. A wry smile crossed his lips, the irony of this laboratory reopening to study prions not lost on him.

He turned a corner and was surprised to see a uniformed guard sitting next to a closed door. "Good morning, sir. Please identify yourself."

Lars showed her his university badge, which she briefly studied before turning to a list on her desk. "Yes, Dr. Sorenson, you are expected." She opened the door and ushered him into the newly renovated building. "Sorry the tunnel entrance is still in the primitive nineties."

They walked over to an impressive instrument; she obtained finger-prints and a retinal scan. "Access to the laboratory here will soon be controlled electronically. Only a few people, such as yourself, will be authorized to enter by this route. The main entrance upstairs is more elaborately secured."

Lars glanced up to see an outsized camera monitoring his presence.

"The new cameras are on back order," the guard commented. "God knows when these clunkers will be replaced."

The young woman spoke into her headset. Shortly thereafter, Jenna appeared with a bright smile on her face. "Welcome to the new laboratory, Dr. Sorenson." She extended her hand in formal greeting, which he accepted.

"Thank you, Dr. McDaniel. I've just arrived, and I must say I'm impressed."

"Come upstairs with me. Dr. Latchfield is waiting for us. We're eager to show you the new digs."

"Good morning, Lars," Norma Latchfield greeted Lars at the top of the stairs. "Welcome to our humble laboratory. Can I get you a cup of coffee?"

Lars looked around, mouth open in amazement. "Ah, hi, Norma. Please, black with no sugar."

She quickly poured the coffee and handed it to Lars. "Pretty neat, huh? We're standing in the central area, which contains offices along with supplies and services for the research program. It also houses the mainframe computer that serves the network within the building and the Pathology Department. The latter's participation in the network was in deference to me. I'll maintain tight security within my department; the laboratory director will do the same here. The principal investigator gets access by virtue of office."

She nodded to Lars and continued, "Specialized laboratories come off the central area like spokes on a wheel. Each of those labs has a biological containment hood. Some rooms have positive pressure to keep bad things out; others have negative pressure to keep them in. We have both scanning and transmission electron microscopy, along with specialized instruments to study nucleic acids, proteins, and lipids."

"It's spectacular. And you did it so quickly."

"Well, not really. We had a lot to work with. The CDC spared no expense in building this place. We had state-of-the-art construction from that era. They were paranoid about security. They didn't want the public in or mad cow disease out. They were also fastidious about cleanliness. Prions are hard to destroy—"

Lars couldn't contain himself. "I'll be honest. The two of you fooled me. I thought there'd be issues that would keep you from working together effectively."

"Dr. Latchfield and I were able to come to terms quickly. I must say, she drives a hard bargain. She demanded most of the instrumentation you see in exchange for ElijahCo leasing the building and facilitating the company's scientists getting academic appointments. Those appointments are necessary to conduct research here."

"Dr. McDaniel gives me too much credit. The Pathology Department is in it for the long haul. I hope the same is true for ElijahCo. However, if we part company, the technology in this space will revert to the university. This state-of-the-art equipment can be applied to any number of research projects. It can act as a magnet to draw the best minds to our department. My predecessors failed to do the same with the CDC. So when they left, they took their equipment with them, leaving what amounted to a gorgeous shell."

Jenna nodded. "Like I said, she drives a hard bargain."

The three of them walked through the facility, respecting the safety and sterility of the specialized labs. One room caught Lars's eye. "What's with this?" he asked. "It looks like Fort Knox."

Jenna spoke up. "That room houses EJ 75 and 181."

"So when I order one of the drugs for a patient, it isn't flown in from Silicon Valley?"

"Hardly. We have strict rules of accountability. Only a few people have access to the room. You're one of them. Your retinal scan is the key to getting in."

Lars couldn't contain his curiosity. "Do you mind if I test drive my retina?"

Jenna smiled. "But of course."

The door opened into a small anteroom and then into a long, wide room with a biological containment hood at the far end. Open shelves lined the walls leading to the hood. Vials of drugs stood like soldiers in formation on the shelves. Lars looked confused, and Jenna volunteered, "This room was used as a cattle morgue by the CDC scientists. The room had air filtration and negative pressure to keep the rogue prions imprisoned here. We replaced the autopsy table with a hood for mixing drugs in a sterile environment. The shelves were used to store cattle brains preserved in formalin. We modified the shelves to be pressure sensitive, like a hotel mini bar. When a vial is removed, that information's recorded for inventory control and, of course, security."

"Pretty slick, ladies. I continue to be impressed by your creative renovation. Any chance I could get your help renovating my home?"

The two women looked pleased, but before they could reply, Dr. Latchfield's cell rang. She stepped aside to answer it and returned saying, "Sorry, I have to run. Duty calls."

Lars gave a chivalrous bow. "Thank you, Norma, for the tour—more than that, thank you for your part in making this project possible."

"I'll second that," Jenna said. "Speaking for ElijahCo, we thank you for your cooperation."

Norma graciously accepted the accolades and departed.

"Lars, would you stay for a few more minutes?" Jenna asked.

"Sure, what's on your mind?"

"The deal we worked out with Norma included a laboratory director appointed by ElijahCo. Remember the postdoctoral fellow I told you about, the one who discovered that prions were absent in the long-living mice?"

"Vaguely."

"He's the laboratory director. Dr. Aak is native Thai and has a work visa. His surname is a mile long and impossible to pronounce. Anyway, Aak is quiet and deferential to Norma, which iced the deal. Her tough negotiations played nicely into our hands. The technology she insisted upon will serve Aak well in his advanced prion research. He has been instructed to keep a separate set of notes which Norma will not see."

"When I asked you how you proposed to study EJ 181's effect on aging, you said something about that being on a need-to-know basis. Why are you telling me this now?"

"Well, Lars, now you have skin in the game. You're one of us."

"Good morning, Dr. McDaniel."

The voice startled Lars, and he turned to find a thin, bearded man in black scrubs. Jenna smiled and replied, "Good morning to you too. Thank you for coming in early. Lars, this is Dr. Aak, our new laboratory director. Dr. Aak, meet Dr. Sorenson, principal investigator for our projects at High Plains."

The two shook hands, with Aak giving a quick bow. "It's my pleasure to meet you sir. I have heard much about you."

"Should I be worried about that?"

"No, no, it's all good." He turned to Jenna. "I have preliminary results of the first six patient specimens. I ran the numbers last night." He glanced warily at Lars.

"He's okay, Aak. You can tell both of us."

Aak looked relieved. "Let me preface this by saying the results are on just six patients treated with a low dose of EJ 181. I compared the membrane prion count on the pretreatment tissue with that of tissue taken after four and eight weekly doses of EJ 181. We also examined each specimen for evidence of immune system activation.

"We documented immune activation in all specimens taken after EJ 181 treatment. We also saw a statistically significant decrease in the number of membrane prions in all six patients after four weekly doses, with a further reduction after eight weekly doses. Considering we have only six patients, a statistically significant response is remarkable."

Jenna and Lars looked at each other with pleasant surprise.

"What have you observed clinically, Lars?" Jenna asked. "I know you don't have patient charts with you, but at least give us your impressions."

"All six had low-grade fever and malaise, what you would expect to see from immune activation. We see the same thing with patients after influenza or measles vaccination. None showed a reduction in the size of their cancers. Two of the patients died of their cancer. Remember, all of the patients treated with EJ 181 have far-advanced cancer and have had a lot of treatment. I have several more patients coming up for their eight-week biopsies. An additional cohort of patients has been started on the next-higher dose of EJ 181 and will be due shortly for their four-week biopsy."

"Good, that will help us see if there is a dose response—"

Jenna interrupted Aak: "Excuse me, gentlemen, while I make a quick call. There is a certain party in Silicon Valley waiting impatiently for this information." She went into an office and closed the door.

Aak looked pensive and then asked Lars, "Is your wife's name Katherine Jane Sorenson?"

"Why, yes, it is. How do you know that?"

"Did she have tissue biopsies sent to ElijahCo for analysis?"

"I really don't know. She has a mysterious disease that's defied diagnosis. Tissue was sent to a number of laboratories looking for help. Some may have come your way."

"I had the opportunity to examine her tissue, looking for prions."

"And . . . ?"

"Her cells are loaded with membrane prions. I've never seen so many."

Lars's heart skipped a beat. "Are you certain?"

Aak looked insulted. "Of course I'm certain. I sent my report to her doctor a month ago. I'm surprised he hasn't contacted her."

Lars tried to rein in his growing excitement. "I don't think he connected the dots. An increased number of prions probably wouldn't arouse his curiosity."

"Well, Dr. Sorenson, now you know. I'm sure you will be, how did you say it, connecting the dots?"

"Connecting what dots?" Jenna interrupted.

"Oh, nothing, Jenna. Dr. Aak and I were just talking prions." He rose from his chair. "I have to be in clinic thirty minutes ago. Dr. Aak, let's get together as soon as you have the next batch of results. Of course, Jenna, you're invited to join us."

"I wouldn't miss it. Thank you, Lars, for accepting our invitation to tour the lab."

"The pleasure's mine. Love your new digs. I just hope it's not Pandora's box circa twenty-first century."

Lars couldn't concentrate on clinic. His flow of thoughts had become a torrent of prions. Hour two brought his third mistake.

Sally shook her head in disbelief. "Your mind is elsewhere this morning. Let your body join it. We have two no-shows. Dr. Excitement and I can handle the rest."

"No, Sal, I'll keep my focus on clinic—"

"Sorry, but you've had three strikes. You're out of here today."

"What—now we're working by baseball rules?"

"Nope, the stakes are higher than a child's game. Trust me, when mind and body are not joined, judgment follows the path leading to perdition."

"Another Chinese proverb?"

"In a way, yes. I made it up on the fly. Now why don't you leave, and meditate undisturbed? Bring your mind, body, and judgment back together before clinic tomorrow."

Lars signed out to Dr. Thorndike and left. He continued to obsess over Kate's disease. He convinced himself that prions were the masters of aging, and that 181 would have a cross-species effect. What remained was convincing Kate (okay, and himself) that giving her EJ 181 was morally justified. This would be a hard task, considering the ramifications of making her the first amortal human being.

He found himself walking through the High Plains University Memorial Park. It was a clear, chilly day, and he buttoned his coat against the ever-present wind whistling off the prairie. The odor of distant cattle feedlots tainted the fresh air; he didn't notice. He focused on the busts of the university's founders and past presidents. Each had his dates of birth and death, as if they were all that mattered. The lives of the founders were short, with the succession of presidents living longer and longer, a testimony to progress in medicine. Lars's mind was churning. But they all died, every one of them. Death was their curse, but the university's blessing. If none had aged, the founders would still be here, and running the university. I can't imagine such proud men ceding power. The university would be denied each succeeding president and the innovation he would bring. It would mire in the founders' rut.

Kate's different. Power isn't what drives her. Amortality won't change that. She'll relinquish power to the next generation when they mature. The lesson learned is to carefully select those who receive the drug. Kate is an excellent first choice.

This rationale helped Lars bring mind and body back together and fortify his resolve to save Kate. Some would argue that his perspective and judgment had indeed taken the path to perdition.

Lars drove home to catch up on emails. He wouldn't be disturbed since Kate, who had returned to work weeks ago, wouldn't finish for another six hours. He took leftovers out of the refrigerator and ate them, but with little enthusiasm. Bartholomeow jumped up on the kitchen table to investigate. "Come on, Bart, get down. You know better than that." The cat sensed his lack of resolve and brushed up against him, trying to coax out a tummy rub. "Okay, but just this one time, and don't tell anyone." The cat purred his approval.

They were interrupted by Kate coming in the door. "Hi, Lars. I thought you had clinic this afternoon."

"I toured the new lab this morning and decided to take the rest of the day off. And you—what are you doing home so early?"

"Bartholomeow doesn't belong on the kitchen table, particularly getting a tummy rub." She glared at the two of them.

Lars looked sheepish. "Uh-oh, Bart, we've been busted." The cat jumped to the floor and left the room. "Kate, hon, I think you're avoiding my question."

"I quit my job."

"You did what?"

"You heard me. I'm officially unemployed. I feel like an old lady, so I decided to start my retirement today."

"Don't play games with me. Why did you quit, and why didn't you discuss it with me?"

Kate sat down next to Lars. Fear and frustration crossed her wrinkled brown. "I'm slipping mentally. Most of the time, I'm exhausted and just want to sleep. When I'm awake, my mind is cloudy. I'm having trouble with names, particularly new ones."

"But—"

"No buts, Lars. Just listen. The other evening, I stopped by the grocery store to pick up a few things for dinner. When I walked in, I forgot why I was there. Three things, Lars, just three damned items—"

"We all—"

"No, no, that's not the half of it. When I left the store, I forgot where I'd parked the car. I wandered around till I finally found it by pressing my fob till the car I passed chirped. Even then, for a moment, I didn't recognize it." She was starting to become agitated. "When I got in the car, I realized I was lost. I forgot how to get home. A lady finally came to my rescue and helped me locate my address on the car's GPS."

She inhaled deeply and then continued: "I've been thinking about quitting my job for a while. Today I made a mistake. I made a wrong diagnosis. Fortunately, it was caught before anyone suffered from it. That forced me to face reality, and I resigned.

"I've kept my secret—okay, I'll say it—my dementia from you because

I was afraid you wouldn't accept it. Rejecting my dementia would be rejecting me. Unfortunately, we're inseparable."

"Oh, Jesus, Kate, I'll accept you no matter what."

Tears came to her eyes. "I can handle the gray, and even the wrinkles, but not losing my mind! I thought about driving off a bridge or taking pills, but killing myself wouldn't be fair to you. Besides, this damned disease is doing the job for me."

Lars was speechless for a moment and then responded: "Are you sure about the dementia? You've been under a lot of stress."

"That's why I didn't tell you sooner. You really aren't accepting . . ."

"You're right. I'm not accepting the dementia without doing something to stop it. I firmly believe I can do that, and without rejecting you as a person."

"I guess it really makes no difference what we believe. Nothing's going to slow my pace to death."

"Don't be so sure. I met Dr. Aak, the new laboratory director, this morning. He looked at your tissue specimens—"

"I know. I got a copy of his report from my endocrinologist."

"Come on, Kate. Transparency has to go both ways. Or did you just forget to tell me?"

"I'm not that far gone. I didn't tell you because prions causing aging may be just a pipe dream."

"Instead, they offer hope. You have accelerated aging, and you have too many prions. Aak told me today that EJ 181 reduced the number of prions in our first six patients. It's all coming together, Kate. It's as though fate—"

"You're right, but I don't care if it is. So few patients have taken the drug, EJ-whatever. So what dose do I get? Do you know what I can expect? Do I just stop aging, or do I get younger?" Kate was getting worked up again.

And . . . and . . . is it really ethical for me to get the drug in the first place. That will have to be dealt with. So by the time I get my first dose of EJ 181, I'll be dead. Or worse yet, a demented glob of humanity drooling my life away in a memory care unit. I have to be realistic. Time is as much my enemy as aging, and I'll be running out of it long before I could receive EJ 181."

"So we just give up?"

"False hope is worse than no hope."

Lars thought for a minute. "What if I can accelerate the pace of research so you could receive EJ 181 in months, not years? Would you take it?"

"How could you possibly do that?"

"That's my challenge, Kate. However, if you won't take the drug, speeding up research will be a fool's errand."

Kate's mind was slowing from thought fatigue. She was having trouble finding words.

Lars leaped to her rescue. "I know what you're going to say. It's the ethical issue that troubles you the most, isn't it?"

"Yes, it does. We could discuss it till we're blue in the face, but the bottom line is that the morality of what you're doing hasn't been vetted. There are, ah, things about all of this that seem wrong. However, the reality of my dementia has shaken my moral foundations. I'm floundering.

Do I accept the life preserver if it's sullied? Another time, another place, I would have said no, of course not. Now I'm not so sure."

Lars was becoming impatient. "I see the issue through a different lens. You have a disease. I'm a doctor. How can I ethically deny you treatment? Would I withhold penicillin if you had pneumonia?"

"If it were only that simple, I'd have no qualms about taking EJ 181."

"Perhaps you're making the whole thing too damned complicated! Come on, Kate, if we waited for every discovery to be ethically vetted, we'd be in caves debating the promise of fire. Science has always shattered the status quo, leaving ethicists to pick up the pieces."

"Oh, Lars, I don't want to be remembered as morally challenged. I've always been the good girl. But the thought of dementia pulling me away from you and leaving but a shell of the person you married is breaking my heart." She took a deep breath. "I'll take that life preserver, sullied or not. God forgive me."

5

THE WEEKS PASSED quickly, and things were going smoothly. Kate's dementia appeared to have stabilized for the moment. She did a pretty good job of hiding her gray hair and wrinkles, but she moved slower than most twenty-eight-year-old women, and she still tired easily. When Lars worked late, he had grown accustomed to Kate being in bed, sleeping soundly, when he arrived home.

Patient accrual to protocol was brisk, keeping the oncology team at full throttle. Lars was amazed at the number of patients responding to EJ 75, including patients with historically resistant cancers.

As Lars and Sally were finishing clinic one afternoon, Sally left an exam room with a big grin on her face. Lars glanced up. "Did you win the lottery or something?"

"Better than that. I saw Eddie Kolinsky. He's now in complete remission. I cross my fingers every time I see him."

"Good for him," Lars replied with little enthusiasm.

"What's the matter with Dr. Grumpy?"

"Oh, the last patient I saw is on the 181 study. She's getting the highest dose of drug we've given so far and is showing tumor growth after only two treatments. To top it off, she's getting unacceptable side effects. So I think we've gone beyond the maximum dose of EJ 181 that we can safely give. We'll have to drop back a little with subsequent patients. Damn! The preclinical data looked so good . . ."

"Mice are not men, and for that matter, not women either," Sally said. "Before you ask, that's just a casual observation on my part. Look, how many times have we seen drugs that will cure a mouse cancer only to fail when tested on humans?"

"Then why is EJ 75 doing so well, while 181 is falling flat on its face?" Lars said. "The two drugs are just not that different."

"So, should we proceed with Phase 2 trials of 181? You said we have a dose we can give. Maybe patients with less disease and fewer prior treatments will fare better."

"I'd like to give it a try. I'm not sure ElijahCo wants to make that kind of investment, since EJ 75 is a potential blockbuster. I'll be meeting with Jenna and Aak. She'll have the results from the other centers testing 75. If they're doing as well as we are, I think ElijahCo will cancel further studies of EJ 181."

"Well, keep me posted. I'll be waiting with bated breath. Oh yeah, the chemotherapy nurses were wondering why you want 181's empty vials. They're afraid to ask you, so I volunteered."

"You might say they're collectibles from our first clinical trial. I can't forget that my mother threw away all of my comic books. I don't want to repeat that mistake."

"Really, Lars, the empty vials are worthless and always will be."

"That's what Mother said about my comic books. Who knows what we might get for those vials some day?"

Sally finished clinic and went home. She felt unsettled by Lars suddenly becoming a hoarder.

Meanwhile, he was mulling over the data when his cell phone rang.

"It's Norma Latchfield. Are you still on campus?"

"Hi, Norma, I'm in clinic. What's up?"

"I have something I need to show you in my office. It's private."

"I'll be right over."

Dr. Latchfield's office was befitting a departmental chairperson. It was spacious with beige and soft wood tones, giving it an air of dignity. Norma was fastidious to a fault, with everything in its place, except for the pictures lining her walls. They showed her children at various stages of their lives, including adulthood. However, uneven gaps between pictures marred their symmetry. Norma had removed pictures of Jack. She still couldn't face him each morning she came to work. The divorce was too fresh in her memory.

She was sitting at her computer when Lars knocked. He let himself in at her request. She beckoned him to sit next to her. "I found some irregularities in the EJ 181 trial."

Lars felt his pulse quicken. "What? We've been meticulous about consent forms, documenting dose escalations, and patient toxicities. Responses haven't been recorded because there are none."

"No, no, that's not what I mean. Everything is fine on the clinical side of the trial. I'm concerned about what's going on in my laboratory. I'm chairman, and in the end, I'm responsible for policing it."

"What's with the lab?"

"Well, I found a number of encrypted folders on the laboratory computer. I initially thought it was one of the lab techs trying to pull a fast one. Then I noticed all of them had been generated from Dr. Aak's workstation. I'm blocked from seeing the data, even though we're in the same network."

"I don't see that as unusual. You know how paranoid Big Pharma is about their proprietary information."

"True, and that was my first thought as well. However, when I reviewed Aak's unencrypted folders, the entire patient laboratory database was present. Nothing that was required by the protocol was missing. So what the hell is he concealing—and why? If it's data gathered on protocol patients that have not been approved by the university's scientific and human trials committees, then Dr. Aak is guilty of protocol violations and ElijahCo is guilty of violating its contract with the university."

Lars was starting to sweat. "That's disconcerting. However, going from encrypted data to contract violations is a pretty big jump."

"You're right, but I'm not finished. You don't keep secrets from Momma Latchfield in her own laboratory. So, I went sleuthing and found a locked drawer in Aak's desk. My master key opens pretty much every lock in the department, including that one. I found Aak's handwritten notes. Let me say that penmanship is a lost art, and I don't read or speak Thai. However, the word 'prion' was mentioned over and over again in those notes. Now what the hell does a prion have to do with EJ 181?"

Lars was getting anxious and blurted out, "Well, Dr. Aak is some sort of authority on prions."

"I know. I read his CV. I have this gut feeling that ElijahCo has an ongoing shadow study with 181, and, who knows, maybe with 75 as well. They seduced us with megadollars, playing us for fools. We run a drug trial that acts as a cover for their true intentions."

Nearly breathless, Lars inquired, "And what might that be?"

"I don't have a clue, but I sure as hell am going to find out."

"I don't know what to say, Norma. I feel blindsided."

"I'm confronting Dr. Aak tomorrow morning. He better have an answer, or I'm telling the dean and the human trials committee. They may get away with shadow studies in Thailand, but not here in the US. I'll let you know how it goes. Thanks for listening to me. It helps to have someone I can trust."

Lars left, overcome with self-loathing. The little half-truths he'd been telling were about to be exposed for what they were—lies!

He got into his car and began the short trip home, thinking out loud in an attempt to organize his thoughts. "Norma is no fool. She knows Aak's shown deference to authority figures and will crumble under pressure, so she'll push him hard. What will Aak confess to Norma? Hmm . . . what was it Jenna said? Oh yeah, 'ElijahCo provides information on a need-to-know basis.' Then Aak really won't be able to say much of anything about the shadow study we're conducting. He's a lab jockey, not a clinician. His job is to count prions and not make clinical correlations. Consequently, he'll divert the finger of accusation toward me. Shit. I'm gonna have to come up with a good cover story."

He pulled into the driveway. The lights were on in the family room, and that's where Lars found Kate mindlessly watching TV.

She looked up when he walked in. "Lars, you look terrible. What's wrong?" she asked.

"Norma Latchfield called me to her office. She knows about Aak studying prions and suspects a shadow study. She's going to confront him in the morning."

"She told you this?"

Lars sighed and broke eye contact. "Yes, she trusts me. She wanted to give me a heads-up. I feel like a total asshole."

Kate went to the bar and poured Lars a double scotch on the rocks. "Here, take it."

He took a sip and motioned to the glass. "Thank you. This is just what I needed."

"What are you going to do if what's-his-name—Aak—dumps on you? After all, you're the principal investigator."

"Theoretically, I can come forward with the whole truth and face the consequences. But we both know I can't do that. Now even more is riding on the results of EJ 181." He looked at Kate; her eyes met his. "So that leaves me continuing to tell my little half-truths," he said.

"And what would they be?"

"Well, my wife Kate has a mysterious disease. She's undergone countless blood and radiographic tests, and her disease has yet to get a name. Without knowing what it is, treatment can only be directed at symptoms, with no chance for cure. In desperation, tissue samples were obtained and sent to various laboratories around the world, including ElijahCo. Dr. Aak was one of their scientists who looked at Kate's tissues and noticed a large number of membrane prions. He sent a report to her doctors, who then forwarded it to Kate without comment. No one really knows the clinical significance of an excess number of membrane prions. I took it upon myself to find out."

"So far, I think you may be telling the truth."

"Bear with me. High Plains Medical Center has a growing bank of tissue samples taken of cancer patients in various stages of treatment with EJ 181. I'm principal investigator of the 181 trials and therefore have access to the tissue bank. Dr. Aak graciously agreed to count the membrane prions in those tissues. I was hoping they might give me a clue to the significance of the prions in my wife's body. I can't say whether my request was right or wrong. It was merely a fishing expedition using tissue sample fragments that would have otherwise been destroyed."

"I don't know what you're saying, but it sounds pretty good."

Lars was going to stop there since Kate was clearly not able to follow his thinking. However, she was at least engaged and enjoying the conversation, so he continued, changing tactics.

"So, my dear Kate, I suppose you're wondering what I hoped to find on my so-called fishing expedition. I figuratively threw my line out, hoping to catch something—anything. My wife was slowly dying in front of me. I had access to cancer patient tissue. I was also in a unique position because I had access to the patients' clinical records as well. So if we did catch something in the laboratory, I could review the patient record for what we call clinical pathologic correlation.

"Your next question might be, What did you find?"

Kate stared at him blankly but smiled.

"We're very early on in the pathology review, far too early, I'm afraid, to make any conclusions." Lars paused a moment before continuing, "I suspect they'll start trying to trick me."

Kate looked concerned.

"Have no fear, honey, I'm ready for them. They'll ask something like, What was I planning to do if I found something? My answer will be 'I was planning to make a formal research proposal.' Then, here's the toughy: Why didn't you do that before embarking on your fishing trip?

"This is where I come clean and confess. 'In retrospect, I should have done that, but I guess anybody caught doing something irregular would say the same thing. Please remember my desperation and the red tape associated with any human trial. I was also using tissue fragments that would have otherwise gone down the garbage disposal.'"

Kate brightened up and spoke: "I'm following some things, but I don't understand why they won't want to punish you."

"I hope they do."

"Why would you want that?"

He grinned deviously. "So, are they going to fire me for such a minor thing? We're talking about a megamillion-dollar grant. I go and it goes. It may also be to our advantage to have them dwell on my fishing expedition. It will divert their attention from the real shadow study."

"My goodness, you are positively . . ."

"Machiavellian? I love you, hon. I'll do anything to save you." Lars sniffed the air. "I smell smoke," he said, jumping up.

"Oh dear! I forgot. I have dinner in the oven!"

Lars ran into the kitchen and rescued the chicken from a fiery fate. They sat down to a crusty dinner while Kate flogged herself for forgetting. He held her hand in his. "It's okay. No harm was done. But I do think it's time to get you some help. I'll arrange for someone to be with you during the day while I'm at work."

Kate resisted, but with little enthusiasm.

Sleep was a unicorn that night. Lars got up early and made breakfast, which he shared with Kate before heading off to work.

Dr. Thorndike was on service this month, allowing Lars respite from rounding with house staff. He stopped by the office before going to clinic. He noted that Patty's blue hair clashed with her outfit but held his tongue.

"Morning, Dr. Lars," Patty said. "I see you've cleared your email already. Good job! You get a gold star. Here's your snail mail and clinic schedule, and no, Sally's not in yet. She had to take Fred to urgent care."

"I hope it's nothing serious."

"She didn't think so, but didn't want to take any chances, you know, with his health and all."

"Let me know when she gets in."

"Will do."

Lars sat at his desk, leafing through his mail. He looked up to find Patty at his office door with two large, serious-looking men in tow. "Dr. Sorenson," Patty announced in her most formal voice, "these, ah, gentlemen are from the police department. They insisted on seeing you." She quickly returned to her desk.

Lars motioned them into the room. The first man wore an ill-fitting brown suit and was well on his way to metabolic syndrome. He produced his shield. "I'm Lieutenant Ray Garcia, and this is my partner, Detective Hal Kramer." Hal wore a tailored blue suit that partially concealed a buff body. Ray continued, "We're from the High Plains Police Department."

Lars was near panic. He came from behind his desk, his mind reeling. My God, what did Aak tell Norma?

He shook hands with the two, hiding his fear in a friendly smile. "I'm Dr. Lars Sorenson. Why am I getting this unexpected visit?"

Lieutenant Garcia responded while Detective Kramer took out pen and notepad. "Do you know a Dr. Norma Latchfield?"

"Yes, of course I do. She's chairperson of the Pathology Department. Why do you ask?"

The lieutenant said solemnly, "I'm sorry to inform you, she was found dead this morning." He paused to maximize the impact of his news.

Lars sat down in his chair, fearing collapse if he didn't. He tried to respond but failed to find words.

Lieutenant Garcia continued, "We checked her cell phone, and yours was the last number she called."

Lars found words and blurted out, "I'm shocked! I mean, I can't believe Norma is dead! What happened? She looked perfectly healthy last night." Lars noted raised eyebrows and cursed himself for providing too much information.

Garcia took note of Lars having been with the deceased, but decided to answer his question. "We're not certain. That's why we're here. What we do know is that she was found by the neighborhood watch some time after midnight. She was in her car, which was parked in her closed garage with the engine running. She had a bottle of vodka in her hand, and she reeked of alcohol."

Lars was gaining composure. "Norma didn't drink. Oh, she'd nurse a glass of wine at university functions, but vodka? No way, and certainly not getting drunk on it."

Detective Kramer looked up from his notepad. "That's what her daughter said when we notified her—"

Lieutenant Garcia glared at him, giving the nonverbal cue "I'm doing the interview; you're taking the notes." He turned back to Lars. "Like I said, the last call she made was to your cell phone. That was about seven p.m. Can you tell me about her state of mind?"

Lars took a moment to choose his words. "She seemed okay. She asked me to come over to her office. We've been working together on a research project, and she wanted to go over some data."

"Go over data that late? Wasn't that unusual?"

"Oh, no, we both keep late hours, what with our other responsibilities. We frequently have to meet at odd times."

"Did she seem depressed?"

Lars looked pensive as he appeared to search his mind for clues. "It would have been hard to tell with Norma. She is—ah, was guarded in her dealings with other faculty members."

"Why so, Doc?"

"I've not known her that long, but through interactions with her and others, it's become clear to me she's had a tough go of it. High Plains has a good-old-boy network, and until the time Dr. Latchfield came here, it also had a low glass ceiling for women. She shattered that ceiling and managed to dodge the shards—"

"Whaddya mean, Doc?"

"She was the first woman to become a departmental chairperson. Rumor has it she was in line to become dean of the medical school when the current dean died, but was passed over in favor of another man."

"How did she take that?"

"She was stoic and gracious. She supported the other guy despite her probable resentment."

"How did she take her divorce?"

"Norma was hurt but never showed the extent of her injury." Lars saw a way to deflect questioning away from his meeting with Norma and took it. "There was a rumor that she was having an affair with Dean Hanley before he was tragically killed in an auto accident. So lots of bad things appeared to be going on in her life, and none of us can compartmentalize stress."

"What's your point, Doc?"

"It's possible all those bad things mounted until, well, she couldn't handle it anymore. She lived alone, and her kids are on both coasts. As far as I know, she had no shoulder to cry on."

The room was quiet for a moment as Lieutenant Garcia mulled over the growing possibility of Dr. Latchfield having committed suicide, and Detective Kramer finished scribbling his notes.

Lars was gaining confidence and broke the silence: "That's about all I know, gentlemen. If you have no further questions, I have cancer patients to treat."

Both officers thanked Lars for his cooperation. He escorted them to the door and returned to his desk.

He half-heartedly proceeded with going over his mail but then stopped and stared off into space, trying to make sense of recent events. EJ 181 and the prions had miraculously escaped public exposure—or was it a miracle? They were safely ensconced in a laboratory built like a fortress, while two high-profile academics had perished under mysterious circumstances. Had they gotten too close to the shadow study, or were they just unlucky? Lars snorted. Maybe Kate's right. This collaboration of academia and Big Pharma may indeed have a dark side. My collaborators encourage the half-truths I tell in the service of amortality. When those lies fail to conceal the promise of EJ 181, would they resort to murder? Have I become an accessory by telling more half-truths to the police? I wove a tale to support the ruse of Norma committing suicide. Have I stooped so low as to betray a dead friend and colleague?

But then again, maybe my tale was truth in disguise. Norma could have killed herself. More than one depressed alcoholic has led a double life. Yes, indeed, God knows she was under a lot of pressure and could have succumbed to the temptation to escape. Then again, she could have been a careless drunk who forgot to turn off her engine. I'll never know for sure where the truth lies. However, if I'm to play it safe, I have to assume Norma was murdered and that the promise of 181 saving Kate carries a great risk to both of us, particularly if I stop enabling Norma's killers. They have to be connected somehow to ElijahCo. Half-truths beget half-truths and now beget death. Lars began to sweat. I am so out of my depth.

Patty's voice startled him. "Are you okay, Dr. Lars? Whoops! I didn't mean to startle you."

"I'm fine. The police just left me a little unnerved."

"What did they want?"

"Dr. Latchfield was found dead last night."

"Oh, no! She was such a nice lady!" Ever in search of grist for the gossip mill, she continued, "So why did they want to question you?"

"She died under unusual circumstances. Since I worked closely with her on the drug trials, they thought I could be of help."

"Were you? I mean, were you of help?"

"Who are you working for, the university or the High Plains Police Department?"

"Sorry, I was just curious. By the way, Sally's on her way in. Fred's being admitted for observation. Sally didn't say why, but with his health and all . . ."

"I'm sure they admitted him for a good reason. Now, please give me a minute; I need to go to the men's room."

Patty nearly blurted out, "Number one or number two?" but she contented herself with a smile and returned to her desk.

Lars splashed water on his face, staring at the desperate man in the mirror. *I can't pretend nothing happened last night. There's no more whistling in the dark. I have to confront Jenna.*

He dialed her personal cell. "Jenna, I need to meet with you—"

"Oh, Lars, I heard about Norma. It's all over the news. We're getting together with Aak later today. I'll see you then."

"No, I need to see you now. I got a visit from High Plains' finest this morning."

"Okay, okay, I can break loose."

"Good, but I don't want to meet in the lab." Lars took a deep breath and tried to lighten up. "How about joining me at the Morning Grind? I'll even spring for the coffee."

"Okay. I can be there in thirty minutes."

Lars arrived early. After ordering a double espresso for himself and coffee for Jenna, he took a seat away from the speakers emitting New Age music. Seeing Jenna enter, he signaled her to join him.

He held a chair for her, and she sat down to her coffee. "Skim milk and no sweetener?"

"Would I get you anything else?"

"Holding my chair and getting my favorite coffee—chivalry is not dead."

"I do fear it's on life support."

"So what's this about the police?"

"My cell was the last number she called. They wanted to know why."

"So do I."

"Norma called in near panic wanting me to come to her office, which I did. To make a long story short, she found files on the lab computer which Aak had encrypted. She became suspicious and ferreted out his lab book. It contained notes written in Thai, but she managed to make out frequent references to EJ 181 and prions. She suspected Aak was conducting unauthorized human research, a shadow study being covered by the drug trials. She told me she was going to confront Aak in the morning. She conveniently died before she could do that."

Jenna frowned. "What do you mean, 'conveniently died'?"

"Come on, Jenna. Norma's about to reopen the box, and she's found dead by alcohol and carbon monoxide poisoning? Think maybe there just might be a connection between the two?"

Jenna angrily replied, "What are you inferring?"

"Okay, I'll say it in plain English. I think ElijahCo was involved in her death, and maybe, just maybe, in the death of Jim Hanley as well."

"Come on, Lars. Conspiracy theories don't become you. Do you think ElijahCo has a team of hit men on call?"

Lars shrugged his shoulders and maintained eye contact.

Jenna, now furious, continued, "Yeah, just sound the alarm and a team of ruffians will slide down the figurative fire pole and be off to the killing field."

It was Lars's turn to get pissed off. "Don't ridicule me!"

"I'm not ridiculing you; I'm debunking your preposterous conspiracy theory." Jenna took a sip of coffee to settle down.

Lars toyed with his cup. "So tell me how you think Norma died, and no fair invoking little green men from another planet."

"Girls talk."

"What do you mean by that?"

"Days get long in the lab. Dr. Aak is a nice guy, but he's no one to tell your troubles to. So Norma and I found common cause. A woman in power can't show weakness on the job, not to her boss or her minions. She'll be eaten alive if she does. Norma found me to be neither of the above. She felt comfortable showing me her private face."

"So Dr. Jekyll had her Ms. Hyde?"

"Yes, but her monster struck inward. She was a terribly depressed woman. Her career had consumed her and her marriage. Her children learned early to live independent of Mommy. She was too busy to care until it was too late. Now they live on opposite coasts."

"What about her grandchildren? Norma spoke warmly of them."

"That was a part of her persona. Reality had them learning early that Grandma was aloof and not to be trusted with feelings."

"So she had no one?"

"Let's just say she was lonely . . . and found me."

"Oh," Lars said when the light bulb went on. "I thought you had a stable relationship with, ah, what's her name?"

"You mean Kendra. And we do. However, she's a world away in Silicon Valley, and Norma was such a beautiful, lonely woman."

"Did she find comfort in the relationship with you?"

"I'd like to think she did, but I'm a realist. Sex with another woman violated a taboo."

"Was there enough guilt for her to kill herself?"

"No, and in retrospect I think her death was a work in progress until last night. Her divorce highlighted her alienation from her children, as they sided with Daddy. She still had an upwardly mobile career until Jim Hanley died and she was passed over for promotion. She knew she'd never get beyond departmental chairman at High Plains. The good-old-boy network would see to that. Then ElijahCo came along with the new lab, enabling her to build a powerhouse department. Her career was resuscitated."

"I remember what she said on my tour of the new lab . . . ," Lars said.

"Yes, the space and equipment were her tickets to stardom."

"I think I see where you're going with this. Aak's shadow study was a threat to her career."

"More than you know, Lars. A clause in ElijahCo's contract with the university states that failure to complete the drug studies will terminate the contract, with all equipment and supplies returned to ElijahCo."

"She told me the lab would revert to the university. You were there. It was the day of my tour."

"It would revert to the university only if ElijahCo left the scene. The clause I'm talking about relates to failure to complete the studies."

"Damned technicalities. Do you think she knew anything more than she told me?"

"I don't think so. If she did, she wouldn't have trusted you and wouldn't have asked you to come over to her office last night. I think she believed Aak went rogue, which placed her on the horns of a dilemma. Exposing Aak would be an academic disaster. Allowing him to continue would cost her control of her department and make her dependent on his guile for her future success. She'd found him out, which meant he was vulnerable to other probing eyes. She'd have a ticking time bomb in her department."

"So you think this dilemma pushed her over the edge, resulting in her suicide?"

"No, I don't think she intentionally killed herself. I think she accidentally overmedicated herself."

"You mean she got drunk."

"She had talked to me about her ongoing use of alcohol. She had a growing dependency. Bluntly speaking, she was a closet alcoholic. I believe she misjudged her intake last night and passed out in the garage."

"So there's no conspiracy."

"Only in your mind if you choose to believe it. Look, Norma was a flawed woman who died tragically, either by accident or by her own hand. We'll never—"

"I want to believe you, Jenna."

"When have I lied to you? I promised ElijahCo's money and the drug studies—you got them. I promised you'd be principal investigator of those studies—you got it. I promised you exclusivity in your pursuit of amortality—you got it."

"I must admit those are compelling reasons to trust you."

"Then don't fight it; just let trust happen."

She glanced at her watch and announced, "Look, I've got damage control duty. Norma's death left a ton of fallout, including a void at the top of the Pathology Department. I need to meet ASAP with Henry about appointing an interim chairman. You've been here long enough to know the herd. Any thoughts?"

"I was thinking Jasmine Washington. She has excellent credentials. She'd also be a woman replacing a woman in authority. That wouldn't go over well with the good old boys, but the rest of the med school would eat it up."

"She was my first thought as well. However, she's too bright and too inquisitive. I think we want someone you and I can control. We don't want another Norma Latchfield nosing about, do we?"

"You don't mean—"

"Yes, I do. I want Dr. Aak as interim chairman of the Department of Pathology."

"There'll be a revolt."

"Then what, the whole department quits? Come on, Lars, they have research space and equipment of their dreams and money that Aak will hand out for pet projects. Oh, there'll be howls of protest, but only half-hearted. In fact, they may secretly agree with us that a nonmeddling chairman will be good for everyone."

"Will Henry go for it?"

Jenna took out her phone, punched speed dial, and replied, "That's why I'm setting up a meeting with him now." She motioned Lars to hush as she spoke to her called party. "Henry, this is Jenna. Yes, I know, and that's why I'm calling you. Yes, we need to meet. I'm with Lars now. I can be in your office in fifteen minutes." She gave Lars a thumbs-up and ended her call. She slipped on her jacket and turned to Lars. "Are we still on for this evening? Aak and I have new data that you'll find interesting. I'm looking forward to hearing your clinical correlations as well."

"Uh-oh. Now you've replaced skepticism with curiosity. See you at six."

Lars watched Jenna leave, and mused, Why in the hell does she have the dean's cell phone on speed dial? He finished his espresso, then glanced at his watch. Damn, I should have called Kate after the police visit. He tried her cell, but his call went to her voice mail. He left a message to call him back and then hurried off to clinic. He so wanted to believe Jenna, but doubts lingered.

Getting to clinic was a perp walk for Lars. Eyes and whispers followed him into the building and down the hall. He sought refuge in the area marked Clinical Personnel Only, but was accosted by Sally. "Lars, what the hell's going on? Dr. Latchfield is dead, you're visited by the police, and then you disappear for more than an hour . . ."

"Good morning to you too, Ms. Ming-Davis. How's Fred?"

"Don't pull this nonchalant act with me. I know you too well."

Lars slumped into a chair and then looked around to be sure they were alone. "This has been a god-awful morning. Please don't make it worse."

"How can I make 'it' worse when I don't even know what 'it' is?"

"The less you know, the better off we both are. Why don't you content yourself with speculating like the gossip mongers outside?"

"So I'm a gossip monger? That's a low blow, Lars. I thought we were friends and you could trust me."

"You are my friend, and I do trust you. I also care about you, and that's why I'm going to end this discussion and start seeing patients." He turned his back on Sally and opened his computer. Sally muttered something about friendship, but it fell on deaf ears.

Arctic winter settled over the clinic. The usual friendly banter was replaced by terse exchanges. Sally was anything but inscrutable when angry; today she was livid.

Sally broke for lunch and a quick check on Fred. She was nearing the cafeteria when she was surprised by Lars. "Please step outside with me. We need to talk."

Her reactive glower faded when she saw his anxious face. The two stepped out into the garden. "I purposely acted like an asshole in clinic today because I'm afraid we may be bugged."

"What? Are you getting paranoid?"

"Maybe. I don't know, but Norma's death last night and the cops today have really freaked me out."

"You're not making a whole lot of sense."

Lars looked around. "Will you promise not to breathe a word of this to anyone?"

Sally rolled her eyes. "Okay, but if you killed Norma, I'm going straight to the police."

"Good Lord, Sally, how could you even think—?"

"Well, you've been acting weird lately, and I don't mean just today. Come on, saving empty vials?"

"I'm sure as hell not a killer."

"Okay, then your secrets are safe with me."

"Dr. Aak has—well, actually, Aak and I have been doing some extra work with EJ 181."

"What kind of work are you doing?"

"It may not be the best cancer drug in the world, but it has, let's just say, some interesting properties. ElijahCo would prefer them to be kept out of the public eye."

"You mean you're doing human research not sanctioned by the university?"

"It may not be explicitly sanctioned, but it's not really forbidden. As you know, the drug trial specifically allows us to take patient tissue to study the cancer-killing effects of EJ 181. We're merely taking discarded scraps of that tissue and looking for other effects."

"Smells fishy to me. Why in the world would you push the envelope of acceptable research, and why would ElijahCo support you doing it?"

"I'm doing it because it might help Kate. What ElijahCo does is their business."

"Help Kate'? What are you talking about?"

"We still have a lot to learn about EJ 181, so talking details would be pure speculation and would also violate the letter of confidentiality I signed. Please trust me. I'm only in this for Kate."

"So, man of mystery, what has Dr. Latchfield's death got to do with this clandestine research? Cable news says it was suicide or a drunken accident."

"Norma found Aak's research notes and called me to her office last night. She suspected he was conducting a shadow study that was being masked by the legitimate drug trial. She was going to confront him today and wanted to give me a heads-up."

"So she didn't know you were working with Aak?"

Lars winced. "God help me, no."

Sally frowned. "What about the police?"

"The alcohol and carbon monoxide poisoning demanded an explanation. The last call Norma made was to my cell. So they talked to me."

"What did you say?"

"I told them what I knew about her death—which is a big, fat nothing."

"But obviously you suspect something."

"I'm suspicious as hell. Norma is about to blow the whistle on ElijahCo's scientist, and she turns up dead. Yeah, I know what everyone's saying, but I'm worried there was foul play."

"Aside from this confession to Mother Ming-Davis, what are you going to do about it?"

"For starters, I'm going to keep you out of it. That's why we're out here where it's bugproof. No pun intended."

"Good, because that would even be beneath your humor."

"Seriously, though, I'll have to continue working with Aak. I've come too far and risked too much to walk away from the only hope Kate has. This should also keep the bad guys at bay, should they be out there."

"Bad gals may also be involved—think Jenna and dear Debby Steiner. I've never liked either one of them."

They stopped, and Sally gave him a hug. "I'm scared for you, Lars. You've dug yourself a deep hole, and contrary to the law of holes, you're still digging."

"I've no choice."

"Perhaps none that you can see. I know you adore your Kate, but I fear you've gone beyond the bounds of rationality in your attempt to save her. Admitting helplessness can be empowering."

"Is this another proverb?"

"No, just a friend trying to be the best friend she can be."

Lars smiled and returned the hug. "I'll spring for lunch, but not that god-awful hospital cafeteria food."

"How about we go to the Asian fusion restaurant across campus?"

"I hear you eat bison steak with chopsticks."

"You're hopeless."

"Why don't you check on Fred? I'll get carryout and meet you back in clinic. Oh, and give him my best."

Afternoon clinic passed quickly and more comfortably as the arctic chill had melted. Lars excused himself early to prepare for his meeting with Jenna and Aak. He tried to reach Kate again, but his call went directly to her voice mail.

He arrived early and found Aak working alone. He was greeted with a polite bow and "Good evening, Dr. Sorenson."

Lars sensed trepidation, which would benefit no one. He casually returned the greeting with his own bow. "Good evening to you too. Tell me what's new in the wonderful world of prions?"

Aak appeared confused and responded, "I didn't know prions had a world, Dr. Sorenson. None of my studies—"

"Sorry, Dr. Aak, it's just an idiom, a foolish American expression. We're all distressed by Dr. Latchfield's death. I just wanted to reassure you. Now, please tell me the latest results of your prion studies."

Aak seemed to brighten with the reassurance and proceeded with his report. "Dr. Jenna has been delayed. The results of EJ 75 studies at the other centers came in this afternoon. She's in the midst of correlating them. She told me we could proceed with the results from EJ 181. Please tell me about your clinical data. I'll follow with the laboratory report."

Lars sat across from the more relaxed Aak. He purposely slowed the process of removing the papers from his briefcase to enhance the new mood. "The good news is we've found the proper dose for further clinical trials of EJ 181," he said. "The toxicity is pretty much as we expected from a drug activating the immune system, mainly chills and fever. We also had three patients with a rash. Over half had some redness and itching at the injection site. None had more than what would be seen with an influenza vaccination. A single patient was given a dose level higher. She had rigors, high fever, and a seizure. This was deemed unacceptable toxicity, and no further patients were given that high a dose.

"The bad news is we saw no anti-cancer effect of EJ 181 at any dose level. This was surprising and deeply disappointing to me."

"But not to me."

Lars was caught off guard. "What the hell do you mean by that?"

"EJ 181 was able to kill the mouse cancer because of a ubiquitin mutation." Aak briefly paused to allow his revelation to sink in. Savoring his newfound power, he continued, "The original EJ 181 trial was on tumor-laden mice. EJ 181 showed three principal effects. The first was a loss of membrane prions. The second was mouse survival without aging. The third effect was eradication of cancer in the treated mice."

"Yes, of course, Dr. Aak. That's why I expected some human cancer cell destruction."

Aak stood up, exercising both physical and intellectual superiority over Lars. "Ubiquitin is a protein found in almost all cells, including mouse and human cancers." He nodded toward Lars and continued, "The name 'ubiquitin' is of course, derived from 'ubiquitous.' It plays many roles, chief of which is to mark defective proteins for destruction."

Lars chafed at his demeaning explanation. "That's Biology 101, Dr. Aak. Please get to the point."

Aak remained standing. "I have been studying the mouse cancer that

181 so ably dispatched. One of the four genes coding for ubiquitin has a unique mutation. The resulting ubiquitin protein marks a number of normal cell repair proteins for destruction. This creates a cell which is vulnerable to attack from EJ 181, and for that matter, many other drugs as well—"

Lars interrupted: "I'm confused. EJ 75 is such a great cancer killer, yet it's almost identical in structure to 181, which can only destroy mutant cells."

"True, Dr. Sorenson, but the key word is 'almost.' Something that differentiates 75 from 181 enables 75 to destroy tumor cells—"

"That's obvious," Lars interjected. "So what is that something?"

"We don't know that. It's a work in progress."

"EJ 181 eliminates membrane prions more effectively than 75 by a factor of a thousand. Why?"

"We don't know that either."

Lars sighed. "I'm sure you can't answer this question, but I need to ask it. EJ 181 seems to allow cancer cells to escape destruction. Will patients receiving this drug inevitably develop cancer?"

Humbled by his lack of answers, Dr. Aak sat down and replied, "You're correct, Dr. Sorenson: I don't know. However, I suspect 181 may greatly increase the risk of cancer—"

Jenna overheard Aak's speculation and chose to break in with a cheery "Of course you don't know that, Dr. Aak. Perhaps we should focus on what we do know about our two drugs." She did not wait for consensus but proceeded: "First, let me report on the clinical trials of EJ 75. They are unprecedented in the history of treating human cancers. We have

DAN W LUEDKE MD

a blockbuster drug, gentlemen. No, it's more than a blockbuster. It's a game changer. The details from the participating centers are contained in a new folder which you can download at your convenience."

Lars perked up. "Can High Plains University participate in the Phase 3 trials?"

"I'm sure something can be arranged. Meanwhile, ElijahCo is applying for early FDA approval."

Lars frowned at the slow no. He said nothing, but was thinking, *Early FDA approval would short-circuit expensive Phase 3 trials and ElijahCo could begin charging for the drug. Any oncologist treating cancer would have access to the drug, denying High Plains University any special status.*

Jenna was all smiles and went on, "You two have explored EJ 181's failure as a cancer killer. Let's explore what it can do to prions—I think you'll like this, Lars. Go ahead, Dr. Aak."

"Thank you, Dr. Jenna. As you recall, the findings presented at our last meeting suggested that the higher the dose of EJ 181, the more prions are eliminated from the cell membrane. Unfortunately, as Dr. Sorenson said earlier, higher doses of the drug produce greater toxicity." Aak paused for effect and then continued with a wide grin: "I'm pleased to report that at the maximum tolerated doses of EJ 181 there was total eradication of membrane prions. This effect was seen after only four weekly doses—"

Lars broke in: "So we know how many weekly doses it takes to eradicate prions, but we don't know if we can stop at four doses and have a permanent effect, or whether we need maintenance treatment. A study designed to answer those questions would be complex and costly. We would need a large number of patients and frequent monitoring of the membrane prion count in all of them. This would require frequent biopsies, which would be painful. I doubt you could get such a study approved by the university, even if we would reveal the true reason for doing it—i.e., the search for amortality." He turned to Jenna. "Is ElijahCo willing to design and finance such a study?"

Jenna motioned for Dr. Aak to speak.

"I have developed a blood test to determine the total-body prion burden," Aak said. "It's as simple as testing for blood sugar. The quantity of blood I need for the assay I can get from a mere pin prick. I have tested the assay on your cancer patients and found a remarkable correlation between membrane prion count in tissue samples and the prion level in the blood samples. We won't need tissue samples anymore."

Control of the conversation was a bouncing ball; Lars grabbed it. "Yes, Dr. Aak, that is a remarkable breakthrough and will greatly simplify further studies. However, it will still take a large study with many patients—and it will have to last a long time to see whether eliminating prions will produce amortality—"

Jenna interrupted: "Thank you, Dr. Aak. You're excused from the meeting. Dr. Sorenson and I have clinical issues to discuss which will only bore you."

Lars was about to add something when he felt a sharp pain from a kick in the shin. He took the hint and kept quiet.

Dr. Aak left the room as Lars rubbed his shin.

"Sorry about the kick," Jenna said, without remorse. "Remember, we're on a need-to-know basis. It's best if Aak doesn't contemplate the clinical implications of his work. Think of what might have happened this morning if Norma had lived to interrogate him."

Lars nodded. "So, what have the gods at ElijahCo got up their sleeves? We can't ignore what we know about 181. Then again, that's my opinion, and what I think doesn't matter. They have the money and will have tons more once EJ 75 hits the market."

Jenna carefully crafted her response. "ElijahCo considers the pursuit of amortality with EJ 181 a top priority. Two more studies are in the pipeline. The first is an extension of the dose-finding study, which we have completed. It addresses the question of maintenance therapy. The second is an efficacy study. It addresses the question of whether eliminating prions can slow or even reverse the aging process. This will be an extremely large clinical trial. We know that determining the effect of 181 on aging will take years, perhaps even decades, to complete."

"Jenna, you've left out the elephant in the living room: institutional approval to conduct those trials. You can tell the gods for me it's not gonna happen here at High Plains University. We burned the human trials committee once with our half-truths. It ain't gonna happen again." Lars paused a moment and slapped his forehead. "Duh! I was thinking like a scientist. Our biggest problems will be the ethical and social implications of our findings if EJ 181 produces amortality. How do we keep the old box closed?"

Jenna slowly stood up and peered down at Lars. "We're moving EJ 181 to Thailand."

A cold chill ran through Lars's body. "What do you mean?"

"Dr. Aak wasn't hired for his pretty face. He is, of course, a Thai nationalist working here on a visa. He has strong ties to a backwater university on the outskirts of Bangkok. Think High Plains University goes Asian. The university sits adjacent to a sprawling slum and serves the medical needs of its poverty-stricken population."

"I see where you're going. The slum will be an ideal source of patients for the 181 trials. Pay the peasants a few bucks, and they're yours for life. Who'll know or care if they age or not? I doubt CNN or Fox News has a strong presence there."

"Dr. Aak's brother is a ranking member of the Thai Food and Drug Administration. He can assure rapid approval of the trials and turn a blind eye to the effects of EJ 181."

"Very clever. The gods of ElijahCo are omniscient. I'm curious: How do they intend to get 181 out of the US without gaining attention from the feds or the public?"

"It's just another anti-cancer drug that looked good in animals but fell on its face in human trials. Oh! I almost forgot to tell you: Dr. Aak is now the interim director of the High Plains University Pathology Department."

"So, you did it. You got Mitchell to approve his appointment."

"Yep, he saw the light. Aak will remove the encrypted files and polish the rest of the data for your approval. You can bundle his report with yours, submit it to the scientific committee, and EJ 181 is in the university's rearview mirror. Dr. Aak will be responsible for disposal of the remaining stores of drug at the university."

Lars struggled to respond. "But what about those patients still receiving 181? Will ElijahCo just cut them off?"

"Why not? The drug isn't helping them; you have conclusively demonstrated that. The longer the drug is here in the US, the greater the chance it will fall into the wrong hands."

Jenna noted Lars becoming progressively more worked up and needing reassurance. "Ye of little faith, the gods have not forgotten your fealty."

"What are you talking about?"

"ElijahCo is not going to just dump you."

"Golly gee, that's mighty nice of them."

Jenna frowned, and Lars backed away from humor. "Seriously, I'm having trouble understanding why ElijahCo didn't conduct all of the 181 human trials in Thailand. It would have been cheaper and subjected to less scrutiny."

"I told you at the beginning of this venture that ElijahCo needed your expertise in conducting drug trials. Dose-finding studies are tricky and need close attention. The need for proper tissue acquisition and processing adds a new level of complexity. The sophistication necessary to conduct such a trial is not present at the university in Bangkok. Dr. Aak also needed the instrumentation in this lab to devise his blood prion assay. Now that we have it, trial complexity drops dramatically and off we go to Bangkok."

"So what do I do now, ma'am? Submit my report and ride off into the sunset?"

Jenna elected to support his humor. "No, Shane. You can put your horse back in the barn, and you're not going out to pasture. We need you to be principal investigator of the 181 trials in Thailand."

"Why me, and why can't Chuck Thorndike do it?"

"Dr. Thorndike will be boots on the ground in Thailand. He'll supervise the trials there. However, he'll continue to report to you. All of the data will flow through you for interpretation and correlation. After all, you know EJ 181 better than anyone in the world. We don't want to lose your expertise."

"I don't think Kate's up for another move."

"Who said anything about moving? It's an electronic world. We can run studies from anywhere. Of course, you'll need face time with Chuck and Aak, but most of that can be via Skype. Look, I know it's been a long day, and you must be exhausted. Go home. Talk it over with Kate. We can work out the details of your co-appointments with ElijahCo and the university later. I can't imagine the dean having any problems with such an arrangement." She gave him a reassuring pat on the shoulder, but no hug this time, and then left him alone to brood.

Lars removed his engraved Montblanc pen from his coat pocket and tucked it under the cushion of a conference room chair. He made another futile effort to reach Kate. He was near panic with worry, but he couldn't go home right then. He had to visit a patient first.

6

LARS KNOCKED ON the half-open door of hospital room 638. A thin, grizzled man in his late sixties looked up from his e-book and grinned. "Hi, Lars. What the hell are you doing here this time of night?"

"Hey, man, I work here. So why are you taking up a bed some sick bastard should be occupying?"

Two fist bumps later, Fred Davis sighed. "It's the pacemaker. I shoulda paid retail instead of going on eBay."

"Don't blame yourself. It's the women in our lives, always looking for a bargain."

"Speaking of women, Sally was here earlier. It sounds like you've got problems."

Lars was startled. "She . . . she promised . . ."

"Sally and I don't keep secrets. Never have and never will. Don't worry. It goes no further."

Lars settled into a chair. "It's okay. Kate and I have promised to share as well. Ours, however, is a work in progress. Oh, Fred, I wish life was a trout stream on a sunny day."

"Is there anything I can do to help, at least anything from a chair? It's not like I can punch out the bad guys."

"It's best I say no. I'd be afraid for the two of you if you got involved."

"So Sally told me, but I'm not clear why we'd be in danger."

"Honestly, Fred, I don't even know if you would be in danger. I just can't take the chance."

"Friendship carries risk. We want to help."

Lars hesitated for a moment before proceeding. "What I need is your IT expertise. ElijahCo has a drug that may help my Kate get better."

"Are you talking about EJ 181? Sally told me it's not such a good cancer drug."

"That's right, but it does other things that may help Kate. Tonight I learned ElijahCo is going to halt studies of the drug and destroy the existing stock."

"Bummer. No drug means no help for Kate."

"I need to get hold of some before that happens."

"I got an idea. You're the principal investigator. Why don't you just order a six-pack to go?"

"I wish it were that simple. ElijahCo is paranoid about 181 getting into anyone's hands, including mine. It's held under tight security."

"So where do they keep it?"

"It's in a locked room in the refurbished CDC lab adjacent to the Path Department."

"I know the place; in fact, I was in the lab when I worked for the company installing security back when they built it."

"Well, security's been upgraded big time, including fingerprint and retinal scan technology."

"You got my attention. Tell me more."

"I have access to the lab, the mainframe computer, and the room where 181 is stored. However, who comes and goes and when they do so are closely monitored. If I make an unauthorized visit to the storeroom, they'll know it."

"Plus they'll know you bagged the goodies when they discover the missing inventory."

"I've got that covered. I just need to get in and out of the 181 storeroom without being detected."

Fred scratched his chin and cleared his throat. "I'll bet they grafted the new security system onto the old one."

"So how does that help us, Fred?"

"The sensors are new and transmit information lickety-split. However, once they reach the old circuits, information transfer is slowed due to a narrower bandwidth."

"Huh? Come on, Fred, no techy-talk."

"Okay, then think of what happens when traffic on a four-lane highway is choked down to two lanes," Fred said.

"Traffic is slowed down."

"Right you are. Now add rush hour, and traffic comes to a halt or just crawls along—at least for a while."

"I see where you're coming from, but how do we get rush hour?"

"That's my job, but I'll need to hack into the lab's mainframe."

"Like I said, I have computer access. I can just give it to you. My gift."

"Good, that'll make my job easier. In any case, I'll erase the presence of your gift when I'm done. No one will know I've even been there."

Fred paused for a moment. "I'll need to have communication with you at all times. I can't hold traffic back forever. I'll need to warn you when I lose control. So I'll pick up a couple of throwaway cell phones when Sally springs me tomorrow."

"And what about Sally?" Lars asked.

"Don't worry. She won't rat us out. When we gonna do this heist?"

"I'm not sure, but I'll keep in touch."

Lars gave Fred a man-hug. "You're a true friend."

Fred pulled away. "Careful of my wires . . ."

"Whoops! I forgot about your heart monitor."

The two said their goodbyes. Fred was worried. IT is all about details, and he wasn't sure about how his new partner would perform.

On the way out of the hospital Lars reached for his phone, but then thought better of it. Why bother to call? I'll just get more frustrated when she doesn't answer. I'll get carryout on my way home and wait for her there. But why in the hell doesn't she answer her damned phone?

Lars pulled up to his darkened house. He sighed heavily and opened the back door.

"Don't turn on the light!"

"Whoa, Kate! You scared the bejesus out of me!"

The gloom was broken by a streetlight. Kate sat at the kitchen table hunched over a cup of coffee. She lit a cigarette and took a long drag.

"What are you doing, Kate? Do you have some kind of death wish?

You quit smoking years ago. Why start back now?"

"I'm in mourning."

"So you heard about Norma."

"How could I avoid it? She's a tawdry feast for a slow news day. Every cable news jackal has been tearing her apart. Why can't they let her rest in peace? Why do they need to destroy her reputation?"

"I don't know. I haven't seen the news. I've been . . . well, kind of busy."

"They got it wrong, Lars, so damned wrong. Norma was a troubled soul, but she wasn't a closet alcoholic. She wasn't enraged over Mitchell's promotion, and she sure as hell was not a suicidal maniac. No, Lars, no . . . As sure as I'm sitting here, Norma Latchfield was murdered." She paused to further fog the room.

"You don't know that. She may have had a dark side she didn't—"

"She friended me on Facebook, Lars. Norma and I IM, and lately we've shared a lot. That damned ElijahCo somehow got to her." She sighed. "And you know, we're accessories to her murder. The conniving and the half-truths set that brave woman up for the kill. Anywhere along the line we could have saved her by simply telling the truth. Oh yes, it would have cost us dearly, but Norma would still be alive." Kate ended her tirade by smashing the cup and ashtray against the wall.

"Kate—"

"I need to be alone. I'm going to bed. Maybe we can talk tomorrow, but not now. Jesus! I hate you, I hate me, and I despise the day we let ElijahCo into our lives."

She stormed off, leaving Lars bewildered. He sat down and opened the carryout. Bartholomeow smelled the food and jumped up on the table.

"Bad cat! Get off the table. You know what happened the last time you did this."

Bart ignored him and nosed the bag. Lars smiled and reached over to pet him. "Silly me, calling you bad. You're an animal responding to the smell of food. A cat behaving like a cat. Good and bad doesn't apply."

Maybe Kate's exaggerating. The conniving and the half-truths may not be evil after all. Maybe I'm no different than an animal that is instinctively saving its mate. Perhaps I'm nothing but a human behaving like a human.

Lars began to eat his Chinese carryout. He gave Bart a piece of chicken. They both felt better.

He finished eating and went to his basement workbench. He took out his stash of empty vials. One of them contained residual EJ 181. He carefully matched the color of the drug, using food coloring and water. When he was satisfied, he filled the remainder of the vials with the colored water and sealed them. He took his fishing vest out of the closet and filled the many pockets with the vials of imitation 181. He returned the vest to the closet and hung it next to a fresh white lab coat, smiling with satisfaction. All was ready. He yawned and went upstairs to sleep alone on the couch.

Lars rose early the following morning and showered in the guest bathroom, then tiptoed into the master bedroom closet to get clothes. Kate was fast asleep with Bart cuddled up next to her. He opened one eye and then closed it, content he had made the better choice of bed buddies.

Lars drove directly to the hospital and made quick rounds, seeing only the few inpatients that were on study. Dr. Thorndike and the house staff would follow up later. This gave Lars free time before clinic. He settled into his desk chair and mindlessly scanned his email. He tried to put aside Kate's rant, but her words rang true.

Patty's voice broke the silence: "Dr. Lars, are you hiding in there?"

Roused from his reverie, Lars replied sharply, "No, I'm not hiding; I'm simply trying to get some work done before clinic."

Oblivious to the rebuff, Patty said, "I just wanted to remind you of your appointment with Deborah Steiner. You're to meet her at the Morning Grind in fifteen minutes. Better leave now if you're gonna be on time."

He grabbed his coat, thinking, That woman's voice would shatter glass. If it weren't so much work to replace a university employee, she and her rainbow hair would be out of here. Pushing that thought aside, he replied, "Thanks for reminding me. I'm on my way."

"Oh, and by the way, Dr. Lars, I would love a skinny double latte with vanilla soy milk; hold the sugar."

Shaking his head in disgust, Lars walked out the hall door, avoiding Patty.

"Thank you for meeting me here, Lars. Office walls have ears."

"Yes, they do. I commend your caution. What's on your mind?"

"I have major concerns with what's going on between the university and ElijahCo. I felt you would be the best one to share them with."

"I'm all ears."

"I was hired to be special projects manager and the university liaison with ElijahCo. I see myself as the administrative counterpart to your medical role. You're principal investigator for the drug studies. This makes you the university medical liaison to ElijahCo. Does that make any sense?"

Lars nodded. "I think that's a fair assessment."

"I embraced my duties and felt supported as the two of us presented our drug study proposals to the human trials committee. I felt a sense of accomplishment when they were unanimously approved. I also provided Dean Mitchell valuable assistance getting the approval of the university's scientific committee. He thanked me for my services, adding to my sense of accomplishment."

"To be honest, Debbie, I was intimidated by your handling of both committees. I suspect the members were as well. You steamrolled the proposals—"

"No, Lars, not me, but we presented sound proposals which we vigorously championed."

"Call it what you may, but you were impressive."

"Thank you, I appreciate that."

"So, what are your concerns?"

"I thought we made a great team, and I was looking forward to continuing my work with you. However, after the trials started, I became marginalized. Dr. Latchfield negotiated the deal with Dr. McDaniel to renovate the old CDC laboratory. I played a bit part at best."

She paused to suppress her emotions. "I arranged for your tour of the facility when it was completed. I was not invited to accompany you. The numerous meetings in the lab included Drs. McDaniel and Aak and of course you. I was never included. Everything was done behind my back or over my head. Records of the meetings and the ongoing studies were encrypted, leaving me totally in the dark."

Lars shook his head. "Honestly, Debbie, I didn't purposely exclude you. I thought Jenna was ElijahCo's administrative liaison to the university and that she kept you abreast of what was happening. I figured those scientific meetings would bore you, and you had better things to do. So Jenna didn't keep you in the loop?"

"Hardly. I believe she's the one responsible for marginalizing me. She even had the gall to go over my head and directly lobby the dean for Dr. Aak's appointment as interim chair of Pathology. Jesus, Lars, she has Mitchell on speed dial."

"Whoa, Debbie, you may be making this whole thing a little too personal."

"'Too personal'? You're damned straight I'm making it personal! Come on, Lars, you know university protocol as well as I do. Jenna has replaced it with her own agenda."

The two sat in silence. Lars sipped his coffee; Debbie stirred hers. Both were lost in thought.

Lars found words first: "You have valid concerns. Have you spoken to Henry?"

"I haven't been able to catch up to him. I think he's avoiding me. If I were able to tell him, I think he'd say that I was a big girl and should handle issues with Jenna myself." A sardonic grin crossed her face. "I don't think he wants to get in the middle of a catfight."

"Is there something I can do?"

Debbie paused briefly. "If you mean, Can you do something to put me back in the picture here at the university? I think the answer's no. I'm telling you all of this so you'll understand why I'm looking elsewhere for a fulfilling job. I'll add our accomplishments to my résumé. I may also embellish my role in the laboratory renovation. What you can do"— Debbie hesitated a moment—"is write a letter of recommendation—but only if you're comfortable doing it."

"Yes, I certainly will do that for you. I'm flattered that you asked."

"Thank you. Please keep what I've said confidential. I could be fired if certain parties found out. Meanwhile, I'll have a lot of time on my hands. I'm curious about Dr. McDaniel and the secrecy surrounding the drug trials. Oh, I'm not asking you for information. I know you're bound by a letter of confidentiality. Besides, I'll enjoy being a sleuth."

"Just be careful, Debbie."

"What do you mean by that?"

"You said at the beginning of our conversation that walls have ears. Those ears may belong to people who play hardball."

"That's cryptic."

"Consider it a gift from me."

Debbie put on her coat and paused. "Good heavens, I almost forgot! Jenna asked me to invite you to a meeting in the dean's office. Of course, I don't know the agenda. She said there is nothing you have to do to prepare for it." She frowned. "It's just another Jenna secret."

"I'll make myself available. Just text me the time and I'll put it on my calendar."

Debbie nodded, gathered her things, and left.

Lars made his way to clinic via the Oncology Division office. Patty greeted him as a brunette with conventional highlights. Lars couldn't resist: "Your hair today lacks its usual pigmented punctuation. Why the change?"

"Funny story, Dr. Lars. I've always been kind of a free spirit," Patty said. "I like spreading a little cheer wherever I can. I thought my frequently changing hair color might boost people's spirits, but instead, most people just make fun of me. So I decided to return to what nature gave me, with just a hint of joy with the highlights. Now you're seeing the real me."

"I like the real you."

"Thank you. And no, Sally is not in the bullpen or the clinic. She's taking Fred home from the hospital. However, Dr. Thorndike has started clinic. I'm sure he'll appreciate you joining him.

"Speaking of Dr. Thorndike and hair, he certainly is a quiet one. My colored hair had no effect on his bland expression. He didn't even notice when I returned to hair au naturel. So I checked my sources and just got shrugs. I googled him, and there is nothing on him except for the CV we got from ElijahCo. He's either lacking a third dimension or he's hiding it from the rest of the world."

"Maybe it's the former," Lars said. "I'm sure if he had a third dimension, you would have found it by now. You're the master miner of the human spirit."

"You flatter me, Dr. Lars."

"I speak the truth. Now, I'm off to assist the good Dr. Bland."

While on his way to clinic, Lars thought, I loved my euphemism for queen of gossip. That thought brought a smile to his lips.

Thorndike and Sorenson greeted each other with a grunt and went to work. The two plowed through the patient load, constantly behind schedule and losing ground. Sally finally arrived and signaled Lars to step out into the hall. Holding out a small package, she said, "Fred told me to give this to you. It's a throwaway cell phone. He told me about your intended caper—damned crazy if you ask me."

"Is Fred okay with it? I mean, he's an honest man agreeing to do a dishonest deed."

"He's fine. His rationale is that you're the boss man of the drug study. EJ 181 is your drug, so you are entitled to it. ElijahCo is just a paranoid company with greedy fingers trying to hold on to everything it can."

"I'm trying to protect him by minimizing his exposure."

"I'm not worried about Fred. He can hold his own in the world of hacking. He'll remain an anonymous, shadowy figure. You, on the other hand, are risking everything. Is 181 really worth it?"

"Who knows? I feel like a character in a Greek tragedy. I play my role but am ignorant of my outcome. I'm not in control. I'm merely responding to the will of the gods. I can only hope they know what they're doing."

"Here's another loosely translated Chinese proverb for you: If you don't do stupid things, you won't end up in tragedy."

"So you think I'm doing stupid things?"

"I think you've relinquished control of your life to an obsession to help Kate. Your dream of building a cancer center has morphed into a nightmare of intrigue and possibly murder. Don't let the gods, as you call them, trick you into doing stupid things. I don't want your life to end in tragedy."

Lars started to reply but was stopped by Sally placing a hand on his shoulder and guiding him back to clinic. As they walked in she said, "Let me get to work before the two of you get even further behind."

Shortly after lunch Lars got a terse text from Debbie: "The meeting will be 9 AM tomorrow in the dean's office."

Lars drove home with trepidation. He muttered to himself, "I'm not sure I can handle more of Kate's rage. This is so unlike her . . . Well, time to face the music."

The house was lit up when he arrived home. He pulled into the garage and entered the kitchen to find that the remnants of the ashtray had been swept away. He sniffed the air and there was no smoke. He walked into the great room, where Kate was reading with Bart cuddled up in her lap. She looked up and said, "Hi, you."

"Hi, yourself. Are you okay?"

"I want to apologize for last night. I wasn't smoking or throwing the ashtray. It certainly wasn't me spewing hate."

"Yes, I know it was your illness."

"Let's call a spade a spade, Lars. The psychiatrists call it 'dementia with behavioral issues.' Rage is one of the behaviors. It's a horrible feeling being out of control, shrieking at the one I love the most."

"Hey, hon, no harm done. I adore you and will continue to be here, whatever your behavior."

"Please don't lock me up in some memory unit."

"I promise."

"Please let me starve when I can no longer feed myself. I don't want this to go on any longer than it has to."

"Let's talk about that later. How about we go out to dinner? I'm starved."

Kate sighed. "I don't feel hungry, Lars, just exhausted. Why don't you order in for yourself?"

Lars kissed her goodnight and sat down on the couch with scotch and water. Bart sat next to him and loudly meowed as he headbutted him. Lars reached over and scratched him behind the ears. "Okay, okay, little buddy. It's not like you don't get plenty of affection." Bart continued to headbutt him. "All right, already. Let me check your food bowl. Maybe Kate forgot to feed you."

He walked into the kitchen and found the freezer door open with the food inside melting. He glanced at the stove, where a burner had been left on. Bart walked over to his empty food bowl and gave Lars a harsh meow. Lars shook his head. "Sorry she forgot to feed you. It wasn't intentional. The dementia's getting worse, and at an accelerated pace." He turned off the burner, closed the freezer door, and filled the empty food bowl. "Things will be better tomorrow. A woman is coming from the agency. At least the two of you will be safe."

* * *

The atmosphere in the dean's office the next morning was convivial. ElijahCo was doing a victory lap with the success of EJ 75. The university joined in the celebration, with an eye toward future trials. Both parties were eager to show transparency going forward. The rumor mill could destroy the relationship.

Jenna, Dr. Aak, and Dr. Thorndike were present, representing Elijah-Co. The dean, Lars, and Debbie were present, representing senior university administration. Pharmacists, nurses, and laboratory technicians were present as well. All were smiles, even Dr. Thorndike, as they sipped a common Kool-Aid—or so rumor had it.

Dean Mitchell stood up and tapped his cup to bring order. "I'm not one for speeches . . ." That brought a collective chuckle. "Well, maybe just a little, but I'll make this one brief, as we all have work to do."

He turned to Jenna and raised his cup. "Here's to ElijahCo and the exciting research it's brought to our fine campus."

Jenna smiled, raising her cup in response.

Henry continued, "Before I turn this meeting over to Dr. McDaniel, I want to thank all of you for your part in the execution of the EJ 75 drug trial. Cancer patients will enjoy many more days thanks to your efforts and those of your colleagues in the other participating centers. ElijahCo and High Plains University have forged a bond that will be of benefit to all parties concerned. Let me turn over the gavel to Dr. McDaniel."

"Thank you, Dean Mitchell. I would like to echo your thanks to those assembled here." She gave a bow and proceeded as a smile crossed her face. "I would like to announce here that EJ 75 will be on the shelves of cancer centers nationwide. The FDA has granted the drug expedited approval. The brand name we've chosen for EJ 75 will be Ejectica, a fitting name for a drug that so effectively removes cancer from the human body. A press conference will come later today from our Silicon Valley headquarters."

Jenna paused for effect and received polite applause. "ElijahCo will give special consideration for those centers participating in the Ejectica trials, including High Plains University. Of course, those considerations will be in compliance with state and federal laws."

She paused again and received more-enthusiastic applause. "Before I let you good people return to work, I want to assure you that ElijahCo has a new and promising cancer-killing drug: EJ 445. It will be ready for human trials soon. Dr. Sorenson and I will be working out the details." She exchanged nods with a surprised Lars. "So, again, my thanks for your efforts. ElijahCo looks forward to a bright future with High Plains University."

Lars approached Jenna as she was leaving the room. "This is a totally different meeting than I expected. There wasn't a word about EJ 181."

"I found out about the FDA approval late yesterday. I spoke with Henry, and we decided to change the direction of the meeting by having it be more inclusive and keeping it upbeat. I purposely left out 181 and focused on 75—excuse me, Ejectica. I'm hoping the big splash from that drug will drown out the ripple from 181."

"I hope you're right."

"Have you thought about the job offer from ElijahCo? I know I surprised you by adding EJ 445 to your plate. I wanted to show you that High Plains Cancer Center will continue to thrive, and we need your leadership. You and Kate can remain here, while your reach will extend across an ocean."

Lars realized that he couldn't talk to Kate about Jenna's offer. She would become confused and angry because she couldn't wrap her poor brain around it. He had to make an executive decision.

"Well, what do you say?"

"That's an offer I can't refuse. Show me a contract, and I'll sign on the dotted line."

"Good, I'll let the gods in Silicon Valley know you're on board. Two more things you need to know: The first is that Dr. Aak has submitted his resignation to Henry. He's cleaned up the lab data on 181 and will be forwarding to you. He'll destroy the remaining stock of drug tomorrow."

Lars expressed no surprise.

Jenna continued, "The other thing is EJ 181 is getting a new name when it gets to Thailand—"

"So, EJ 181 disappears from the face of the earth. Have you selected the new name?"

"Yes, but it's known to only a few."

"Come on, Jenna, tell me. After all, I'm the principal investigator of the damned drug; I should at least know its name."

Jenna feigned thoughtfulness; she couldn't resist a little teasing. "You make a good point. I guess you do have the need to know. EJ 181 will become Somitra."

"That's a nice name. It just rolls off the tongue."

"Well, it's a person's name in India, which will disguise its true meaning. Somitra is a portmanteau of the Buddhist 'amrita' and the Hindu 'soma.' The words are synonyms for the celestial drink that confers immortality upon the gods and humans alike."

Lars furrowed his brow. "That's clever. Now, is there a portmanteau of EJ 181 and Somitra? That would really conceal the drug from hungry eyes."

Jenna was confused for a moment, then grinned. "You goofball! For a moment I thought you were serious."

"I'm just trying to be helpful. You wanted an upbeat meeting. I'm just going with the flow."

"I'll put together your new contract and send it to you and Henry. Debbie will not be a part of it. She's not one who needs to know."

Lars left the room, thinking, The heist will have to be tonight. I need to finalize plans.

Lars walked over to clinic, speed-dialing Fred on the way.

"Yeah, it's me. We go fishing tonight. Uh-huh. It's gotta be tonight. The trout season ends tomorrow."

The rest of the day passed on turtle legs, and clinic lasted a lifetime. Lars called the agency nurse and apologized for running late. She was angry and threatened to leave, until she was promised a generous gratuity.

Lars didn't pull into his driveway until seven p.m. Kate had prepared Crock-Pot stew with the help of the nurse. It was one of his favorites.

He'd been on pins and needles all day in anticipation of the caper. As time grew near, his anxiety escalated. He took a bite of stew and began to chew. The chunk of beef swelled in his mouth and tasted like sawdust. He bragged on the stew, knowing it would please Kate. She answered with another generous helping. He gave a silent groan and munched on.

Kate returned from the sink, where she had piled dirty dishes. "Is there anything wrong?" she asked. "You seem to be struggling with the stew."

"Oh, no, honey. I'm just savoring every bite."

Fred called right on time, rescuing Lars from the sawdust. "Yes, operator, this is Dr. Sorenson. Please put her on." He paused, pretending to listen. "Yes. Yes, I understand. I'll be over in just a few minutes."

"Don't tell me you have to go back to the hospital? Why can't Chuck Thorndike handle the problem?"

"He had an urgent personal problem to deal with. I volunteered to cover for him. I'm sorry. It seems that no good deed goes unpunished. I really have to go."

"I was hoping we could cuddle tonight. It makes me feel warm and safe."

"I'll make it up to you when I get home."

"Promise you'll wake me?"

"Cross my heart."

Kate retreated to the bedroom. Lately, she was sleeping more and more, courtesy of the dementia. He tucked her in, gave her a kiss, and went to the basement. He put on his fishing vest after assuring himself the vials were safely there, then donned the white lab coat and pocketed the throwaway phone. Before leaving the house, he made certain Kate was asleep. There was a risk to leaving her alone, but he had to do it.

He arrived at the medical center and made the Bluetooth connection, putting the earpiece in place. He chuckled, recalling how he ridiculed people walking down the street in apparent conversations with themselves. Ironically, he was about to join those loonies. He made contact with Fred. "Testing, testing. Am I coming through okay, Fred?"

"I read you loud and clear. Are you hearing me?"

"Yup. I'm so nervous my knees are knocking. Do you mind if I keep talking? It'll help calm me down."

"Not a problem, my friend. I'll keep listening."

"I'm walking down the hall past the dean's office . . . I'm now walking past Pathology and entering the tunnel. Thank God there's no one around . . . I'm walking through the tunnel . . . Talk to me, Fred. I'm feeling scared . . . No joking, Fred! Just talk to me!"

There was no answer. Lars was truly alone.

Jesus, I never thought about losing the signal. He began to feel short of breath and light-headed. His legs felt like lead. Come on, Lars, get hold of yourself. You're hyperventilating. You can do this. Just settle down and pray we get reception back when I really need Fred. Think positive thoughts, like it's good you haven't been caught and you're now at the end of the tunnel. Aha, here's the back door. Now let's get your fingerprints. Good boy. Now open your eye for the retina scanner. Okay, you opened the door. Now let's go up the stairs and down the hall.

His cell phone began to vibrate. "Fred, is that you?"

"I thought something happened to you when your cell went dead," Fred replied.

"It would have happened if I hadn't gone to the men's room earlier. Where in hell did you get these phones?"

"It's not the phones. The tunnel was built like a brick outhouse. We should have expected the outage. Now keep talking. I want to be sure I don't lose you again."

Lars continued to walk, turning his head away from the upcoming cameras. He replied in a hushed voice, "Okay, I'm now in the lab. The cameras see me; I'm doing my best to ignore them. Yes, cameras—I'm just looking for something I lost . . . I'm firing up the mainframe and putting in a couple commands, and now you bucket of chips are under the control of Uncle Fred."

"Good Job, Lars. I'll make a geek out of you yet. Now walk over to the storage room and show it an eyeball. If I start the party too soon, you may not be able to get inside."

"The door's open, and I'm inside the storage closet. It's time for the traffic jam."

"Okay, all signals from the lab are now blocked. Do your thing and do it quickly. I don't know how long I can keep the computer jammed."

Lars began carefully removing the vials of EJ 181, replacing them with the vials in his vest. His hands shook, and he paused a moment. "Settle down, Lars, and for Christ's sake, stop with the hyperventilation."

"Are you finished?" Fred asked, sounding a little frantic. "The traffic is starting to move. It's still piecemeal and garbled, but that won't last long."

"I'm working as fast as my nerves will allow."

"Well, work faster; I'm beginning to see images on the monitor."

Lars felt like he was moving in slow motion, but finally finished the job.

"Lars, you gotta do something, anything, to mess up the computer, or you're dead meat!"

"Damn it! I'm gonna get caught red-handed!" Looking for some way to prolong the traffic jam, he spotted a loose bracket holding up the top shelf. He grabbed it and pulled hard, tearing it loose from the wall. The top shelf dropped onto the second shelf, creating a cascade of broken shelves and shattered vials.

"Lars, what have you done? We've got the mother of all traffic jams."

"I'll tell you later. I'm getting out of here."

Lars walked out of the storage room and closed the door. He disconnected the Bluetooth and put the earpiece in his pocket. He walked nonchalantly toward the conference room, only to be greeted by a security guard coming in the front door. She challenged him, brandishing a Taser. "Who are you and what are you doing here?"

Lars raised his hands in surrender. "I'm Dr. Sorenson, and I was looking for something I lost."

"Let me see your ID."

Lars complied and she studied it carefully. "Okay, you seem to be who you say you are, but how do I know you belong here?"

"Well, for one thing, you can check the list of those with permits."

"I know that, but I can't do it. The computer's down."

Lars breathed a sigh of relief and began to gain confidence. "Then why don't you check with your supervisor? And, if it's not too presumptuous of me, if I promise not to bite, will you put away that Taser?"

"Oh, sorry. I forgot about it."

She was getting frazzled and still held the Taser in a death grip, but, fortunately, pointing it downward. He looked at her name tag and gently addressed her: "Rhonda, take your time getting your super. She'll be able to find my name on her list, and we can both relax."

Rhonda nodded. "I will, but he's a man." She got him on the phone, while keeping an eye on Lars. "Jess, it's me. I've got a situation here in the lab. I was sitting at the reception desk, keeping an eye on the main entrance, when out of the blue, the monitor went dead. I checked the computer, and it was showing gibberish I'd never seen before. I checked the security office. All the monitors were down. So I tried to get into the lab to see if something in there was haywire. The retina scan didn't work, so I had to use the manual override."

She paused to listen to Jess. Lars couldn't have been happier hearing Rhonda's tale of woe.

She continued her conversation with Jess: "Yeah, and that's not the half of it. I got into the lab, and there's this guy in a white coat just casually walking toward the conference room. He must have gotten in through the back door before the network went down. He says his name is Dr. Sorenson and is on the list of those with permits to get into the lab; can you check it for me?" She paused. "Oh, okay. Yeah, I'll see if he'll stay until you get here."

Rhonda relaxed and put away her Taser. "Jess says you're okay and asked if you would—"

"I overheard. I'll stay if it's not too long. I have no intention of spending the night here in the lab."

"He won't be long. He just lives a couple blocks from here. Say, did you happen to see or hear something that might have messed with the system?"

Lars scratched his chin in fake contemplation. "Well, I did hear noise coming from one of the storage rooms."

"Will you show me which one?"

"It's right down the hall."

Rhonda followed closely, taking out her Taser. Lars frowned.

"Don't worry, Dr. Sorenson, it's not meant for you. You know, someone could be hiding in there."

"It's this one, Rhonda."

She paled. "Oh, I'm not authorized to go in there. It's above my pay grade. Let's wait for Jess." She stood guard at the door with Taser in hand.

"That's fine. I don't think I can get you in there now anyway. The retina sensor is still down."

Jess appeared within a few minutes. Lars explained, "I was walking toward the conference room, and I heard a noise coming from in there. About then Rhonda came in and, well, you know the rest."

Meanwhile the system reset itself, and they were able to access the room. Jess was a little tentative. "I'm authorized to enter that room only in a dire emergency."

Jess and Rhonda both turned to Lars, who volunteered, "I'll verify that this is a genuine emergency."

Jess looked relieved and glanced at his watch. "I'm entering the room at eleven hundred hours." He looked at Lars. "The sensors will report me."

Lars nodded. "Go for it, Jess."

The door opened to reveal broken shelves and shattered vials covering the floor.

Lars shook his head. "What a mess!" He restrained the two guards. "Don't go in there without proper protective clothing. It's a chemical spill. You won't need masks or respirators. EJ 181 is not a volatile chemical. But you will need to glove and gown."

Rhonda backed away. "Sorry, I don't want a chemical exposure. I'm trying to get pregnant."

Jess donned the protective clothing and in a manly voice said, "Well, I'm not worried about getting pregnant." He entered the room and studied the scene. "It looks like one of the struts buckled and the whole thing toppled over. Putting in the sensors must have weakened the system. It just happened to give way tonight. Each of the vials that fell out tripped its sensor. The sum of the signals from all those sensors overloaded the system." Jess closed the door. "Let's wait until tomorrow and let the professionals clean up the mess. Oh, and, Dr. Sorenson, just for the record, why did you come here tonight?"

"Thanks for reminding me, Jess." He walked into the conference room. The others followed. He searched the chair cushions. "Aha, here it is." He showed them the pen he found, an engraved Montblanc. "This pen was given to me by my wife on our anniversary. Do you know the trouble I'd be in if I hadn't found it?"

Rhonda volunteered, "If you were my husband, I'd take my Taser to you."

Lars laughed and took his leave. He and Fred kept telephone silence until he got to his car.

Fred broke silence first. "Lars, I'm dying to know what you did in that storage room."

"Well, each of the vials is sitting on a sensor, and—"

"I see where you're going with this. You toppled the shelves, and the sensors went wild. That was quick thinking, my friend. I was concerned you'd panic in a clutch situation. I guess I underestimated you, Mr. Bond; James Bond." The two laughed like schoolboys.

Lars went home and put the 181, aka Somitra, in safe storage. He was exhausted. He crawled into bed and kept his promise. He pushed Bart away and gently awakened Kate. He cuddled her as never before. She gave him a kiss, and both fell asleep. Bart did not share the love and left the room, looking for trouble.

7

LARS GOT UP the next day later than usual. Despite the added sleep, he still felt exhausted. Bart had knocked the place mats and runner off the kitchen table. Salt, pepper, and sugar were scattered on the floor. He cleaned up the mess, cursing the damned cat. Meanwhile, Bart had slipped back into the bedroom, taking his place next to Kate.

Lars just shook his head. A shower, a hot cup of coffee, and memories from his escapade lifted his mood. He woke Kate before leaving. Her gray hair was thinning, and the wrinkles grew deeper and more pronounced. He would have to push the issue of taking Somitra soon, but not this morning. Despite having the drug, he hesitated to give it to her. He would discuss it with her this evening. She was still capable of making her own decisions.

He was entering the physician's parking lot when Jenna called. He put her on Bluetooth. "So, Jenna, what's on your mind this morning?"

"You were a busy boy last night."

"I got my pen back, if that's what you mean."

"Rhonda and Jess told me a wild tale of shattering vials, falling shelves, and disrupted security. Ah, the powers you must possess to create such calamity. I'm impressed."

"I didn't create calamity. I just happened to walk by when it occurred."

"Come on, Lars. You know I'm not a fan of coincidence."

"And I'm not a fan of innuendo. What are you trying to say?"

"My, we are defensive this morning. Lighten up. I was just making a joke."

"If I'm being defensive, I've earned the right, with all the shit that's been flying around here."

"Have you listened to the news this morning?"

"No, I savored the quiet of my Tesla."

"Then prepare to duck more flying feces. Deborah Steiner was struck by a car last night."

"Stop joking around. That's just not funny."

"I'm afraid it's true, Lars. She's in serious but stable condition in University Hospital. It was hit and run. The police are looking for the driver. They think he's a drunk who panicked."

"Once again, the old adage comes true: 'Cars and alcohol don't mix.' Then again, cars and university employment don't mix either. She's the third victim in less than a year."

"Maybe that's just coincidence."

"Jenna, you just told me you weren't a fan of coincidence."

"I'm not, but I must admit there are times when even random events that coincide can appear related—like last night when you walked by the storeroom and the shelves collapsed. You had no motive to cause calamity. Jess said all the vials of 181 were accounted for, and Dr. Aak was going to destroy them anyway. So, fan or no fan, I've got to chalk one up to coincidence."

Lars started to reply, but Jenna cut him off.

"I've got to run. Talk to you later. Try to stay out of trouble, and look both ways before crossing the street."

Lars walked down the hall and was nearing his office when Patty appeared. "Dr. Lars, I came to warn you. The cops that came after Dr. Latchfield died are back. I let them wait in your office, as if I had a choice." She frowned. "It must be about Deborah Steiner's accident—if it was an accident."

"Do you think it was intentional?"

"Twitter's alive with conspiracy theories. Of course, I had to read them all, but I couldn't find one that made a lot of sense. Anyway, let's go to your office through the bullpen. You can grab a cup of coffee and prepare for the grilling. The house staff are rounding with Dr. Charles, and Sally has started clinic, so no one's around but me.

"Oh, with your memory for names, the cops are Ray Garcia and Hal Kramer."

She poured a cup of coffee, and Lars picked it up with shaking hands. Patty noticed and took the cup away. "Maybe coffee's not a good idea. The shakes are not the image you want to convey."

Lars was moved. Patty was showing greater loyalty than just to her next paycheck. He smiled. "Thank you, Ms. Patricia." She gave a nod and went to her desk.

He greeted the officers with a firm handshake. "Good morning, Lieutenant Garcia and Detective Kramer. To what do I owe this second visit?"

Both men fell into their roles: Garcia the inquisitor, and Kramer the note-taker.

"I'm sure you've heard by now that Deborah Steiner was seriously injured last night in a hit-and-run accident," Lieutenant Garcia said. "The media are screaming drunken driver. We suspect foul play. I mean, this is the third high-level university employee to be involved in a fatal or near-fatal automobile incident in less than a year."

"Why come to me with your suspicions?"

"Well, for starters, you spoke to all three victims shortly before their unhappy events."

Lars feigned thoughtfulness. "You keep saying three; I count only two: Dr. Latchfield and now Ms. Steiner. Who's the third victim?"

"The late Dean Hanley is number three. We've been reviewing all the evidence in his case, including his cell phone records. Sure enough, he spoke with you less than twelve hours before his death."

"Should I get an attorney before we talk further?"

"No, no, Doc, we don't suspect you of foul play. We're just hoping you can help piece things together. Did the three victims have a common party that might want to do them harm?"

"Academic medicine is full of intrigue," Lars replied. "One day you and your colleagues are supporting the same cause. The next day you're bitter rivals. In this ever-changing environment, it's hard to know who would do what to whom. That being said, I'm not aware of a person who would wish any of them harm, and certainly no one who would resort to violence."

"You and Ms. Steiner had a conversation shortly before her incident. Can I ask what that conversation was about?"

Lars, remembering his promise to keep her resignation a secret, struggled with Garcia's question. "Deborah Steiner and I worked closely getting university approval for two chemotherapy drug trials. After we got approval, I got busy conducting those trials, and our work relationship essentially ended. Rumor has it we're getting a new drug to study. She wanted to be sure we would work together on that project. We parted with a handshake and a promise to do just that."

"Did she seem frightened, or maybe suspicious of wrongdoing by one of her colleagues?"

Lars paused. "No, she didn't mention anything that frightened her. She's a curious person, but I wouldn't call her suspicious."

"Was there anything going on outside of work that may have been troubling her?"

"Lieutenant Garcia, her personal life never came up in conversation between us. Our relationship was strictly professional. However, life outside the office may be a fruitful area of investigation if you're looking for treachery. I doubt you'll find it in her professional life here at the university."

"Just for the record, Doc, and you don't have to answer, but where were you last night?"

Lars smiled. "I was in our cancer research lab looking for my pen. Two security guards saw me. Believe me, they won't forget my visit."

Garcia turned to Kramer, who was closing his notebook. "Have you got any questions before we let the doc get back to stomping out disease?"

"Yeah, just one. The name ElijahCo keeps popping up. Does Elijah-Co have anything to do with our three victims?"

"ElijahCo is the pharmaceutical company that sponsored the cancer drug trials I spoke about earlier. It was one of their new drugs that brought Deborah Steiner and me together for our most recent conversation."

The detective opened his notebook and began writing again. He looked up for a moment. "Is there anything suspicious about this Elijah-Co company or their drug studies?"

Lars wanted Kramer to stop the fishing expedition. "I'm not aware of anything, and I work closely with their representatives. Detective Kramer, I thought you had just one question. I've counted two. I'm late for clinic; my patients will not be pleased. If you don't mind, I'll be on my way. My secretary will see you to the elevator."

Garcia intervened: "Thanks for your time, Dr. Sorenson. If anything pops up that we should know about, here's another one of my cards. It has my cell number. You can call me anytime.

"Don't bother with the escort. We can find our own way out."

Sally was at her computer when Lars arrived. "Where have you been? Clinic started a half hour ago."

She was pissed, and Lars ruled out a humorous response. It would only fan the fire. So he told the truth. "The boys in blue paid me another visit."

"What?" She turned on music and upped the sound on her monitor.

"Did last night's caper go south? Fred said it was a clean snatch. He kept me up half the night bragging about it."

"No, no, everything's still cool. They questioned me about Debbie Steiner's accident, or should I say non-accident. They're thinking it was foul play."

"Cable news is buzzing about it, and Twitter is lit up with theories."

"So I've heard."

"I'm sure you'll become grist for the gossip mill if a certain party I know was at her desk when the cops came."

"I'm afraid she was. It's possible she'll be discreet about the visit. I saw a different side of her today. One that was thoughtful and, dare I say, loyal."

"You wish! She's addicted to gossip, and you gave her a fix. No, sir, you'll make a splash on Twitter and maybe even twenty seconds of innuendo on cable news."

"Remind me to turn off my television."

"I'll forget because I'll be glued to mine."

"Oh, no, not you too?"

"Gossip goes well with lo mein."

The two paused for a moment.

"Well, Lars, are you going to tell me, or do I have to beg?"

"Tell you what?"

"Chuck's in a family conference. They're really upset about taking away their loved one's EJ 181. They think it's the only thing that can save him from his cancer."

"That drug isn't going to do their loved one a lick of good."

"You know that, I know that, and so does Chuck. He's in there trying to change the minds of a determined patient and family."

"So what does that have to do with me telling you something?"

"I'm trying to assure you we're alone and you can tell me about your visit with the police."

"Sometimes your conversations are nonlinear. You go from A to Q before ever touching B."

"And your point is?"

"I have a hard time following you."

"Maybe I should give you a road map."

"That would help. Let's step into the hall; I'm not sure your music will drown out our voices." Lars found a quiet corner and continued: "The cops are trying to connect the dots."

"And you think I'm nonlinear? What are you talking about?"

"Dean Hanley, Norma Latchfield, and now Debbie were all upper-echelon university employees. All were involved in an automobile-related injury or death. They're looking for a common denominator that might lead them to a serial killer. A detective by the name of Kramer went fishing and found the name ElijahCo. I tried to brush him off, but he's nobody's fool."

"So what are you going to do?"

Lars shrugged. "I think Kramer will run into a roadblock when he finds out Dean Hanley died before ElijahCo came to High Plains. So I'll just watch and wait. Meanwhile, thanks to Fred, I have 181. I need to give it to Kate soon. Probably tonight. Her dementia is spiraling out of control."

"Do you really think that 181 can reverse her dementia?"

"I don't know for sure, and I can't say anything more about the drug to you. In fact, I may be violating my letter of confidentiality right now."

"Damn that letter! Someday I'll use Chinese water torture and get the whole truth out of you, and I don't mean just 181. A few drops of water will be devoted to finding out your true relationship with ElijahCo."

"Does Chinese water torture really work, or is it just another Asian myth?"

"It works on Fred. Now let's get back to killing cancer cells."

Clinic provided Lars a diversion from his growing angst. That relief ended at six o'clock, when he left work and headed home. He walked to his car in deep thought.

Before I had my hands on 181, I could fantasize injecting it into Kate and watching the miracle occur. Now that I can actually treat her, doubts are making a coward of me. What if she doesn't benefit from the drug but suffers terrible toxicity? It may shorten her life, rather than prolong it. My God, I could even kill my wife with it!

Lars opened the car door and began feeling light-headed and dizzy. He gasped for breath as he sat behind the wheel. Get a grip on yourself, Lars, and stop the hyperventilating. He continued his battle for self-control. You risked everything to get 181. Don't squander the opportunity to save Kate. Side effects will be there, and you'll deal with them, just as you have with your study patients. You've strayed beyond the ethical boundaries to get 181. Forget her informed consent. It would be lip service to your flawed morality. Get on with it, man. You're doing this to save her life.

He arrived home and dismissed the nurse, then went to the basement to retrieve the EJ 181. He drew the therapeutic dose into a syringe, capped the needle, and put it into his pocket. He found Kate in bed asleep. He pulled her arm out from under the covers and swabbed her deltoid with alcohol. He only hesitated a moment before injecting the full measure of 181.

"Ouch!" Her eyes opened in fear and pain. "Oh, Lars, it's you! Why did my arm hurt?"

"Everything's going to be all right. I killed the bee that stung you. Go back to sleep. I'll stay here with you." She fell back asleep, and he spent the night by her side.

Early morning found Lars dozing. He awakened when Kate began shivering. She had a shaking chill and awakened with a start. "Lars, I'm so cold. What's happening to me?"

He felt her forehead. "You've got a fever. Maybe you've caught a virus. You'll be fine. I'll get you another blanket and some Tylenol." He slipped into the bathroom and opened the medicine cabinet. He heard a cry from the bedroom and found Kate in the midst of a grand mal seizure.

"Oh my God, Kate! What have I done to you?"

He raced over to the bed to keep Kate from throwing her body to the floor. After an endless three minutes, she stopped seizing. She gasped and started breathing again but didn't respond to him. He stroked her cheek, saying over and over as much to himself as to Kate, "You'll be okay. You've had a seizure. You'll wake up soon. You'll be fine."

But she wasn't all right. She cried out and began to seize again. Lars called 911 and remained with Kate to prevent injury.

His mind switched to doctor mode. Yes, one patient had a seizure after taking 181, and that's why we lowered all subsequent doses, including the one Kate received. Think, Lars, think! Why did Kate have two seizures? And God knows she'll have more if she isn't medicated soon. Why is she different from all the others? Ah, you fool, Lars, you stupid fool! Kate's cells are loaded with prions. You should have known her reaction to 181 would be violent. You should have given her a lower dose.

Again, Kate gasped and resumed breathing, only to start a third seizure. EMS arrived as she ended the third seizure. The paramedic, per protocol, started an IV and medicated her. She had no further seizures but remained unresponsive. She was whisked off to the hospital, accompanied by Lars. Feeling guilty and terribly alone, he phoned Sally from the ambulance and asked her to meet them in the ER.

Sally was just minutes behind the ambulance. She walked into the ER and found Lars off in a corner of the waiting room, alone and forlorn.

"Lars, what's going on? You were incoherent over the phone."

Lars spoke quietly. "I did it. I did it . . ."

"What did you do?"

"I almost killed the person I love more than anything in the world."

"Snap out of it, Lars! You're acting like a driveling idiot!"

Lars looked into Sally's eyes. "Oh, Sally, I gave Kate 181. She was fine for a while and then had a shaking chill and spiked fever. When I went to get her Tylenol, she began having one seizure right after another. It was a nightmare that just wouldn't stop."

Sally was about to reprimand him but decided against it. He was beating himself up and didn't need her to pile on. Putting an arm around him, she gently asked, "Is she okay now?"

"Who knows? She's postictal and heavily medicated. She's unresponsive."

"How much did you give her?"

"The dose level we decided was safe."

"Then why did she have the seizure?"

"I don't know," Lars lied.

Their conversation was interrupted by the emergency room doctor. "Hi, Sally. I didn't recognize you for a moment, probably because you're not wearing your white coat."

"That's okay, Erv. Lars and I are the loved ones this morning. How's Kate doing?"

Erv glanced at Lars.

"It's okay," Lars said. "Sally's permitted to know."

"Well, vital signs are good. The combination of seizures and medication will keep her asleep for a while. Based on what you said, Lars, I think she had febrile seizures. I'm a little concerned about their repetitive nature and the fact that she's an adult, but I think her dementia contributed to the problem. You know, abnormal brain cells subjected to stress, like high fever, can do bad things."

Lars nodded, but Sally pressed the issue. "Then why did she have the fever?"

"That's a good question. We're doing blood studies, looking for a possible infection. It was probably some virus, but we may never know. I'm also getting an MRI. It's routine with first seizures, particularly when they're repetitive. She'll also be our guest in the ICU. I don't want her on the general neurology floor. She has just too many unsolved problems, like the fever. I want her monitored closely."

Sally and Lars went straight to the ICU to await Kate's arrival. A smiling nurse greeted them in the waiting room. "Sally, it's good to see you again! We need to get together for coffee. We have a lot of catching up to do."

She turned to Lars. "Dr. Sorenson, I'm so sorry to hear about your wife. I can assure you we'll take good care of her. Radiology called to let us know her MRI has been delayed a few minutes. Meanwhile, you can wait in your wife's room."

"Thank you."

The nurse guided them into the ICU proper. It consisted of a long, wide corridor with patient rooms on either side. A nurses' station was positioned facing the corridor across from Kate's room. The ward secretary waved to the nurse. "Whoops, I have to go. It's change of shift, and I need to give report." She pulled an extra guest chair into the room and said, "Make yourselves comfortable while you wait." She pulled the curtain shut as she left.

Sally sat; Lars paced. "I should never have done it. I acted like a fool, obsessed with the impossible . . ."

"Desperation clouds the clearest of minds. And that's not a proverb, Chinese or otherwise. I've merely been listening to you obsess—

Sally was interrupted as the curtain abruptly parted. Kate came rolling in on a stretcher, unconscious and with a tube sticking out of her nose. A nurse pumped life-giving oxygen into the tube. Kate was quickly transferred to the waiting bed. A cadre of ICU personnel went into action. One of them guided Lars and Sally into the waiting room, admonishing, "Wait here. Dr. White will be with you as soon as possible. Right now, she has her hands full with your wife." Before Lars could respond, she was gone.

Lars crumbled into a chair and looked to Sally with pleading eyes. "What is happening to my Kate?"

Sally frowned and shook her head. "I'm as much in the dark as you are. Whatever is going on in there can't be good."

"Maybe I can help. I know 181 better than anyone in the world—

Sally restrained him. "You're Kate's husband; you'd be a useless emotional mess. What's the old saying? 'Lord, defend me from my family and friends. My enemies I can handle myself.'" She stopped, realizing she was making matters worse.

Lars, the man who was always in charge, was rendered helpless by the situation. He needed to get back at least a measure of control. Sally took his hand, as if to guide him.

"But you're right," she said. "You do know 181. You can best serve Kate by trying to figure out what 181 is doing to her. Think out loud. It will help you focus. Besides, I need to know more about that damned drug if I'm going to be of help. So talk to me about what it's doing to Kate, and that letter of confidentiality be damned."

Lars switched from helpless husband mode to controlling doctor. He was silent for a moment, calculating how much he should tell her. "I hate it when you're right, Sal. I'd make a fool of myself in there. And yes, I need to share with you what I know about 181. You can put away the water torture."

Mission accomplished, Sally released his hand and waited for him to start his tutorial.

"EJ 181 is a complicated molecule that doesn't give up its secrets easily," he began. "It's an immune modulator. That is, it turns on parts of the immune system while turning off others—"

Sally interrupted: "So 181 is turning on the part of Kate's immune system causing fever and chills?"

"Well, not directly. Her fever and chills are the result of an interaction between the drug and an unknown protein. Dr. Aak is still working on that."

Sally unconsciously raised her hand. "Is the intensity of the reaction to 181 related to how much of that yet-to-be determined protein is in her body? She must have more of it than normal, since only one of our patients had a febrile seizure. That patient was given a higher dose than what you said you gave Kate."

Sally's speculations were too close to 181's true effect. Lars initiated diversion tactics. "I'm afraid that's too simplistic. It fails to consider the modulating effect 181 has on other parts of the immune system, which may directly or indirectly cause fever. The drug may also have interactions with extraneous proteins such as antibodies generated by Kate's influenza vaccine this year or the venom from the bee sting she had last summer." He sighed. "That's what I mean about EJ 181 keeping its secrets."

An imposing woman in scrubs entered the waiting room and walked toward them. "I'm Dr. Shanice White, one of the new intensivists. You must be Dr. Sorenson."

Lars acknowledged her and introduced Sally. "Please tell me what's going on with my wife," he said.

"Well, as Erv told you earlier, we'd been operating under the assumption your wife had febrile seizures, probably related to a viral infection. However, we started getting lab results back, and I've begun to doubt that diagnosis. Every organ in her body appears to be inflamed. We didn't want to delay treating her, so we got a quick CT scan of her head, rather than an MRI. It shows her brain to be swollen, no doubt a response to the same process affecting the rest of her organs."

Lars was frightened but also intrigued. "What's causing the inflammation?"

"It's as if she's allergic to her own body. It's bizarre. Frankly, I've never seen anything quite like this before. However, speculating on the cause of her illness can wait. Treating her can't. As you well know, inflamed organs don't function properly—"

Lars interrupted: "Are you telling me Kate's dying?"

"Her condition is critical, and we need guidance from you on how aggressive to be—"

"What do you mean, how aggressive you should be? She's my wife; she means everything to me!"

"Well, I've reviewed her advance directives, and she was clear about no heroics if her condition was hopeless."

"You said she was critical but nothing about hopeless."

"Her condition is not entirely hopeless, but she has the underlying dementia. The severe insult her brain is now suffering can only aggravate her dementia and potentially leave her in a vegetative state."

"Do you mean she may never wake up?"

"I'm afraid that's a real possibility. In my opinion, the best we can hope for is her awakening with more problems thinking and remembering. Her dementia is bound to be worse."

Lars paused to collect his thoughts.

"Dr. White, what I'm hearing from you is only the worst-case scenarios. Allow me to present another possibility. I have a friend who's a physicist. We got to talking about the differences between the physical and the biological sciences. My friend lives in the comfort of immutable laws. Take gravity, for instance. Every single time my friend drops an apple, it falls to the earth. The certainty of gravity provides predictability with no room for an alternate outcome.

"On the other hand, our current knowledge of biological systems does not provide such predictability. Replace the apple with a human body and replace the certainty of gravity with our fragmented knowledge of biology, and we'll get some surprises. The human body will fall to earth on a regular basis. However, periodically, and with no apparent reason, that body will rise into the air, leaving us in awe of our ignorance."

"That's called a miracle, Dr. Sorenson."

"It's comforting to appeal to the supernatural when transgressing the boundaries of our understanding. Please proceed with full effort to save my wife's life."

"Then I'll get the consent for hemodialysis. Your wife's body desperately needs help clearing waste products from itself." She turned on her heel and walked away.

"Nice job pissing her off, Lars," Sally said.

"I have to give 181 a chance to show its therapeutic potential."

"Let's hope there is one."

Four hours and too much coffee later, Lars sat vigil at Kate's bedside. Sally had gone to salvage clinic by enlisting the aid of Dr. Thorndike and the senior resident on service.

The mechanical sounds of the dialysis machine blended with the rhythmic tones of Kate's ventilator to produce a hypnotic effect on an exhausted Lars. The voice of the dialysis technician awakened him with a start. "I'm finishing up here—oh, I'm sorry I disturbed you, Dr. Sorenson. I'll get another set of vital signs and draw blood for post-dialysis lab studies. I won't unhook your wife from the machine until I get the go-ahead from Dr. White. I'm sure she'll want to give you an update once those labs are back."

He disappeared and returned with a fresh cup of coffee. "This should get the cobwebs out. I thought you'd want to be alert when Dr. White comes to see you."

Kate's nurse came in to take her own set of vital signs and to check the ventilator settings. Lars gave up trying to remember her name and just blurted out, "How's she doing?"

The nurse glanced over at the exhausted man and took pity. "Her vital signs are good, and we've been able to lower the ventilator settings."

"And?"

She feigned ignorance, trying to spare him bad news. "And what?"

"What about her neuro checks?"

She sighed. "I'm afraid I've seen no improvement. She's as flaccid as a ragdoll."

Lars couldn't hide his disappointment. He slumped back into his chair and said, as much to himself as to the nurse, "I can't give up now. I have to give her a chance. Is that so unreasonable?"

The nurse chose not to answer his question. "I'll see if her lab results are back." She stepped out of the room, leaving him terribly alone with Kate.

A few minutes later, Dr. White came into the room with nurse in tow. "We have Kate's lab results."

Lars stood up and braced himself for the worst.

"Actually, they look pretty good. She's making urine now, and we turned down the ventilator," Dr. White said. "My major concern is her brain. It's not showing us any function by clinical examination."

"You mean she may be brain dead?"

"I'm getting a neurology consult. I have no choice at this time. I have to initiate our brain death protocol."

Lars sat down to keep from falling.

"Oh my God!" he croaked, and broke into tears. The nurse put a hand on his shoulder and offered a tissue.

Dr. White maintained her distance. "The neurologist will be seeing her later this afternoon. Meanwhile, I'll order an EEG and a repeat CT scan of her brain. I'll let the neurologist order anything else she might like.

"You look totally exhausted, Dr. Sorenson. Your wife is stable, and I'll meet you after the neurologist sees her."

Lars stiffened his spine. "Who's the neurologist?"

"It will be Dr. Changchang O'Reilly."

"Good. I want to meet with her as well—alone."

"Of course you can, Dr. Sorenson." Her prickly response was almost palpable, but Lars needed to reassert control. He was not about to let Shanice White railroad Kate into an early trip to the morgue. She didn't know about EJ 181. He couldn't share that information with her. He could only dig in his heels and buy time with the hope that Kate would recover.

His thoughts were interrupted by Dr. White. "The point I was trying to make is that you need some rest. We'll be in contact with you if something unexpected happens. Later today you may have to make some hard decisions. They will be better, if not easier, decisions if you get some rest. Let's meet about seven this evening. That will also give you time to meet with Changchang. If you have no further questions, I'll see you at seven."

Dr. White returned to the ICU. The nurse lingered. "She's right: you need rest. You also need time out of here to help gain perspective. Don't worry; I'll take good care of your Kate."

Lars found himself in the doctor's parking lot looking for his car. He was about to report it stolen when the thought struck him: Oh, for heaven's sake, I rode in the ambulance with Kate. My car's at home.

His cell shattered the silence with the theme song from Chinatown. "Sally, what's up?"

"I haven't heard from you for hours."

"Kate made it through dialysis. Her lungs and kidneys seem to be recovering." He hesitated. "They're worried about her brain. Dr. White initiated the brain death protocol."

"Oh, Lars, I'm so sorry. Where are you? You shouldn't be alone, not now."

"I'm in the parking lot. I was looking for my car . . ."

"Your ride today was the ambulance, with Kate."

"Yeah, I just figured that out. I'm trying to get home. Changchang O'Reilly is seeing Kate later today. After that, I'm going to powwow with her and then meet with White at seven this evening." Lars yawned. "After my auto adventure, I realize how wasted I am. I'm going home for a nap."

"Okay, but I'll be at your meeting with Dr. White. I don't want you to be alone, no matter what she has to say."

"You must be exhausted as well."

"We had a short clinic today. I'll be there tonight with bells on my toes."

"Thanks, Sal. You're a real pal. See you at seven."

Lars dialed Uber and went home.

Two hours later, Lars awoke to a loud meow, followed by crushing chest pain.

"Jesus, Bart, why did you do that?"

The cat continued scolding him as Lars pushed him off his chest and onto the floor.

"Oh, I get it. Your food bowl is empty. Sorry, buddy. Kate's in charge of that. But honestly, couldn't you have been more subtle than the high dive from my dresser?" He went into the kitchen, yawning and doing the baseball pitcher's scratch. Bart followed, continuing his reprimand.

"Here's food and water, so stop with the yowling. You'd think you owned the place."

After making coffee and sitting down at the kitchen table, he glanced at his watch. "There's no going back to sleep after your wake-up call, Bart. So what do I do before seeing Changchang?" He sighed. "No way am I going to the office; Patty would drive me nuts with the questions. Going to the lab is out of the question; I'm not up for verbal jousting with Jenna. I can't stay here; I don't want to be with the horrible memories of this morning." He nodded his head. "I know: I'll go see Debbie Steiner. I've been meaning to do that since her accident. I heard she was out of the ICU."

Bart stopped eating long enough to give a grateful purr. Lars scratched his ear and remarked as he headed for the shower, "You're about as useful as a bra at a mammogram, but I still love you, little guy."

"Knock, knock." Lars addressed the half-open door to Debbie's room.

A surprised voice greeted him: "Is that you, Lars?"

"Yup. Are you up for a visit?"

"Only if you want to see The Wreck of the Hesperus."

Lars walked in to find a battered woman, bruised, bandaged, and cast from head to toe.

"You're the last person I expected to see." Debbie's tongue was thickened by morphine.

"Why do you say that? I thought we were friends."

"You warned me and I didn't listen. This is the price I paid."

"I don't know if it's me or your pain meds, but I still don't understand."

Debbie groaned as she struggled to get comfortable. "Remember the last time we met, when I asked you for a letter of recommendation?"

"Yes, and I agreed. I'm feeling guilty, but I haven't written it yet. Then again, you never got back to me about who and where I should send it."

"Never mind that. I told you I had suspicions about Jenna McDaniel, and I liked being a sleuth—"

"I remember, and I told you to be careful."

"You said that was your gift to me. Well, I ignored your warning, and here I am, damned near dead."

"You don't think I had anything to do with this?"

"No, no, but somebody did. My professed accident was a purposeful attempt to kill me. I caught my heel on the curb. Jesus, I don't know why we women torture ourselves with spiked heels. But that's for another day. Where was I? Oh, yes, I caught my heel on the curb, slowing me down. The van sped up too soon and hit me with a glancing blow. Otherwise, I would have walked into the street and the asshole would have hit me straight on. I'd be dead for sure." She licked her lips. "Damn, if it's not pain, it's cotton mouth from the pain meds. Would you give me my water?"

Lars put the straw to her lips, and she drew water, rinsing her mouth. "That's better. Thank you."

"It's the least I can do."

"I don't know how much sense I'm making with this narco-fog, but

I'm damned scared they're going to finish the job. You warned me, so you knew I was in danger. I don't know how you knew that, and I'm not asking for details. What I am asking is that you get word back to whoever needs to know that I'm off the case. No more sleuthing for this girl. I learned my lesson. I'm going to get rehabilitation as far away from High Plains as I can get—and forgive me for not saying where. I don't know what kind of shape I'll be in after therapy, but I think it will be retirement with disability. So there's really no reason for them to finish the job."

She began to weep. "They don't have to kill me. The part of me that would pursue them was killed by that van. I just want the rest of me to live in peace."

She coughed and groaned. "Tell them I even told the police it was an accident, that my tripping on the curb caused me to fall into traffic."

Lars was uncertain whether the version of the story she told him was the truth, or the version she told the police. When bodies are mangled, minds become muddled. She needed reassurance that she was safe. That was his second gift to her. He left her room as she was falling asleep.

8

LARS FOUND DR. Changchang O'Reilly hunched over an EEG machine at Kate's bedside. She was a study in contrasts, having her father's height and her mother's features. A second generation Irish Chinese American, she claimed her parents had met on a boat bound for America, leaving those listening to wonder where that boat might have come from. Lars found her to be a brilliant, witty neurologist.

"Oh, hi, Lars. Your wife and I are having a conversation." She noted his surprised look and explained, "Well, not a conversation in the usual sense, as she can't speak, but she's definitely communicating with me. Her brain waves speak volumes."

"You mean she's not brain dead?"

"Whoever said she was?"

"Well, Dr. White initiated the brain death protocol."

"Brain death is a bunch of nonsense. If the rest of you is dead, so is your brain. If your brain is dead, so is the rest of you. We're a set of organs connected in series, like cheap Christmas tree lights. We're not a house full of appliances to be turned off individually, with the last one being the brain. But enough of my polemic. To answer your question, no, your wife is not brain dead."

"But her neurological exam earlier showed no signs of life."

"I came right over when I got the consult and did a quick EEG. Brain waves don't lie if you can read their truth."

"And Kate's truth is what, Changchang?"

She replied with mild arrogance, "Your wife was having closely spaced seizures, leaving her no time to recover. She appeared dead, at least to the casual examiner."

He gave a sigh of relief and walked over to Dr. O'Reilly.

"See, Lars, now that I have her seizures under control, she has diffuse slowing of her brain waves. She is telling us her brain had a nasty insult, but there's still life."

His heart quickened. "You mean she may recover?"

"I don't know. She hasn't been able to tell me one way or the other. She keeps repeating over and over that her brain has suffered terribly."

"So what do we do?"

"Wait to see if her communication can go beyond repetitive complaints."

"And if she can't?"

"Well, let's not go down the road of ifs; it only leads to frustration. You have a meeting with Shanice White at seven tonight. Meanwhile, Kate will be on continuous EEG monitoring.

"Oh, by the way, her repeat CT scan showed much improvement. That's of limited prognostic value. It tells us the tornado is gone but says little about the damage done. The whole thing is damned confusing, if you ask me. So many whats and whys remain. We may never understand the evolution of your wife's illness. One day, I want to discuss with you in detail the events leading up to Kate's seizures. There are missing pieces that you may be able to provide . . ."

Lars started to respond, but Changchang put a firm hand on his shoulder. "Not now. You've been through too much today—with more to follow at seven. Shanice invited me to your meeting with her. Do you mind?"

"By all means, please be there."

Changchang released her grip. "I have to finish rounds, but I'll be here at seven."

Lars wondered what she meant by "missing pieces that he might provide," but he put it aside. There was enough to worry about. He remained at bedside. Where else could he go?

Sally showed up early and gave Lars a hug. "What did Dr. O'Reilly have to say?"

"Kate's still alive, but her brain is only sending out injury signals. Her apparent lifelessness was due to subclinical seizures, which Changchang has under control. Kate needs time to recover from the seizures to see what brain function remains. It's kind of like rebooting a computer: we can't tell how much damage has been done to the hard drive until the computer is up and running again. Meanwhile, I'm just sitting here watching brain waves on the monitor."

Sally felt encouraged by the news but could see Lars wasn't sharing that feeling. If she were too upbeat, she would drive him away. It was the control thing—and the waiting. Everyone knew Dr. Lars Sorenson did not do wait well, even if he had brain waves to entertain him.

"I can understand your frustration, Lars. This waiting helplessly is getting to me as well."

"It's not just the waiting. Dr. White acts like Kate's already in the past tense. She's convinced that Godot will never arrive, so let's close the curtain and move on to another play."

"I'm not taking sides, but I can understand where she's coming from. Shanice sees you as just another husband who refuses to let go of a dying wife. You and I have seen that over and over with the families of our cancer patients. The family just wants one more treatment for their loved one, interpreting terminal restlessness as an encouraging sign."

Lars shook his head. "You have a point, but I'm not budging. Kate gets her chance."

Sally could see the conversation was going nowhere, but at least Lars felt empowered fighting the angel of death. She moved to a neutral topic. "Did you get some rest, or have you been sitting here all afternoon staring at the monitor?"

"Yeah, I got enough to keep going. I also visited Debbie Steiner."

"How's my not-so-much BFF doing?"

"She's a mess, physically and mentally. She's getting as far away from High Plains as possible, and as soon as possible. I think she has the makings for a bad case of PTSD."

"Did someone really try to kill her, or did she just have a horrible accident?"

"She doesn't know and, for that matter, may never know. Right now, her world is occupied by pain and narcotics. What little space that remains is occupied by sheer terror. Trauma does bad things to people."

"Now you've got me on a guilt trip."

"You bought the ticket, Sal."

"Is that a jigger of cowboy wisdom?"

"Nope, I'm sticking to your metaphor."

Changchang walked in with a Mandarin greeting, "Nín ho, Sally, and hello again, Lars."

Sally responded with a polite nod, "Nín ho, Dr. O'Reilly."

Changchang studied the EEG monitor. "I see Kate's still complaining. I can't say I blame her."

Dr. White walked in quietly without interrupting Changchang.

"The question becomes whether that's all she'll ever be able to tell us. Prognostication is a murky art at best. However, recent studies suggest that trying to evoke a response may be helpful."

Lars perked up. "So we don't just sit here and watch the monitor?"

"Oh, we continue to watch the monitor, but with a focus on the signals coming from her parietal lobes. They're the parts of the brain that make a human experience out of information coming in through our senses. If we can evoke a response from the parietal lobe, it tells us someone is in there capable of more than just complaining of injury. It predicts recovery."

Lars was quick to respond. "What do we do, pinch her or yell at her?"

"Nothing so violent. It appears the best way to evoke a response from Kate's parietal lobe is for someone she loves to express her name, and that, my friend, would be you. Let me adjust the electrodes so we can tune in to the proper site in her brain."

Changchang quickly went about her task, which Lars felt took a lifetime. "Okay, Lars, you're on."

"Kate . . . Kate. It's Lars, honey. I adore you."

Changchang studied the EEG for a moment and then announced, "Someone's home. Kate's in there and appears to be able to create an experience from your voice, Lars. Nothing is one hundred percent, but this suggests strongly that recovery is possible."

Dr. White chimed in: "Recovery to what? A demented state?"

"I don't know. I've not examined this woman or treated her before this afternoon. I don't know whether she was irreversibly demented or suffering from a reversible delirium before the events of today. We need, or rather she needs, time to declare herself."

All were speechless until Dr. White spoke again: "You heard the doctor. Let's give the lady a chance."

Those words danced into Lars's head, bringing relief from the burden of his guilt. "Just maybe EJ 181 will keep its promise," he whispered to Sally. She gave him a knowing look and with a half-smile replied, "Here's hoping, my friend."

The two of them walked to the parking lot in silence. They reached Sally's car, and she drove off, leaving him alone. He checked his voice mail. He'd missed six calls, all from Jenna. He returned her call, and she immediately answered. "I've heard rumors about Kate. I hope they're not true."

"She had seizures, probably related to fever and underlying mental condition." Lars had stopped using the term dementia.

"Is she okay?" Jenna's voice had an unusual urgent quality.

"She's critical but appears to be recovering. It's too soon to know for certain."

"Hey, no more sending me to voice mail." Her voice had changed to a sharp tone. "I need you to keep me posted." She paused.

"Hmm, fever and seizure—that sounds like a familiar combination of symptoms. Didn't one of our Somitra study patients have them?" she asked.

"Somitra?"

"You still can't get used to EJ 181's new name."

Lars was starting to feel defensive. "Lots of things can cause fever and seizures."

"I'm not an MD, so please indulge me. Give me some examples."

"Taking Kate's illness into consideration, that symptom complex could be caused by a kidney infection, pneumonia, or influenza."

"Does she have any of those maladies?"

"No, she doesn't." Lars was trying not to let anger cloud his judgment.

Jenna kept pushing. "Have you eliminated the possibility of a Somitra overdose?"

"How could she get the drug? The inventory of 181 has been destroyed. Come on, Jenna, I've had one hell of a time. My wife is on a ventilator in the ICU, and you're implying I put her there."

"You know me and coincidence."

"And now you know me and innuendo."

Jenna could hear Lars fraying and backed off.

"I'm not implying anything, Lars. I know you would never intentionally hurt Kate. I think we ought to leave this conversation where it stands. You've had a tough time of it, and I'm frustrated from futile attempts to reach you today. Speaking of which, I wanted to let you know we've had new developments. I was going to go over them with you this evening, but that can wait. Get some sleep, and meet me in the lab tomorrow morning at seven thirty. Dr. Thorndike can cover rounds. We'll be done in plenty of time, so you won't miss clinic. I'll text Sally."

"But I thought Chuck was going to Bangkok to oversee studies there."

"Like I said, there have been new developments. See you at seven thirty."

Lars started to mull over the conversation with Jenna but gave it up. His brain was fried from the day's events. He got in the car and went home.

Lars opened the door to a darkened house and an angry cat. Bartholomeow had turned over his water fountain to protest his empty food bowl. He'd tossed the salt pig on the floor for good measure.

"Bart, you're a self-centered little bastard. You won't get dinner until I clean up your mess . . . Hmm, speaking of dinner, I wonder if there's anything for me to eat."

He found only leftover oatmeal, a package of Oreo cookies, and a can of beer. He put things in order, fed Bart, and poured himself a stiff drink. He slumped into a chair, too exhausted to put together better fare. He sipped his scotch and began eating the oatmeal. "Hey, Bart, you're eating better than I am. Oh well, at least I'm getting fiber."

The day's special, scotch and cereal, left him unsatisfied. He grabbed the cookies and beer and flopped down on the couch. He took a sip of brewsky and gobbled a cookie. "Not bad," he declared. Bart came over and crawled up onto his belly. "Okay, buddy, I'll share." Man and cat finished the cookies before both fell asleep. Bart would only eat the creamy centers.

Lars got up early so he could see Kate before his meeting with Jenna. He made certain Bart had food in his bowl and water in his fountain. He took a moment to hide a few kitty treats for entertainment and to save the salt pig from further calamity.

Driving to the medical center with his YETI cup filled with coffee gave Lars time and a clear head to rerun last evening's conversation with Jenna. She had demanded, not asked, to be kept informed of Kate's progress. This need was fueled by more than just a fondness for Kate. The repeated confrontations about 181 were getting closer to the truth. Jenna was really pissing him off.

Stay cool, Lars; don't let her get to you was becoming his new mantra.

"Good morning, Dr. Sorenson." Kate's night nurse was busy taking vital signs. "Your wife is doing better this morning. After shift change and Dr. White comes in, we're going to extubate her. She no longer needs the ventilator."

"Good news so early in the morning is most welcome."

"She began to fight the respirator during the night and showed spontaneous movement of all four extremities, so we had to sedate her. We'll back off on that once we remove the tube from her airway."

"Good, good . . . I can't stay long. I have a mandatory meeting," he said. "We all have to earn our daily bread. Can I give her a hug before I leave?"

"Of course; you can even give her a kiss. I promise not to look." The nurse smiled as Lars bent over Kate and whispered in her ear. She moved in response to his gesture, which thrilled him.

"My, my, Dr. Sorenson, you do have a way with the ladies. Look at her EEG monitor."

He looked up to see a transient quickening of the brain waves and beamed. "Good, she still likes me. I'll be back later and spend more time with her."

Lars walked over to the lab, dreading the meeting with Jenna. He found her at the computer.

Without looking up, she spoke: "I've heard nothing from you all night, so I assume Kate's okay."

"Her night nurse said they were going to wean her off the respirator this morning. She also had spontaneous movements during the night. So I remain hopeful."

Jenna continued to be occupied by her computer.

Lars started getting impatient. "I hope you didn't set up the meeting so I could watch you answer emails."

"Of course not, and I'm not answering emails. I'm setting up a virtual conference. I want you to get to know the new assistant medical director of the Somitra project in Bangkok. His name is Dr. Armand Cooper. He's an American expat living with his wife in Bangkok. He's retired military—in fact, he briefly served with Charles Thorndike. His wife is Thai, and with the cost of living lower there, they settled in Bangkok. We're lucky to have him. He's an experienced researcher and is, ah, discreet. As a bonus, he speaks the language."

"But I thought we agreed that Chuck would be our man in Bangkok. His experience with 181 is second only to mine."

"You're right; we did. Chuck has personal reasons for wanting to stay here. ElijahCo was going to put pressure on him to go to Bangkok. Then Armand became available, and we grabbed him. Besides, you're going to need Chuck here."

"I don't think so. Things have really slowed down since we closed 75 and 181. We can handle the traffic with our current staff and a little help from the community docs."

"Au contraire, my friend. Traffic will be flowing again soon. The FDA has approved EJ 445 for human trials. ElijahCo is offering High Plains the opportunity to participate in those trials. We just have to get the protocol through the university committees, which shouldn't be a problem if the committees remember the success of Ejectica and have amnesia for the failure of 181. Besides, Dean Mitchell is behind the project, and the committee members won't oppose him."

"That's great news, but it would have been nice if the university's principal investigator was a part of the decision-making process."

"Oh, Lars, you're so sensitive—always the need to be in control. You were busy with Kate, and the gods in Silicon Valley wanted to get things moving. You're still the PI."

Before he could reply, Jenna glanced at her computer monitor and signaled him to come over. "I want you to meet Dr. Armand Cooper."

"Hello from Bangkok!" Dr. Cooper said. "Nice to meet you, Lars. Jenna has nothing but good things to say about you. My friends call me Mando, and I hope you will, too."

The image of a smiling man in his midsixties was on Jenna's monitor. His white hair was combed over, and his face was nicotine wrinkled. The camera caught only his head and neck, but the jowls suggested he never passed up a bowl of sticky rice.

"No formalities at this end either, Mando," Lars said. "Jenna says we have a common acquaintance."

Mando laughed. "You mean Chuck Thorndike? He's quite the party-boy—at least he was when we served together."

Lars was curious about what Mando knew about the man of mystery. "That's certainly not the Dr. Charles Thorndike we know. When and where did the two of you share duty?"

"We met in Afghanistan after 9/11. He was fresh out of training."

Lars continued to pry. "So he was in the medical corps with you?"

"No, no. Neither of us were docs at the time. We were in special ops. We were together only a few months when he got shot up pretty badly in a Taliban ambush. They transferred him stateside. Some folks you never forget, and old Chuck Thorndike is one of them."

Lars just smiled. How people change, he thought. Now old Chuck is as memorable as the hallway rug.

Mando continued, "Enough about the old days. Jenna filled me in on the Somitra project. We're getting our first participant tomorrow."

"I'd recommend getting blood prion levels before giving the first dose of EJ 181—excuse me, Somitra," Lars said. "If levels are high, you might want to start with a lower dose."

Jenna gave Lars a quizzical look but said nothing.

Mando scratched his chin. "It's gonna be tough to do that. The peasant type is not all that reliable, nor mobile for that matter. I plan to get the pretreatment prion blood levels at the time of the first dose of Somitra. I guess we could do it your way, but I'd have to give them more money, which would strain my budget."

"Well, you're boots on the ground in Bangkok, Mando. I'll trust your judgment. If you don't know prion levels prior to the first treatment, at least you'll need to warn them about possible side effects, including fever, chills, and possible seizures." Again, he got the look from Jenna.

"Roger that, Lars." Mando's look suggested otherwise.

Lars decided to end the conversation. Mando was going to do what Mando wanted to do, and he was getting tacit support from Jenna. "Good luck, and please keep me informed. Say hello to Dr. Aak for me."

"I'll do that. Say, listen. When we get together here for a real meeting, I want you to meet the missus; she makes an awesome pad thai. Maybe you can bring your bride with you. ElijahCo ought to spring for the trip."

"I'll hold you to that and will be looking forward to meeting your wife."

The monitor went blank.

"Jenna, I'm getting bad vibes from Bangkok. If Mando's assessment of our study population is accurate, we may have trouble with follow-up."

"Mando knows what he's doing with those people. Money has power, and despite what he says, Mando has a very generous budget." Jenna paused. "What's with your sudden concern about Somitra's toxicity?"

"I keep thinking about the patient of mine who had the seizure and the others who had chills and fever. I'm afraid just one bad event would ripple through the slum population, jeopardizing the study."

"Oh, Lars, you're such a worry wart. Have another cup of coffee, and let's get started on the EJ 445 proposal. The sooner we get it through the committees, the sooner we can start patient accrual. We can get a lot done before your clinic starts."

"Has the dean appointed a replacement for Debbie Steiner? I'm going to need help getting the proposal showtime ready."

"You're looking at her. I think I can comfortably wear her hat and mine, sans scheduling of course. I'll leave that to my secretary. I've made a hard copy of the proposal we submitted for EJ 181. We can use it as a rough draft because that trial was also the first introduction of a drug in human beings. However, we want to make certain there's not a whisper about 181 in the new proposal. We want to draw attention away from it."

Lars was unsettled by Jenna's consolidation of power. On the one hand, it reduced the cast of characters, which was good. The fewer people who knew ElijahCo's business, the safer were the secrets of 181. On the other hand, the old adage held that power is neither created nor destroyed; it just changes hands. Jenna's gain was not just Debbie's loss. He put that thought aside and began working on the EJ 445 proposal.

*   *   *

Lars greeted Sally and Chuck as he entered clinic. "Good news. We got the EJ 445 contract."

"Dr. Thorndike already told me. He also told me he was staying at High Plains and not going to Bangkok," Sally said. She looked up from her computer. "How's Kate doing this morning?"

"I'm surprised you can't tell me. You seem to know everything else that's going on around here," Lars growled.

"Sorry, Lars. I didn't mean to burst your bubble. When Dr. Thorndike showed up this morning, I needed to know why. So, how's Kate?"

"She's better by the hour. At least I want to think so. For starters, they're weaning her off the vent this morning."

He turned to Chuck. "Hey, Chuck, I met an old friend of yours this morning; at least, it was a virtual meeting."

"You met Dr. Armand Cooper. Isn't he quite a character?"

"Have I been asleep for twenty years? News to me is old hat to both of you."

Chuck snickered. "I was the one who recommended Mando to guide the Bangkok project when I asked to bow out. Jenna said she was going to introduce the two of you today."

"Mando told stories about your service in Afghanistan. Why have you never shared that with us?"

"That experience is best left there."

"Is that why you have a time gap in your CV?"

"Yes, and I fill it only on a need-to-know basis."

"Thank you for your service, Dr. Thorndike," Sally said.

He acknowledged her, but his mind drifted elsewhere. Clearly, some things did not remain in Afghanistan.

As the three of them settled down to clinic, Chuck added, "Mando's a fisherman, Lars. You can never tell the size of the fish that got away. It grows bigger each time the story's told."

Clinic consisted mainly of follow-up patients, with only a handful of new ones. Lacking the incentive of a new drug study, referrals to the university had trailed off. Community oncologists could provide conventional care and do so cheaper and more conveniently. So Lars made a token appearance and excused himself to work on the 445 proposal.

He worked quickly and updated the old EJ 181 protocol to reflect the known characteristics of EJ 445. Despite a thorough online literature search, he found little published data on this newest drug in the EJ series, none of which involved human trials. ElijahCo kept most of the information they had as proprietary secrets, revealing only enough information to get approval from research and human studies committees.

Side effects of EJ 445 in animal models were similar to those of both 75 and 181. Upgrading the molecular structure of the EJ drug series was allegedly designed to produce a drug with more anti-cancer benefits than EJ 75. There wasn't a whisper anywhere Lars looked that EJ 445 could affect longevity, except of course, if it killed cancer cells.

Lars went over the details in his mind. I know ElijahCo has hidden the data on EJ 445's effect on the aging process in mice. It must be more effective and less toxic than 181, or they wouldn't bother testing it in humans. I'm not going to ask ElijahCo for that data because I don't want to know about it. I'll make my proposal based on the information I know to be true. We'll be studying EJ 445 to get its toxicity profile in human subjects and to see whether it's better at killing human cancer cells than

EJ 75, Ejectica, or whatever the hell you want to call it. We won't need tissue samples, which will make for a simpler trial as well as making it easier to get through committees. We can divert blood for Dr. Aak's prion assay without suspicion. So I won't have to tell half-truths to the university committees anymore—at least not as many.

Lars completed the 445 draft and, with a flourish, sent it off to Jenna. With no one to listen, he proclaimed, "Have at it, little lady. You can dot your t's and cross your eyes to your heart's content. I've done my part."

Just as he was pressing the send button on his computer, Changchang called.

"This is Lars. I hope nothing—"

"No, Lars; she's much better. I'm with Kate now. Can you break free and join us?"

"Wild horses couldn't stop me."

Kate was awake but delirious. Her eyes furiously scoured the room, though her mind couldn't process what she saw.

Changchang was soothing her. When she saw Lars enter, she spoke quietly to him: "Come over to us, but ever so slowly, and wear your warmest smile. Kate's awakening to a complex world of information and still has limited cognitive ability. We don't want to frighten her more than she is already."

Lars approached the bed as instructed, and Kate began to focus her eyes on him. There was a gleam of recognition, but no words. She reached out her hands, and he gently took them in his, resisting the urge to give her a bear hug. He was speechless, but the tears of joy streaming down his cheeks spoke volumes.

Changchang was touched but preserved professional dignity with humor. "Sorry, Lars, you'll have to wait to kiss the bride. But my, oh my, the lady is coming back to us. I've asked the nurse to give her a mild sedative and start her on Zoloft."

"Why start her on an antidepressant?"

"I'll explain in a few minutes. Why don't the two of you appreciate your moment together? The sedation will take a few minutes to work. Post-seizure delirium is no fun at all."

Kate was soon resting comfortably. Changchang and Lars retreated to the ICU family room.

"I'm overwhelmed. What's happened to resuscitate my Kate?"

"I'm trying to answer that question myself, and I'll need your help. What's really going on with your wife? I mean, she had the heart attack, and now, as I examine her, she doesn't have the figure or features of a twenty-eight-year-old woman. She looks so much older."

"That's funny. No one took notice the whole time she was hospitalized for the MI."

"And you're surprised, Lars? Why examine the patient when you can order scads of tests on your patient and get the results without leaving your computer? Besides, she was in for a heart problem. Why look at the skin?"

"You're preaching to the choir."

"And you, my friend, are avoiding my question. What's really wrong with Kate?"

Lars could no longer divert Changchang. He had to come clean—at least half-clean. "Kate has a yet-to-be-named disease that's causing her to age prematurely."

"She certainly doesn't have progeria or any of its variants."

"Like I said, it has yet to be named. Anyway, she was beginning to feel that her brain was following her body, that she was getting demented. Her memory was slipping, and she was finding it difficult to concentrate at work. She was a bright pathologist but quit her job when she made a diagnostic error."

"Was she having trouble sleeping?"

"No, no, quite the opposite. She was sleeping twelve, maybe fourteen hours a day."

"How about her appetite?"

"It was bad, and the pounds seemed to melt off her body."

"So all of this occurred after she knew about her condition?"

"Yes. It began after her heart attack. That really hit her hard. She realized she would never have babies and our life together would never be normal and, dear God, would be so short."

"You know, Lars, it's tough at times to distinguish depression from dementia."

"Is that why you started her on Zoloft?"

"Yup. My bet is that Kate is a terribly depressed woman."

Lars was shocked. "Oh, Changchang, I feel like such a fool. I should have thought of that."

"Lighten up on yourself. You're her husband, not her doctor."

"So, Kate gets depressed, I mean really depressed. She has the seizure and becomes unresponsive until after the seizures are broken."

Changchang smiled. "The seizures may actually have been therapeutic. They used to treat refractory depression with insulin shock therapy. They still treat it with electroconvulsive therapy. Both mimic epileptic seizures."

"I hope you're right."

"Well, we won't know for a while. Until we do, I'll treat her for depression and for the seizures." Changchang looked thoughtfully at Lars. "What's left to explain is why she had the seizures in the first place."

Their conversation was interrupted as her cell phone sounded an alarm. "Uh-oh, trouble in the neuro-ICU. I gotta run. But, Lars, our conversation's not over . . ."

She hurried away, leaving Lars relieved.

His relief was short-lived. Lars could no longer dodge the oncology office and the queen of gossip. He felt as though all eyes were on him. He wanted to slip into his office through the hall door, but that would only delay the inevitable. He took a deep breath and walked in to find Patty with her hair a rainbow of colors.

"Hello, Dr. Lars," said Patty. "We were about to align our jets and fly the missing man formation." She paused for a moment and then drowned him in a tsunami of questions: "What happened to your poor wife? Is she okay? I mean, I know she's sick, but is she getting better? Where have you been? Why haven't you answered your cell phone? You've got a whole bunch of snail mail—"

Lars struggled for air. "Whoa, slow down. I can answer only one question at a time. Kate had a seizure but is recovering. I've been at her bedside pretty much this whole time. Now answer one question for me:

What's with the hair? I thought you'd given up on coloring it."

"Oh, that: I refuse to let others define me. I am who I am. My hair is my treasure and I choose to flaunt it. If others want to demean themselves by ridicule and jealousy, that's their problem. Now here's your mail, and no, Sally is not here, but Dr. Thorndike still is. Well, he's not here here; I mean he's not leaving High Plains to go to Thailand. I wish someone had told me he was staying, so I could stop sending out his change-of-address cards. I'm always the last one to know."

"Reality check, Patty: you know everything that's going on around here, and even things that are not. As for Dr. Thorndike's change in plans, he's staying to be a part of our new drug trial we got from Elijah-Co."

"I know about the EJ 445 study."

"Did you know the time gap in Dr. Thorndike's CV was due to his service in Afghanistan?"

Patty gave him a smirk. "Oh, that's so last hour's news cycle. I'm working on why he returned to Kabul after his wounds were healed."

"How did you know he was wounded?"

"I can't tell you that, Dr. Lars. I report the news, and a good reporter never gives up her sources."

Lars shook his head. "You never cease to amaze me," he said, and walked into his office to go over his mail.

Patty came in with a load of documents to be reviewed and signed. He groaned, to which she replied, "That's what you get for dodging this office and your administrative duties as chief of oncology."

"Okay, all knowing one, I'll do penance by treating the office to pizza." He did just that and spent the afternoon as administrator-in-chief with the office staff feeling his love.

Five o'clock rolled around, and with it, a merciful end of the day. Lars rubbed the cramp from his writing hand. He checked with Sally to be certain his clinical bases were covered and went over to the hospital to see Kate. He found a new doctor in the room.

"Hi, I'm Kate's husband, Lars, and you are . . . ?"

"I'm Dr. Bruce Javitts. I'm a physiatrist. Dr. White asked me to evaluate your wife for our rehabilitation program."

"So soon? She's not even out of the intensive care unit."

"Oh, that's coming tomorrow if all goes well. You know hospitals—discharge planning starts before the ambulance is parked."

Lars gave Kate a hug and kiss, which she enthusiastically returned. He sat next to her on the edge of the bed, supporting her, as she was a bit wobbly. "So, Dr. Javitts, what do you think?"

"I read in her medical record that she has a bizarre disease of premature aging. I see the effects of that condition in her hair, her skin, and most prominently in her loss of muscle mass. I've never seen such atrophy in a woman her age."

"What about her cognitive function?" He gave Kate a squeeze to help cushion her from a negative opinion.

"I think we need to take into consideration the recent seizures and medications. I also awakened her from a sound sleep. That being said, her cognitive function certainly hasn't kept pace with her physical deterioration. I share Dr. O'Reilly's opinion that what we're seeing is through the fog of her depression. I think she'll benefit from a comprehensive rehabilitation program. Improvement in her physical conditioning will enhance her intellectual and emotional recovery—and vice versa. I don't know how much improvement we'll see, because we don't know the nature of her underlying illness."

A smile crept across Kate's face, and she returned Lars's squeeze. Granted, it was a baby bear hug, but it showed her will to live was back.

*   *   *

Time flew by for Lars. He was able to avoid further interrogation from Changchang, as she had signed off Kate's case while she was in rehab. The EJ 445 research project easily passed muster with the university committees, and initial patient accrual was brisk. Drug dose escalations were well tolerated. EJ 445 appeared to be a disappointing cancer killer, but prion eradication was better than with EJ 181 (Somitra).

On the other hand, time slowed to a crawl for Kate. Rehabilitation proved to be a demanding taskmaster. Initial progress was at a snail's pace but then began to build upon itself. Strength begets strength, which proved to be a powerful tonic for her depression. She looked forward to Lars's visits each morning before rounds and each evening after clinic. She loved hearing stories of Bartholomeow, as he fought a guerrilla war to wrest control of the house from Lars. Her eyes lit up, and her world expanded.

Lars arose early one morning and went to the basement. He drew up a dose of Somitra from his precious stock and went to visit Kate. He heard a girlish giggle as he walked into her room. She was sitting on the edge of her bed, fully clothed, and laughing at something she was holding in her hand. It was too small for Lars to see.

"Looky here! I've found a black hair."

"You've found what?"

"Do you remember the day I found my first gray hair?"

"How could I forget? You were inconsolable."

"Well, today I found my first black hair, and I'm thrilled. Maybe this damned disease of mine has spontaneously disappeared. Maybe I can be normal."

Lars shared her joy. "I'll bronze it."

She caught the humor. "Don't you dare! I want the black to last forever."

Lars grew serious. "You're right; you're getting better. Your wrinkles are fading, and your muscle mass has significantly increased. I'll bet your breasts don't sag anymore."

"You're invited to check that out at a future date."

"Seriously, Kate, you're defying time and the aging process, but ..."

"But what, Lars? What's the 'but' part of my fairy-tale recovery?"

"We both know white hair doesn't become black, and wrinkles don't spontaneously fade away."

"Come on, Lars, spit it out. What's happening to me?"

"EJ 181 is giving your black hair back to you, and your smooth skin and your firm boobs."

"What do you mean? I never got EJ 181. We only talked about it."

Lars studied the floor. "I have a confession to make. I gave you 181 the night before you had the seizures."

"So you lied. The prick was a needle and not a bee sting."

"Yes, it was. Oh, Kate, you were aging in front of my eyes, and I thought your depression was senility. Please forgive me."

Kate's mind was a kaleidoscope. She was speechless.

Lars took her hand. "The fever, the seizures, the brain swelling, the failure of your lungs and kidneys were all from 181. I gave you too much for your body to tolerate. There were too many prions, and they all exploded at once . . ."

Kate regained control. "But I'm better. I'm a younger woman than I was that night. I'm furious you injected me with 181 without my permission, and I hate you for the suffering! So many thoughts and feelings are going through my brain right now. I need time to sort them all out."

Lars sighed. "I don't think we have the luxury of time to do that. I've been monitoring your blood with Aak's assay. The prions were gone from your body after the dialysis. Now they're coming back."

"Oh, God, no! You mean all I went through was in vain? Do I briefly enjoy my youth only to have it snatched away? That's just not fair."

"You'll need periodic injections of 181 to keep aging at bay."

"I can't go through the suffering again. My body just won't tolerate it."

"I'll give you lower doses, and it won't happen again."

"I don't know, Lars . . ."

"You'll have to trust that I do know what's best. I have a dose in my coat pocket. I can give it to you now."

She looked at him clear eyed. "I remember the woman I was, dying too soon. My joy was gone. I couldn't concentrate; I couldn't do the things I used to do. I felt like a shadow of myself." She began to weep.

"I can't go back. I have little choice but to trust you." She rolled up her sleeve. "Let's get it over with."

Lars briefly studied the room, assuring himself they were alone and no cameras were present. He took a deep breath and plunged the needle into her arm, murmuring, "I love you so much."

He stayed with her all day waiting for the horrible side effects—which never came.

Lars walked out of the rehab unit into the evening air. He felt good, better than he had in forever. He walked by a woman in a motorized wheelchair, whose face was in the shadows of the setting sun. She called out to him, "Lars, it's me."

"Debbie!" Lars was surprised. "Wow! You look so much better. I hope that reflects what you're feeling."

"I've come a long way in a short time. I'm in rehab and making improvements every day."

"Good for you."

An awkward silence was broken by Debbie: "I want to apologize for my behavior last time. I don't remember a whole lot of our conversation, but I do know I acted like a blubbering idiot."

"No need for an apology. You were one miserable cookie."

"I remember telling you about that awful night. Things were a blur. I'm seeing more clearly now. The driver of the van that struck me was a man; I'm sure of it. He aimed the van at me. He intentionally tried to kill me."

"Have you told the police?"

"No, I didn't," she scoffed. "What good would it have done? If I recanted my original story, I'd be just another victim lacking credibility. Even if they found my story believable, what would I have gained? There are a lot of male drivers in this city. They would never have found the one who did it. I would have put myself in further danger and gained nothing for my effort."

"Why are you telling me this?"

"We both know the woman behind these purported accidents. So be careful. Watch your back, and don't trust her for a moment." She put her wheelchair in gear and headed toward the rehab entrance. Lars could barely hear her call out above the hum of the motor, "I'm just returning your favor."

Lars pondered Debbie's words. They had changed nothing. She was still a frightened woman with a whodunit story. Should he believe her, and did it really matter? Still, he felt unsettled by their encounter and would watch his back.

Lars drove over to the laboratory. Jenna's secretary had scheduled a virtual meeting with Mando for tomorrow morning. He put on his principal investigator hat and settled in to review the Somitra data coming out of Bangkok. He noted that blood prion levels before subjects ever received Somitra were within the normal range. He was disappointed not to find another Kate, but that was to be expected since her disease was so rare. After subjects had received Somitra, blood prion levels were scattered all over the place. Prions were undetectable in some but not in others. Some cases showed prion levels dropping after the first dose and then popping back up after the second.

"This doesn't make a damned bit of sense," he muttered. He looked at the data from every angle he knew and subjected it to all forms of statistical analyses, and still he couldn't make sense of it. "What the hell is going on?"

The answer came to him just as Jenna walked in for the meeting. Lars glanced at his watch and realized he'd been at this the whole night. "Damn it," he whispered. "I wanted to be fresh when I get Kate."

"Good morning, Lars. Were you talking to me?"

"No, Jenna. I was talking to myself. I've spent the whole night going over the Bangkok data."

"I only had time for a cursory review. It's very confusing . . . I trust Kate is doing well."

Lars flashed a big grin. "I get to take her home today."

While Jenna made coffee and checked into the virtual meeting, Lars made a final review of the data. He poured coffee for the two of them and joined Jenna at her computer monitor.

"Hello from High Plains," she greeted the face in the monitor.

"Hello from Bangkok," he replied. "I brought Dr. Aak with me this evening." Aak had a silly grin on his face and waved.

Jenna opened the meeting: "Thank you for providing us with the So-mitra data. Lars has taken the opportunity to study it, so I'll turn the meeting over to him."

"Thank you, Jenna." He turned to the monitor. "May I extend my greetings to the two of you as well."

Lars got down to business. "Dr. Aak, have you had any problems with your blood prion assay?"

The silly grin on Dr. Aak's face was replaced by a serious look. "I had been concerned that the difference in climates would have an effect on the results. But the controls I brought with me to Bangkok produced the same results as they did in High Plains. So I have a very high level of confidence in the assay results. I know the data we sent you is . . . well, irregular, but it's through no fault of the assay."

"Thank you," Lars replied. "I'm pleased to hear the assay is performing well. Mando, what steps have you taken to confirm the identities of your subjects? Do you have retinal scans or fingerprints?"

Mando snorted. "We're not that sophisticated. We're using picture IDs."

"Who verifies the identity of subjects when they come in for blood testing and Somitra injections?"

"We've hired a local security firm to do that work." He gave a nervous laugh and added, "It helps the local economy."

"So the guards are hired from the same slum population as your test subjects—is that correct?"

"I haven't checked the security firm's hiring practices, if that's what you mean."

Lars sighed. "To paraphrase an astronaut, Bangkok, we have a problem."

Mando went silent.

Jenna broke in: "You mean to tell me the identities of the study population haven't been confirmed?"

"Bingo," Lars replied. "Money is a powerful tool. I'm not accusing anybody of dishonesty, but I suspect the guards have been lax in verifying the identities at the time of follow-up visits."

Jenna jumped up and threw her hands in the air. "So this whole damned project has been compromised! Mando, your data is worthless! This meeting is adjourned!" She shut down the call.

Jenna sat back down, face in her hands, murmuring, "This won't go over well with the gods in Silicon Valley. They're going to fire Mando's ass and fry mine. How could I have been so stupid as to trust that loud-mouthed moron?"

Lars had never seen Jenna so distraught and tried to help. "Look, Jenna, I'm the principal investigator of this project. Its success or failure is ultimately my responsibility."

Her face still in her hands, she shook her head. "They won't see it that way. They'll review the recordings of the last meeting and find you expressing doubts about follow-up, Mando's arrogant response, and my tacit approval of that damned lout."

She rose and began to nervously pace, grumbling, "We have to salvage the project. It'll prove Somitra's effect on aging. I just know it will be a positive study. I know it will."

"I can go to Bangkok and see what I can do."

Jenna kept pacing. "You're right. We need someone to go there, but not you. We need you here for the 445 study. If that gets screwed up, there'll be a lot more hell to pay. Besides, you have a sick wife." She sighed and continued, "I'm the one responsible for this mess. I should be the one to clean it up." She hesitated for a moment and then said, "I'll get the first available flight. Keep me posted. You have my cell number, and it's a satellite phone. It will find me anywhere, even in a Thai slum."

"Fly safe, Jenna," he called as she hurried out the door.

Lars sat thinking, I should be the one going to Bangkok as the principal investigator trying to save his study. Chuck and Sally can easily shepherd the EJ 445 study, and Kate won't need another injection for a couple of weeks. He snorted. Jenna's in salvage mode, and not just for the sake of the Somitra study. Mando's mess will cause her to lose face and, with it, power, which will flow my way. If she's successful in Bangkok, some of that power will come back her way. On the other hand, if I went to Bangkok and was successful, indeed her ass would be fried.

He checked his watch. The meeting had been a lot shorter than what he had budgeted. He had time for a quick nap and a shower. He walked out of the lab, into the atrium of the building. He was deep in thought and ignored the elaborate security system screening those coming into the building.

"Hello, Dr. Sorenson."

Lars looked around trying to find the source of the cheery greeting.

"Here, Dr. Sorenson. I'm over here. It's Hal Kramer."

Lars saw the man waving and coming his way. He returned the greeting in a chilling tone. "Detective Kramer, I didn't recognize you without your notepad. I'm surprised to see you here. Is that an ElijahCo security uniform you're wearing?"

Hal offered him his hand. Lars shook it without enthusiasm. Hal took him aside to a less crowded area. "I took early retirement from the city and am now working full-time for ElijahCo. I report directly to the vice president in charge of security worldwide. It was too good an opportunity to pass up."

"The last time we talked, or maybe I should say, at the time of my last interrogation, you seemed unfamiliar with ElijahCo."

"Oh, that. I was just testing your loyalty to the company."

"I'm confused. I thought you were a High Plains police detective. You wore the badge."

"I was, but I've been doing special projects for ElijahCo for quite a while. I take PTO from the police force while doing it, just like I would if I were chaperoning a high school prom." He raised his hand in a mocking gesture. "Honest, citizen Sorenson, I never double-dipped. I decided to make the move before Ms. Steiner's unfortunate accident. I just thought I'd take the opportunity to see whose side you were on. It never hurts to know those things when you're in my line of work."

Hal's radio squawked, and he excused himself. "If you have any problems, just give old Hal a holler. I'm here for your security."

A chill ran up and down Lars's spine as he thought, My God, Debbie, I'm a believer—and I think I know who done it.

Lars arrived early to pick up Kate. He silently watched her doing physical therapy and marveled at how strong and agile she'd become. They walked together back to her room. Dr. Javitts was at the bedside computer, completing her discharge summary. He looked up and smiled. "Are you ready to go home, young lady?"

"A team of horses couldn't stop me."

"They probably couldn't. I'm utterly flabbergasted over the progress you've made—"

Lars broke in: "I guess her aging disease went into a spontaneous remission. I guess miracles do occur."

"I reckon you're right. I feel like I'm discharging a different woman from the one I admitted—a more youthful and vibrant one," he added, shaking his head in disbelief.

Kate blushed at his comment and jokingly said, "I bet you say that to all the girls at discharge."

"Frankly, you're the first."

"Do I have any restrictions when I get home?"

"Other than not doing the dishes or laundry, none whatsoever." He gave her a wink.

"Hey, you two, no fair ganging up on me."

The three of them laughed.

Then Bruce became serious. "I do have one request: keep up with your exercise program. Regular exercise is important for all of us, but particularly for you, Kate. You've made astounding progress, and we don't want you to backslide. Oh, and keep up with the antidepressant and seizure meds, at least until your follow-up visit with Dr. O'Reilly. Now, go on, you two. Get out of here and enjoy your life together."

When they got into the car, Kate breathed a sigh of relief. "Alone at last. I felt like I was in a fishbowl."

"Do you think Bruce bought the spontaneous remission story, the miracle?"

Kate thought for a moment. "Yes, I think he did. He has no frame of reference in which to place amortality and EJ 181."

"Like I've said before, it's comforting to appeal to the supernatural when transgressing the boundaries of our understanding."

"Interesting, but I don't remember you saying that."

"Oh, that's right. You were too sick to hear when Dr. White and I had that conversation." He leaned over and gave her a kiss. "Oh, by the way, EJ 181 got a new name while you were out of commission. It's called Somitra."

"Somitra: that's catchy."

"It has symbolic meaning, but let's forget about it for now."

They came home to an angry Bartholomeow who quickly mellowed when he saw Kate. She gave him a tummy rub and his favorite treats. He purred contentedly and went off in search of a sunbeam.

Lars and Kate warmly embraced, which quickly heated up. She put her hand down between their bodies. "My, my, you seem to like the new me."

He stroked her face and slipped a hand inside her bra. "Mmm, such firm tatas. I hope my wife doesn't find out I'm fondling you."

"I won't breathe a word to her."

"You're way overdressed."

"I'm sure you can do something about that."

"Yup, but before I do, let me get the K-Y Jelly."

"I don't think we're going to need that anymore."

"Really? Is your hymen back as well?"

"I'm afraid not. Once it's lost, you can never find it again."

"Do you mind if I try?"

"Please do. I love naughty boys."

* * *

A week later, Lars got a call from Jenna. Her voice was grim. "How about FaceTime tomorrow morning? Things are worse here than what I thought."

"Is six thirty our time good with you?"

"Yeah, that'll be after my day ends. That will assure us privacy."

Lars was too busy to dwell on Jenna's problems. EJ 445 became the same boom to referrals as 75 and 181 had been. He was actively recruiting a new oncologist, expanding the fellowship program, and had convinced one of the local oncologists to come on staff full-time. She had triplets nearing college age. The university tuition reimbursement program was a lure she couldn't resist.

Kate had a follow-up with Changchang, who accommodated them with an end-of-day appointment. Lars left work early so he could drive her.

"Your taxi's here," Lars greeted her.

Kate got into the car and gave him a kiss. "I'm sorry you had to end your day early. I know you've been busy. My sentence to the passenger seat is a real drag."

"Well, the law says no driving for six months after a seizure."

"I know. Maybe I'll get time off for good behavior."

"Fat chance of that occurring. What's in your hand?"

"It's the New York Times crossword puzzle, Sunday edition."

"Whoa, baby, I'm impressed, and you're doing it with a pen, no less. That's confidence."

"Or maybe arrogance. This is the first time I've tried the Sunday puzzle."

When they walked into the office, Kate was handed a detailed questionnaire, which she carefully answered. They were ushered into an exam room by an MA, who took vital signs and reconciled her medications. She left the room saying, "Dr. O'Reilly will be in shortly."

"I'm nervous."

"Why are you nervous? I'm the patient."

"Changchang suspects something's afoot. She was probing me for clues as to why you got sick. I was saved by her cell phone. Since then, I've avoided any one-on-one with her."

"Sorry to keep you waiting." O'Reilly greeted them with her usual verve. "Kate, you look great!"

She glanced at Lars and then back at Kate. "Physical therapy has done miracles for you, my lady." She waved the questionnaire and continued, "I see your depression is under great control. And no more seizures."

"That's right. Maybe we can talk about my driving again?"

"No driving for six months after a seizure is state law. There's nothing I can do about it. On a brighter note, you have a most handsome chauffeur."

She conducted a thorough neurological examination, ending with a cognitive assessment. She took a few handwritten notes, taking care not to get the computer between Kate and her.

After her evaluation, Changchang sat down across from Kate and Lars. A bright smile crossed her face. "Like I said, physical therapy has done miracles for you . . . or has it?"

Lars looked at Kate and then back at Changchang. "What do you mean by that?"

"Tell me about the night Kate became ill."

"I've already told you. She had a chill, then fever and the seizure."

"No, no, I mean before that. I want to know what made her sick."

Lars began phase one of diversion tactics. "You're sailing into troubled waters. If I tell you more, I'll be putting you in danger."

Changchang rolled her eyes. "You're not going to threaten me with the ElijahCo boogeyman crap, are you? I've heard the rumors, like 'Ever since Chuck Thorndike came to town, bad things happen to those prying into ElijahCo's affairs.' How about this one? 'He's doctor by day and predator by night. Thorndike wields the company club.' The best one, I think, is, 'The time gaps in Dr. Thorndike's CV were when he was off somewhere learning his deadly craft.' It's all fabricated by people with too much time on their hands."

"So you know the truth about the accidents befalling Hanley, Latchfield, and Steiner? And please don't give me the coincidence argument. That just doesn't hold water."

"No, I admit that I'm not privy to the truth, but I do know the lies. I also know that Somitra may do more than just kill cancers in mice—"

Kate broke in: "How do you know about Somitra?"

"Pillow talk, Kate. You and I have that in common. I'm sure Lars shares secrets with you."

"Who shares them with you?"

"Chuck Thorndike and I are lovers. That's why Mando is in Bangkok and not Chuck."

Kate was confused. "Bangkok . . . Mando . . . what am I missing?"

Lars put his arm around Kate. "I'll fill you in later. Lots went on while you were sick."

Changchang looked from Lars to Kate and back again. "Look, I'm sorry to unload this information on the two of you, but I need to know what's going on with my patient. Spontaneous remission and miracle cure just won't cut it, Lars. Kate's body is going backwards in time. She has profound changes that have never been seen before. She's growing younger by the day."

Changchang paused and looked directly at Lars. "Kate has received the elixir of youth, hasn't she? Did you give her Somitra?"

Lars tried his standard line: "I have signed a letter of confidentiality with ElijahCo. I can't say any more without violating my contract."

"Oh, for the love of God, that's the same wimpy excuse Chuck gives me. But you're not denying you did it."

Lars went off script: "No, I'm not. You're a brilliant woman who now shares the breathtaking changes that have occurred in Kate's body. She could conceivably achieve amortality. But Changchang—and this is a big but—Somitra has caused these changes in a woman with a rare, yet-to-be-named disease. We don't know if we can generalize her results to a broader population. If her results become grist for the gossip mill or the subject of cable news, you can use your imagination as to what might happen. Record the changes you see, evaluate her response to Somitra in detail, but please keep silent, at least for now. Please preserve patient confidentiality."

Kate was nodding. "I echo Lars's words. I also want to add a personal note. I've lived with the curse of rapid aging and have been denied many of life's pleasures. Now that the curse has been broken, I'd like to enjoy my youth without being a carnival sideshow. Please keep what has transpired today a secret—except, of course, from your pillow partner."

Changchang O'Reilly looked at the two of them. "You have my word. Our conversation will stay in this room. I'll tell Chuck that I've signed a letter of confidentiality. Two can play the cat-and-mouse game. Oh, and, Kate, you better get new makeup. I'm not saying you should go with old-lady blue hair, but you might want to look and dress older."

The three of them hugged. Kate and Lars went home, comfortable that Changchang would keep her promise.

* * *

"Come on! It's me, you damned fool machine." Lars was on his third attempt to get the retina scan to let him into the lab from the tunnel entrance. The fourth time proved successful, and he hurried upstairs for his virtual meeting with Jenna.

"Good morning, Bangkok," Lars said.

"Good grief, High Plains!" was the response.

"Ouch! Are things that bad?"

Jenna appeared exhausted and sounded frustrated. "I don't think they could get much worse, although, given more time, I'm sure Mando could find a way. The scrambled prion data was the introduction to chaos. Pretreatment skin and muscle biopsies were haphazardly processed. Some samples were placed in proper preservative, but others were just dropped into sugar water and set on the counter to rot. Many samples were never taken. One of the supposed lab techs faints at the sight of blood. She just recorded the samples as done. Oh, I almost forgot to mention that the detailed pretreatment photos of the study subjects weren't labeled correctly, so we have a leg here and an arm there with no way in hell to tell who they belong to."

"Why wasn't Mando supervising the study? Is he that incompetent?"

"He was sleeping it off on the job. Our man in Bangkok turns out to be king of the junkies. He's never met a drug he didn't like."

"I'd love to be a fly on the wall when you fire his ass."

"Well, he refuses to be fired. He thinks he can blackmail ElijahCo with information he's gathered. I don't know what that might be, but he stays on the payroll until I find out. I reported him to security here in Bangkok—not the local loonies, but corporate security. We'll see what they can come up with."

Lars thought for a moment. "Before we go further in our conversation, is this video being archived? Could Mondo get hold of it?"

"No, I've scrambled the transmission."

"You're sure?"

"Have you ever tried to unscramble an egg?"

Lars chuckled. "Okay, I feel better. You know, I've been thinking: maybe we should have kept the study simple."

"So, the fallen Christian crucifies himself. Come on, Lars, how do you document aging in a population without pictures? The biopsies are a must for scientific publication. No, the study design is not at fault; it's the conduct of the study. Mando's the asshole, not you."

"The most important question is, Can the study be salvaged? Can you put Humpty Dumpty back together?"

Jenna gave an audible sigh. "I don't think so. I'll have to move the study to a different slum and start over. I'll hire all new help. I don't trust anyone currently involved in it—except, of course, Dr. Aak."

"Is there anyone else who can help you?"

"Aak's looking into that for me. I want to get out of here ASAP. This Northern California girl is withering in the heat and the humidity."

"Maybe Chuck Thorndike would reconsider the assignment; that is, if you can find a position for Changchang O'Reilly."

Jenna brightened. "So you know about the odd couple?"

"Yup, I've got my sources."

"Come to think about it, ElijahCo could use a research neurologist on this project. I don't think we've placed enough emphasis on the effects of Somitra on the aging brain. I'll work on it. Your idea has real possibilities."

"You're going to need big bait to catch a big fish like Changchang," Lars said.

"And that means what?"

"I don't know for sure, but I bet she'll want state-of-the-art equipment, including functional MRI. Of course, she'll need to know Somitra's secrets, since she's going to study it. I really don't know how much you'll have to tell her about Somitra that she doesn't already know. Chuck may be the strong, silent type, but sex has opened the mouth of many men."

"You've made some good points, but I'll get pushback when I ask for another key to that box."

"I know you, Jenna, and if you really buy into the Chuck and Changchang Show, you'll find a way to get that key for her."

Though thousands of miles apart, they stared at each other, both deep thought. Finally Lars said, "I know Mando hurt your credibility with the gods. If it's any consolation, the salvage pathway we're discussing is all your idea. As PI of the Somitra trials, you are presenting it to me for my approval."

"You'd do that for me? I thought you hated me and would gloat over my fall from grace."

"I could never hate you, Jenna. A man's first love stays with him forever. Oh, by the way, you might convince Dean Mitchell to grant Changchang a sabbatical abroad and a promotion to professor of neurology when she returns. I overheard you thinking about that. It was all your idea. I'll sign off now. I hope your day tomorrow will be better than today."

Lars started to leave the lab the way he came in, but then thought better of it. "Whoops. I better report the damned retina scanner to security." So he exited the lab into the atrium and walked over to the security office. He found Hal reading Lonely Planet Thailand.

Hal looked up at Lars. "Hi, Dr. Sorenson. How can I help you?"

"I wanted to let you know the retina scanner in the tunnel entrance is malfunctioning. It took me a number of tries before it recognized me this morning."

Hal laughed. "Yeah. Technology works wonders when it works. If you wait a moment, I'll have one of the techs check it out." He dashed off a text message and waited for a reply.

Lars followed his curiosity. "I see you're reading a tourist guide to Thailand."

"Yeah." Hal grinned. "My boss is sending me on special assignment. It's all hush-hush." He winked at Lars. "I know I can trust you with ElijahCo's secrets. I vetted you in my own way. But don't you worry about security here while I'm gone. I'm putting Jess, our night supervisor, in charge. He's a good man."

Lars smiled back. "Yes, I know Jess. We ran into each other the other night."

"Ah, here's the return text: the tech will check it out within the hour."

"Thank you for being so prompt." He motioned to the book. "I hope you get to try the cuisine in Bangkok. I hear the pad thai alone is worth the trip."

He headed toward the clinic, thinking, Maybe Debbie is wrong. ElijahCo's security may go around and not through Jenna McDaniel.

Sally was reviewing charts and responding to patient emails when Lars walked into clinic. "Good morning. We have a full day ahead of us. Dr. Chuck will join us after rounding with the house staff," she said. "By the way, I spoke to Kate yesterday. She sounds terrific."

"She's amazing. In fact, we'd like to invite you and Fred to join us for dinner this weekend. Kate doesn't feel up to hosting a dinner party just yet, but the Greek restaurant up the street from us has great food. It's informal and it's Kate's favorite. It'll be our treat. Let's just call it a celebration of health."

Sally half smiled, but there was a hint of sadness in her eyes. "We'd love to join you, but I'm afraid Fred can't share in a celebration of health. This time his arthritis is giving him fits. It's a continuing saga of health issues. What's more, he's starting to get discouraged." She sighed in resignation.

"Well, if Fred can't go to the restaurant, let's bring the restaurant to him!" Lars replied. "The Greek place has a pretty good takeout menu, and there's a wine shop around the corner."

Sally's smile grew bigger. "Now that's a great idea. I'll accept your offer for both of us."

"How about Saturday night? Kate will call you this evening to take your orders."

* * *

"Why don't you park curbside? I'll go in and get the carryout."

"Are you sure you're up to it?"

"Good heavens, Lars, you're my husband, not my mother. I feel better than at any time I can remember. I'm counting the days till I can drive again. Besides, I'm just walking in and out of a restaurant, not climbing the Rocky Mountains."

"Sorry to be doting on you. The memory of your seizures still haunts me. I feel so respons—"

"Stop it already. How many times do you have to go through this mea culpa bullshit before you let it go?"

"Okay, okay, I hear you. Do you have money?"

She called back to him as she got out of the car. "Yes, and while you're at it, stop the doting."

Kate returned with her arms full of carryout.

"New subject, Kate; I've been thinking . . . ," Lars began.

"Uh-oh, we're in big trouble."

He took a deep breath. "I want to offer Fred the opportunity to take Somitra. Look what it's done for you."

Kate frowned. "I was right. We're wading into deep doo-doo. Honestly, I can't keep up with your mood changes. Before I walked into the restaurant you were feeling guilty over my seizures. Now I'm hearing excessive hubris over my miraculous recovery. Why not just take a victory lap and enjoy what you've accomplished?"

"Because Fred's my friend and coconspirator in the Somitra heist, and I can potentially relieve his agony from an aging body," Lars said. "He knows very well the side effects of Somitra vicariously through Sally. She was with me that awful night in the ER and the ICU. Both Fred and Sally have seen the salutary effects Somitra has had on your body. Tonight, those effects will be on full display. Do you think parading those benefits in front of them won't induce even a modicum of jealousy and resentment?"

"I'll go—"

"I'm not through. I don't want to risk my friendship with Fred. I think he should at least have the opportunity to say yes or no."

Kate glared at him. "How dare you lecture me on the right to informed consent!"

Lars looked sheepish. "Oops, you're right to nail me on that. Maybe we should drop the subject. I don't want to fight with you. I want to enjoy your company out with dear friends tonight."

"I share your feelings. Just to set the record straight, I'm not flaunting my youth. I've taken Changchang's advice and I'm trying to look older."

"You're not having much success."

"I'll take that as a compliment."

"Please do," Lars said, as they pulled up to their friends' house. "Here we are. I'll take in the wine if you take in the food."

"Agreed. By the way, in the end, it's your drug and your choice."

"Thank you. I may disagree with you and say some things in the heat of debate that I regret later, but I do value your opinion."

"I appreciate that. Now, ring the doorbell. My hands are full."

Fred opened the door, with Sally in tow. She took the food, and he gave Kate a warm hug. Sally had set the dinner table, complete with linen and candles. She and Kate went to the kitchen to plate the food and open the wine.

Fred limped over to the bar and motioned Lars to join him in a drink. Lars sniffed and then savored the Scotch whisky he was given. "It's smoky with a whiff of sea breeze. Very nice pour, my man. Thank you."

Fred sat down with a groan. "Christ, Lars, if it isn't my ass, it's my elbow. My whole body got old on me when I wasn't looking."

Lars felt sympathetic, but could only come up with the trite phrase "They say age is a state of mind."

"I'm here to tell you that's horse hockey. But enough of what ails me. I still chuckle when I think about our ElijahCo caper. You really threw their computers for a loop."

"Well, I learned from the best of them. Here's to our heist." The men raised their glasses and downed the whisky.

Sally called from the kitchen, "Hey, you two, come to the dinner table before you both get schnockered."

Lars helped his friend out of the chair. "You might want to consider one of those power-lift recliners."

Fred snorted. "Those are for old people."

Both men chuckled and joined the ladies for dinner.

Kate poured the wine. When she handed Fred his glass, he took her hand. "I'm not getting fresh with you. I'm just amazed by how youthful your hands look. They've changed so much since I last saw you."

Sally muttered, "That's the lamest pickup line I've ever heard, you old goat."

"Pickup line, nothing. It's the truth. Kate has turned back the hands of time."

There was a collective groan at his pun, which he accepted with a silly grin. The dinner conversation continued with lively discussion that bounced effortlessly from topic to topic. It inevitably returned to the subject of aging.

Lars casually inquired, "Fred, have you ever wanted to return to your youth?" While he waited for a reply, he glanced at a frowning Kate.

"Oh, I guess we've all thought about it, but Kate's the only one to have experienced it. I would like to go back to my youth, but only to right the wrongs and erase those I couldn't change. Then again, doing that might screw things up even more, so I best stay here in the present.

"I'll stop digressing and answer your question by saying my dear wife goes all the way to China seeking wisdom from the philosophers. I prefer to remain in the states. I read an article in the op-ed section of the New York Times a while ago. An Ivy League philosopher was hospitalized for a heart condition. He was ready to meet his maker, having tidied up his will and signed the Do Not Resuscitate papers. Before discharge, he had a cardiac arrest and was mistakenly resuscitated.

"He was furious, and bitterly attacked his rescuers in the article. 'We all have to die, but we should only have to do it once. I'm forced against my will to die a second time.' That started me thinking: I'm not ready for hospice, and I think I have some time left here on Earth. So my condition is not precisely that of the philosopher. I would paraphrase his comment by saying, we all have to live, but we should only have to do it once. Rather than living a second time, the future is best left to the next generation, who, hopefully, will do a better job of it."

The table went silent. Finally, Lars raised his glass. "Here's to the wiser man at this table."

Sally and Kate joined him in the toast.

9

TWO WEEKS LATER, Patty cornered Lars in his office, threatening chains if he didn't exercise his duties as administrator-in-chief. His cell phone vibrated. Still leery that his office was bugged, he turned up the sound on his computer. Cute puppy noises drowned out his conversation. "Changchang, what's up?"

"Good morning, Lars. I hope all's well with Kate."

"She couldn't be better. And you?"

"I'm fine. Big things are happening to me that pertain to you and your research. I was wondering whether we could meet somewhere for a chat."

"I call the Morning Grind my second office. What time's good for you?"

"Is ten o'clock okay? I don't want to take you away—"

"You're rescuing me from a mountain of paperwork, and I thank you very much. See you at ten."

Lars snuck out of the office, avoiding Patty, and walked to the meeting. He joined Changchang at a table in the back. "So, you've roused my curiosity."

"Chuck and I were out to dinner the other night when he broke the news that ElijahCo wanted him in Bangkok to run the Somitra project. It seems his old war buddy Mando had buggered things up big time. Chuck couldn't say no. Well, that soured the wine, and he slept on the couch that night. Now, get this: the very next day I got a call from Jenna McDaniel. I've never met the woman, but Chuck has told me a lot about her, and not all of it warm and fuzzy."

She noticed that Lars's expression had changed. "Whoops! Maybe I said the wrong thing."

"No, no. Jenna can be abrasive. I have no quarrel with that. Feel free to say what you think. I don't bite."

"We met later, and, not to drag things out, she offered me a job. This time I couldn't say no."

"Very good, Changchang!" Lars said. "I'm happy you're joining the project. We need a strong neurology presence. I hope ElijahCo is giving you what you need for a first-rate study."

"They're being more than generous. I'm putting my proposal together and will have a rough draft to you ASAP. I'll need your blessing. I don't want our research goals to clash."

"I'm sure they won't. I look forward to reading it." He paused and looked her straight in the eye. "You do know what you're studying?"

"I'm quite aware of the implications amortality brings. I'm excited to have the opportunity to study Somitra. I think Jenna was right on the mark when she said I was getting a key to Pandora's box."

"Do you have any ethical concerns?"

"I've certainly thought about it, and demanded the whole Somitra story from Jenna. I do see what I'd consider ethical transgressions in the past."

"Tell me more about those transgressions."

"Let's just say a desperate man made a choice that I would not have made and was supported in those choices by an amoral company. I have to qualify that comment by saying I'm neither desperate nor a large pharmaceutical company."

Lars looked troubled.

Changchang thought for a moment and then said, "Both the Chinese and Irish sides of my family are regaled in stories. One side calls them proverbs; the other side calls them fairy stories. Allow me to merge the two as they serve a common purpose.

"A trauma surgeon received an urgent call. A woman was brought to the emergency room with life-threatening injuries that only his skills could save. He raced to the hospital and parked his car in a No Parking Zone fire lane. He saved the woman's life, only to find a parking ticket on his car windshield. He angrily appealed his fine in court, admitting he parked illegally, but said he did so for a noble cause and hence should be exonerated. The judge shook his head and explained, 'You had your job to do, and yes, it was a noble task to save the life of that woman. I have my job to do, which is to enforce the law. At first blush, the law that I'm enforcing is mundane. However, if the hospital had caught fire, first responders would have been blocked by your vehicle, and many could have perished as a result.' He brought down his gavel. 'Now, pay your fine and court costs.'"

"Please explain, Changchang."

"My job is to design and execute a research project studying Somitra's effects on the aging brain. I will do my job as I see fit and let history judge its merits. I'll quit before compromising my moral values. As for the rest of you, you're on your own. I'm neither your mother nor your conscience."

Lars reflected on her words for a moment. He then changed the subject. "When are you and Chuck going to Bangkok?"

"ElijahCo would have us go last week, but there's so much to do in preparation."

They got up from the table to return to their respective offices. Lars extended his hand, but Changchang pushed it aside and gave him a hug. "I look forward to working with you," she said. "We can do FaceTime for progress reports on our research."

"Jenna will get you access to the mainframe in the lab. This is our repository for data, and it's encrypted."

"Good. I shudder when I think about getting hacked."

"Fly safely. I look forward to greeting the new professor of neurology on your return to High Plains."

She looked at him, and a smile crossed her face.

Lars returned to his office, going through the hall door to avoid Patty. No such luck. She was sitting at his desk, entering something into his computer.

Looking up from the screen, she explained herself: "I mean no dis-

DAN W LUEDKE MD

respect, Dr. Lars, but you've got to do your paperwork, and no, buying pizza will not cut it. I mean, supplies have to be ordered, and people have to get paid, including yours truly. I've taken the liberty of writing a job description for a new position, oncology division office manager. I've been taking online courses, and I believe I could comfortably take on the task. I'll need your signature on the cover letter, which I'm finishing now. We'll need to get the department chairman to approve the request. Dr. Chapman drags his feet on new hires, the cheapskate, so I'll need the help of his secretary to move things along. She and I aren't the best of friends, but I heard rumors about an indiscretion or two, so maybe the two of us can play office pool together. I'll be the cue stick, and she can be the cue ball. I'll give her a little bump, which will overcome her inertia, which she will then pass on to Dr. Chapman. Before you know it, we'll have the position we badly need."

"That sounds a lot like blackmail."

"No, no, we're playing friendly office games. Here, sign on the bottom line. Oh, BTW, I heard your desk groaning from the weight of the paperwork. I'll help you get started."

Lars left the office much later with another attack of writer's cramp. Changchang had sent him a rough draft of her proposed research. It looked good, so she didn't have to take time for another meeting with him.

Kate and Lars had an early dinner at home. He was exhausted, and she complained of not feeling well. Despite her wishes, he doted over her. She finally ended that by saying, "Just stop it. Why can't I be sick without you worrying about prions and Somitra?" She pouted off to bed with him not far behind, wisely keeping his thoughts to himself.

Lars was up, dressed, and eating breakfast when Kate came into the kitchen. He mumbled a good morning and returned to his newspaper. He resisted the temptation to inquire about her health.

Kate gave an incoherent greeting and promptly dropped her coffee cup, sending it crashing to the floor.

Lars jumped up and ran over to his wife. "Kate, what's wrong?"

She mumbled senselessly, and her right arm went limp. She struggled to keep her balance as Lars guided her back to bed. A look of terror was on her face. "My God, Kate, what's happening to you?" he asked, sounding as terrified as she looked.

He dialed 911 and then impulsively called Changchang. He was a blubbering idiot, but she was able to understand enough to tell him she'd meet him in the ER. "I'm making hospital rounds. I'll be in the ER to greet the ambulance."

Changchang guided the first responders to an exam room, where Kate was transferred to a waiting bed. She was more coherent and was now able to move her right arm on command. Nursing personnel tried to escort Lars to the waiting room. He flatly refused.

Changchang looked at the nurses and said, "It's okay. He can stay. Oh, and please initiate the stroke protocol while I finish my exam."

She quietly asked questions, and Kate answered with nods and ever-improving speech.

Changchang fired off orders. An IV was started and medication given by vein. Changchang completed her exam, turned off the overhead light, and walked over to an anxious Lars.

"She has a bad case of the raging hormones. She didn't feel well last night because she was getting her menstrual period. It's been so long since she had one, she didn't recognize the symptoms. The period also precipitated a migraine headache. The right-sided weakness and trouble speaking were due to an aura, which can be seen with migraines. Those problems have been replaced by one badass headache. Since she has the cardiac history, we'll complete the stroke protocol and keep her overnight for observation. She'll be fine once the headache subsides."

Lars gave a sigh of relief. "Thank you so much. She had me scared to death."

He started to walk over to his wife but was cautioned by Changchang. "Why don't you let her rest for now? Even quiet words will sound to her like a gong banging in her head."

He nodded, then left and walked out into the morning air, still shaking. He reminded himself that he'd come with Kate in the ambulance, so this time he wouldn't search the parking lot in a futile search for his car.

Lars stopped by the lab before going to clinic and reviewed the latest data from the EJ 445 study. He was about to leave the lab when he got a FaceTime call from Jenna.

"Hello, Bangkok."

"Hello, High Plains."

"You sound a whole lot better today."

Jenna raised her arms in triumph. "We got Changchang!"

"Yes, I know. I spoke with her yesterday. She's excited and has already sent me a rough draft of her research proposal."

"I'm glad to hear that. Did she voice any ethical or social issues with you?"

Lars sighed. "Well, she wasn't thrilled with the way I dealt with the human studies committee getting 181 approved. She won't tolerate such behavior in the future. I didn't tell her about 445's trip to the committee. I figure it's in the rearview mirror and not directly related to her Somi-tra studies, so there's no need to bring it up. She also understands the responsibility she has to keep EJ 181's anti-aging potential under wraps. All in all, I think she'll be a valuable asset to the program."

"Good; I'm glad to hear that, and in more ways than one. This girl wants outta here."

"What's the word on our man in Bangkok?"

Jenna's mouth dropped in shock. "Jesus! How could I forget? He went missing the other night! Rumor has it he was a victim of an auto acci-dent. In the slum, such a victim would quickly lose his Rolex and wallet; his body would be thrown into a dumpster."

"Auto accidents appear to be a recurring theme with ElijahCo," said Lars. "Hmm . . . you go to Bangkok, you get angry with Mando, and he disappears after an auto accident. Is there a possible connection?"

"Really, Lars, how could you suspect me? I'm scared to death of the streets in this place—no pun intended. I told you I had reported him to ElijahCo's security and was waiting for a response."

"Well, honey bun, you sure got one. Bangkok's streets may be scary, but they don't hold a candle to ElijahCo's security team. Remind me to tell you about my encounter with Hal Kramer. He's the new head of security here. I won't waste FaceTime with that story."

"I'll wait with my usual impatience. Let's move on to our research trials."

"Right," Lars said. "The data on EJ 445 is intriguing. The higher the dose of EJ 445, the greater the number of cancer cells killed—"

Jenna interrupted: "A dose-response relationship is what we most often see with cancer-killing drugs."

"Right you are. However, we don't see that with 445's effect on prions. Instead, we see a profound threshold effect. We get little if any elimination of the membrane prions until the third dose level. Then, poof—they're gone. We'll continue to increase the dose of 445 until we reach toxicity, hoping we'll continue to get more tumor cell kill."

"You and Aak voiced concern early on that the lack of an anti-cancer effect of Somitra may enhance its carcinogenic potential."

"I'm still concerned. Rapid proliferation of normal cells occurs with elimination of prions. Witness the increase in number of muscle fibers. Rapid growth favors mistakes in gene coding, which will lead to a greater risk of cancer. That risk may be mitigated if the drug that eradicates prions also eradicates cancer cells."

Jenna nodded. "So you think EJ 445 may act like a hybrid of Somitra and Ejectica?"

"Yup, I'm hoping we'll get the best of both worlds—amortality without the risk of cancer. At the very least, 445 may be a way to gently introduce the world to amortality via the cancer-killing back door."

"We do have a lot to talk about when I'm stateside," Jenna said. "Oops, I better run. As luck would have it, Jefferson Peterson is in town. J. P. is vice president in charge of security worldwide for ElijahCo. He's here to help me recruit more reliable locals for security of the Somitra trial."

Lars glanced at his watch. "You're working late."

"Yeah, he's in town for only a few days, and I want to make best use of his time."

"You might want to ask him about Mando."

"You can count on that. I'm as unhappy as you are about the questionable accidents. I better run. I don't want to keep J. P. waiting."

"Better not; you might be next."

Jenna failed to acknowledge Lars's wry grin.

*   *   *

The next several weeks passed in a blur of activity. Patient numbers escalated. Oncology clinic bulged at the seams, displacing an unhappy rheumatologist. Lars successfully replaced Chuck Thorndike, who then joined Changchang in Bangkok. The community oncologist–cum–university faculty member was working out well. Sally was itching for a clone, and Lars gave her the go-ahead to begin interviewing candidates.

Patty greeted him as he walked into the office one morning. "I've set you up to interview a candidate for the new ODOM position. She'll be with you shortly. Here's your snail mail—"

"Whoa! What's 'ODOM'?"

Patty faked a frown. "Oh, how soon you forget. It's the oncology division office manager position you requested, remember? The university posted the position, and you get to pick from the crop of applicants."

"So, you did it. I didn't think Louis would act on it so quickly. I just hope what's-his-name Lieutenant Garcia doesn't haul you off to the pokey for blackmail."

Patty batted her eyes. "I can't imagine anyone wanting to arrest little old me," she said, and then left Lars to his work.

Lars read his snail mail and was answering emails when Patty came in and handed him a folder.

"What's this?"

"It's the first applicant's CV."

"It has your name on it."

"Yes, and I'm here to interview for the job. I have to say, I'm disappointed. You didn't notice I dressed in my best interview clothes."

"Well, it is difficult to get beyond your colorful hair. However, please have a chair, Ms. Patty, and we'll start the interview."

"How many words a minute do you type, and do you know shorthand?"

She looked puzzled. "Lots of words, but I've never actually counted them. What's shorthand?"

Lars laughed. "Ah, yes, you are a millennial girl. Now, get back to work. You'll get the job, or I'm sure you'll make my life miserable."

Patty smiled whimsically as she stood up and walked toward her desk. "I'm also proficient at the game of office torture."

"Does that include dripping water?"

"You don't want to know."

Lars decided not to go further and shifted topics. "I noticed my calendar is blocked out most of the morning for a meeting with the dean. What do you know about that?"

"His secretary set it up just before the end of yesterday. The only thing I have new on the dean is his absence from the office for a couple weeks." She shrugged her shoulders. "I guess he was on vacation. Please share if you find out otherwise."

Lars arrived for the meeting with Henry a little early. He was promptly ushered into the dean's library, an unusually intimate atmosphere for meeting with a faculty member. He took a seat and waited. Shortly thereafter, Henry emerged from his private bathroom. When he saw Lars, a smile crossed his face, and they exchanged that maddening high five. Lars forced a return smile.

"It's good to see you back, Henry," Lars said. "I hope your vacation was pleasant."

Henry coughed, took a deep breath, and grumbled, "I wouldn't call it a vacation."

"Sorry, I didn't mean to invade your personal life."

Henry waved him off. "No, no, don't be sorry. My personal life is the reason I asked you here. Before we go any further, I want to ask if you would be one of my doctors."

Startled, Lars responded, "I hope you don't have cancer."

"No, but it would almost be better if I did. Please answer my question."

"I'd be honored, sir."

"Okay, I thank you," Henry said, settling into a chair across from Lars. "I almost became a family doctor. The part of medical practice that most attracted me was the patient histories. Everyone has a story to tell, and many are shaped by their health. Think about the effect depression had on Lincoln, and polio on Franklin Roosevelt." Henry paused to take a breath. "So, I guess as much for my own enjoyment as it is for your understanding of my health problems, here's my story. Oh, and if things get confusing, please feel free to interrupt." He hesitated a moment. "Whoops, it's my turn to apologize. I forgot to offer you coffee and danish." He slowly walked over to the table and poured two cups. He then sat down and continued his story.

"I was a member of the team the CDC sent to High Plains to study mad cow disease. The lab was brand-new, with all the bells and whistles that were available at the time. Public record shows the first mouse model for human prion disease was published in 1989. If the truth be known, I had my model up and running at least two years earlier. I moved my laboratory, including the mice, from the CDC headquarters in Atlanta to High Plains. I decided to focus my attention on normal membrane prions. When the CDC closed the lab, I stayed on and moved my lab to its current on-campus location. Over the many years of membrane prion research, evidence mounted that this seemingly harmless protein was responsible for the aging process. So we began our search for the elixir of youth."

Lars interrupted: "Jenna told me it was serendipity that you found EJ 181, akin to Jenner finding penicillin."

Henry laughed. "Fiction is reality on steroids. Eureka moments are much more fun than plodding research. Apparently, Jenna prefers the fictionalized version."

"How do I know what you're telling me now isn't laced with steroids?"

"I guess you don't. Perhaps I might stop here and let you ask questions. Bear in mind that what comes out of my mouth is in the first-person singular. Others would certainly have a different truth, starting, I guess, with Jenna."

"Fair enough. So if you don't have cancer, why do you want me to be your doctor?"

Henry sighed. "The last two weeks, I was not on vacation. I was in a private clinic suffering a flare from a bizarre prion storage disease. Ironically, I acquired it from my lab partners."

"Who were they?"

"Not who, what are they. I got it from the mice I was working with. I actually have a mouse prion disease. I guess working with them so long made me careless. To be fair to myself, no one had described mouse-to-person transmission of a membrane prion disease at the time I got mine—"

Lars interrupted: "And until this day, no one has described a membrane prion disease in a human being, much less a membrane prion disease that has jumped from mouse to man. We are in totally uncharted waters."

Henry coughed and took a deep breath. "Oh, membrane prion disease exists. In fact, I'm not even patient alpha. We may be in uncharted waters, but my navigator will be that person who has successfully treated patient alpha."

Lars looked confused.

"Come on, man! I'm talking about your lovely wife, Kate."

Lars choked on his coffee. "So, Henry, you know about Kate's disease?"

"Of course I do. My job is to know everything that goes on in this medical center. I also know you pilfered the Somitra. We still don't know how you got it without showing a loss of inventory. But you did, and damned near killed Kate with it. By the way, you certainly took your time getting the drug for her. I thought we'd have to send it to her as a Christmas gift, but that's another story . . ."

"When did you learn about Kate's illness?"

"Before you ever came here. Dean Hanley wanted a cancer center; I wanted to move forward with our quest for amortality. It was during that time frame that Dr. Aak examined your wife's biopsy and found the prions. The excitement generated by his findings rippled through ElijahCo. I asked Jenna to get more information on Kate's health. The last name Sorenson rang a bell in her head."

Henry coughed and paused for a sip of water. "Please allow me to shorten my soliloquy. I'm running low on gas; unfortunately, that gas is oxygen."

Another sip of water, and Henry continued, "You pretty much know the rest of the story. Jim got you and the promise of a cancer center; I got Kate and her prions. The marriage of cancer research and the pursuit of amortality was made in heaven—until it wasn't. Things began to fray between Jim and me. He suffered the automobile misadventure, and I became dean."

"Am I to believe Dean Hanley had an accident?"

"Don't go there, Lars . . . at least not for now. Let's just say, epic events are bathed in blood. I've long thought it appropriate that the railroad caboose is painted red."

"I won't pursue the Jim Hanley story, but I'm curious about Kate's and mine. Has coming to High Plains been a saga of deceit and lies?"

"Hardly. The Fletcher Cancer Center was real—until they withdrew the funding. That came as a most unpleasant surprise. Hiding the truth about testing EJ 181 would have been much easier in an independent, well-funded cancer center. ElijahCo took a big financial hit getting things up and running here. Fortunately, EJ 75 proved to be such a terrific cancer killer that it has left ElijahCo awash in cash."

"What else is real?"

Henry coughed and took a sip of coffee. "Sorry, my trip through the truth has been hijacked by my hubris. Your studies of both 75 and 181 represent excellent translational research. Your courage treating Kate and her response to Somitra has been breathtaking. But at this time, proof is lacking that Somitra can actually cause amortality. That's what our work in Bangkok is about. Kate is our proof of principle and provides the incentive to continue those studies. You've also shown that Somitra gives human membrane prions one hell of a punch."

Lars shifted from defensive to doctor mode. "I'll accept that our journey here has been a patchwork of truths and lies. I'd like to check each piece for its veracity, but that can wait for another time. Your breath is short, so let's move on. I'm here at your request, to be your physician. Let me honor that by asking you to tell me more about your illness."

Henry nodded thoughtfully and then spoke: "I don't know when I began collecting the mouse prions. Unlike Kate's generalized problem, mine appears to be organ-specific. I developed a dry cough and shortness of breath when I went out for my daily jog. The symptoms were slowly progressive and finally reached a point where I could no longer ignore them. Routine studies, including bronchoscopy, were inconclusive. I was told that my lungs looked like those of an eighty-year-old. Frustrated by the lack of a diagnosis, I asked Dr. Aak to look at the biopsy specimens. Turns out my lungs were loaded with mouse prions, and the little bastards were aging my lungs faster than a mountain of Marlboros."

"The rest of you appears to be aging appropriately, which supports the idea that prions don't exert a systemic effect. Each cell ages at a rate related to the number of prions present in its membrane," Lars said.

"My original hypothesis was that each prion acts to reduce the ability of a cell to eliminate a toxin that promotes aging. The more prions in the cell membrane, the more crippled the cell's ability to eliminate the toxin. As a consequence, the more prions within a cell membrane, the faster the cell ages."

Lars smiled. "Somitra's the cell's Drano. It's a shame Drackett has the copyright. Drano would have made a great name for EJ 181."

"I've spent years pursing that biochemical clog without finding it," Henry said. "I suspect I've been wrong in searching for a single molecular villain. Drain clogs are made up of hair, soap, dirt, and whatever else may try to go down the drain. I now think multiple different toxins cause the cellular clog. The aging process may well be due to a heterogeneous collection of molecules."

Lars scratched his chin. "Why is the accumulation of prions confined to your lungs?"

"I've asked myself that question a thousand times. I think it may be related to my research. I have used mouse lungs for years to study prions.

The airways are lined with thin, delicate tissue, which is ideal for evaluating membrane molecules. Perhaps, over the years, I have inhaled prions that are attracted by something in lung tissue that's common to mouse and man. Maybe it's surfactant. That's mere speculation on my part."

The two men sat silent for a moment. Lars sighed. "Henry, something else concerns me, and it's potentially a much bigger problem. The prions in your lungs have jumped species. They are no longer just mouse prions that infect mouse lungs. They are now capable of infecting human beings. They're beginning to behave like the influenza virus. The Spanish flu pandemic of 1918 appears to have occurred when the swine influenza virus became capable of infecting humans. This jump from swine to man was followed by the ability of the virus to go from man to man. The virus became highly contagious, resulting in the deaths of millions."

Henry paled. "Oh my God, I never thought of that. Am I contagious?"

"I don't know. Nobody knows, but I would err on the side of caution."

Henry was flummoxed.

Lars gave him an easy out. "Your library is not ideal for a thorough physical examination, so let me continue this visit in the clinic—

Henry waved him off. "No, I don't want to be seen at a university clinic. Academic politics are brutal. Any sign of my weakness will bring out the jackals."

Henry went over to his desk and produced a large envelope. "I have some homework for you. Here are copies of the records from my stay at a private clinic. I'll get you emergency privileges to practice there. How about I see you in a month? My breathing is still pretty good, and we have time before my lungs demand additional treatment. I'll need that time to muzzle the jackals.

"Oh, and, Lars, I'm counting on you to honor patient confidentiality, which means all that was said here today. That's why I made the request that you be my physician at the start of our visit. You can confide in my ElijahCo people; they know about my problem. But don't trust anyone at the university. It's not always clear who is or is not one of the jackals."

"You have my word, Henry. Meanwhile, please take precautions against possible spread of the prions."

"I will."

The men shook hands on their deal.

Lars walked out of the dean's office and found privacy in the courtyard. He took out his cell phone. "Hello, Jenna? Yeah, it's me. I hope I didn't wake you. Can you get Dr. Aak for me right away? Yes, it's that urgent."

* * *

Early the following day, Lars and Jenna were having a virtual meeting. "Good morning, Bangkok."

"Good morning, High Plains." Jenna was smiling and waving something in the air. "I have my bags packed, my e-ticket, and forty-seven hours and twenty-two minutes from now, I am out of here."

"So things are working out with Chuck and Changchang?"

"Yup, Chuck has put the study back together, and we're ready to resume our Somitra trials. Changchang has her new MRI, with all the bells and whistles you can imagine. She's like a little girl with her first Barbie doll."

219

"How are they handling the cultural transplant?"

"They have a taste for pad thai I could never acquire."

Lars smiled and then abruptly turned serious. "I assume from my new-patient visit with Henry that you know about his lung problems."

"Yes, I do. I'm glad Uncle Henry took my advice and sought your help."

"'Uncle Henry'? Should I take you literally, or was that meant to be pejorative?"

"He's my mother's brother."

Lars's face flushed. "You know I don't play hardball well, but I don't do dumb doc well either. I'm damned sick of the half-truths and downright lies that are pervasive at ElijahCo. I parrot the party line, but I don't know when it's truth or lies."

"What are you babbling about?"

"Henry gave me this cockamamie story about the founding of ElijahCo. He said others may have one that's different. But truth isn't a pair of pants that comes in all sizes. You can't just pick one that meets your needs."

Jenna looked confused. "Tell me what he said."

"You speak of ElijahCo as this privately held behemoth, run by the gods in Silicon Valley. Anger the gods, and you risk life and limb. Henry's truth is that ElijahCo is a struggling start-up. Until the largesse of EJ 75—whoops, Ejectica—came along, it could fit nicely in his back pocket. Which is it?"

"Both."

"Oh, for Christ's sake, Jenna, stop with the games!"

"If you think I'm playing games with you and want the true truth about ElijahCo, why don't you just google it?"

"Are you kidding me? The net has every size and color of truth a man could want."

"Well, then listen to me and judge for yourself. My stepfather is Theodore Everett. He and Henry formed ElijahCo just as the CDC was closing the research lab in High Plains."

"Hold on, Jenna. Henry told me Teddy was a classmate in graduate school. He mentioned nothing about family ties."

"They were classmates in Harvard grad school. Henry spoke the truth."

"I'm hearing a half-truth, but please go on."

"As I was saying, ElijahCo was formed after the CDC left town. Both founders were fascinated with the concept of amortality. Henry kept his prion research under wraps. He found out how people age. His next challenge was to find out how to stop it."

"So Henry was right. ElijahCo was a struggling start-up."

"A start-up, yes, but it never struggled. Henry and Teddy are brilliant men. Their search for the secret of amortality was financed by ElijahCo's growing list of patents and products. Henry is the geek, tucked away in his mouse lab making new discoveries, at least until he became dean. Teddy is the entrepreneur who put ElijahCo on the Big Pharma map. The larger it got, the easier it was to finance their common passion and to keep it hidden from public scrutiny."

"So, enter Dean Hanley. Henry told me the cancer center was his dream."

"Yes, it was, and this is where you and Kate came into the picture."

"Henry pleaded poverty and that ElijahCo needed the Fletcher money to finance the EJ 75 and 181 trials."

"Henry was busy with his mice and didn't try to comprehend the size of ElijahCo. He read the balance sheet, but in his heart, it was still a start-up. He did understand the potential of both EJ 75 and 181 and the diverging paths they would take. I'm not sure Henry meant he needed the Fletcher money for the drug trials. I think that was shorthand for needing the cancer center to conceal the true reason for studying 181."

"Why did the rift develop between ElijahCo and Jim Hanley?"

"That was a heartbreaker for me," said Jenna. "Jim was a visionary and ElijahCo's moral compass. He wanted to pursue the cure of cancer and aging as two open and complementary research projects. He believed they would ultimately come together and be one. Henry and Teddy agreed on the complementary and converging parts of Jim's vision. They took sharp issue with the open part. Jim was eager to do battle over the ethics of pursuing amortality. Henry and Teddy viewed Jim as jeopardizing the study. They had worked diligently to keep Henry's research under wraps. No way would they allow Jim to expose the prion and 181 to public scrutiny. They envisioned decades of fruitful research coming to a bitter standstill, waiting for a bloated bureaucracy to pass judgment on their life's work. They were paranoid about the media discovering the potential power of 181 and the battle that would ensue over who should and shouldn't be granted amortality."

"So Jim Hanley had to be eliminated."

Jenna looked Lars straight in the eye. "God's truth, I don't know what happened the night he died."

"So you choose ignorance, rather than confronting the possibility your family may be murder—"

"That's hypocritical. You've turned as much of a blind eye as I have. ElijahCo is a top-down organization, run by Teddy and by Henry, when he chooses to do so. I have ElijahCo's blood flowing through my veins, but I'm still the niece and stepdaughter. I'm being crushed under a low glass ceiling. I'm not a member of the inner circle, and I'm not a part of the decision-making process." Jenna paused and then, with a look of disgust, continued, "Becoming Uncle's doctor has you standing on top of my glass ceiling."

"You met with what's-his-name, the VP for security?"

"Yes, I did. J. P. takes ElijahCo's security very seriously. He is one scary dude."

"Hey, did you ask him about Mando?"

"The look I got could freeze a furnace. I quickly changed topics."

"While I'm on a mission to find truth, I need one more answer from you. I know I shouldn't ask, but did you really seduce Norma Latchfield?"

Jenna's eyes twinkled. "Whether I say yes or no, you won't know if you're hearing the truth. So let me just say, one of my jobs at ElijahCo is diversion. I get the hounds off the scent. My tools are truths, half-truths, lies, and sensationalism."

"I was right; I shouldn't have asked."

"Have a nice day, High Plains. I look forward to my return."

Lars was about to add his concerns over a possible prion pandemic, but instead told Jenna, "Fly safe, Bangkok."

* * *

Lars met with Henry in the private clinic one month later. Henry was wearing an N95 respirator fitted to his face. Lars was surprised at his openness. "I hope the jackals didn't sense weakness," he said.

"No, I deflected their concerns with a great story I concocted. I won't bore you with it."

Lars carefully examined him, while firing off a series of questions. "How is your breathing?"

"Unchanged."

"How about the cough?"

"It's a little better with the codeine."

"Any fever or chills?"

"No, Lars. Aside from the lung problems, I'm feeling better than when you saw me last month."

Lars concluded his examination and stepped back. "Your lungs sound junky, but otherwise you seem fine. The rest of your body appears to be aging normally. I did my homework, and the information you provided at the first visit confirms that."

"So, Professor Sorenson, what can we do about my lungs?"

"It depends on what you want to do about the rest of your body."

"But the rest of my body is aging normally."

"The key word is 'aging.' If I give you an injection of Somitra, as I have been doing with Kate, we may be able to reverse that so-called normal aging process, as well as rid your lungs of the mouse prions. I can't guarantee it, but I'm thinking you would be joining Kate on the road to amortality." He paused for a moment. "Isn't that the true motivation behind your years of research?"

"I never thought of amortality for myself," Henry said. "Prions and the aging process were the subjects of my research, not a part of my personal life. What's the alternative?"

"I asked Dr. Aak to look into insufflations of Somitra."

"You mean I would vape Somitra?"

"Yup, he's come up with a low-concentration formula, which will be rapidly absorbed and quickly metabolized. The mice he tested had no systemic effects. The membrane prions in the rest of their bodies remained unchanged. The experience we had with Kate tells us we have to start low and go slow to avoid her terrible reaction."

Henry rapidly processed the information. "Is there a reason not to start with the vaping? We could go from vaping to injection if I change my mind or it doesn't work."

Lars shrugged. "It's your decision. I'm just giving you options."

A smile crept across Henry's face. "So I join my laboratory mice, but with informed consent. How ironic."

Lars gave a quick smile but then became serious. "You realize what we're doing is dangerous—and illegal. We have journeyed far north of ethical boundaries."

"I've always thought of myself as a moral creature, but with my life on the line, I guess I'm showing my true colors." Henry's voice dropped to a whisper. "Yes, I know, and will be eternally grateful for the opportunity."

Henry was becoming morose, and Lars lightened up. "I didn't know you were a punster."

Henry snickered. "Oh, you mean eternally grateful. There was no pun intended, but it was pretty good. When can we get started?"

"When can you clear your calendar?"

"It's clear."

Lars was taken aback but recovered quickly. "Are you sure you don't want to think about it?"

"There's nothing to think about. I'll be dead unless I get effective treatment soon. Somitra's the only treatment of proven benefit. Let me sign whatever consent you want, and let's get moving."

"We'll need anesthesiology standby. I've learned from my experience with Kate. Let's start low and go slow—maybe once-weekly treatments."

"I've got a better idea. Let's do a test dose today and next week treat with the lowest effective dose in mice. I assume Aak gave that to you. Oh, and I don't want to know if that dose caused any mouse fatalities."

"Yes, Aak did give me the lowest dose, but remember, Kate almost died . . ."

"I'm trying to forget. Besides, Kate had a body full of homegrown prions. I only have mouse prions in my lungs, so I think my risk is a whole lot lower than Kate's."

"You have more faith than I do in Aak's mouse studies translating into a safe dose for humans."

"I have little choice." Henry began choking. He finally caught his breath. "I'm caught between mouse prions and jackals. I can't keep up the appearance of good health for long. The jackals will sense weakness—He interrupted himself with a fit of coughing.

"Yeah, Jim Hanley warned me there was opposition to the cancer center within the faculty ranks," Lars said.

Henry took another sip of water, cleared his throat, and continued: "The search for amortality and the cancer center drug trials are so tightly linked that defunding one would effectively defund the other."

"Why can't ElijahCo make an end run around the opposition and fully fund the cancer center? It has the money."

"I wish it were that simple. ElijahCo's paying the bill for the initial drug trials raised no eyebrows. EJ 75 and 181 need to be tested. So why not at High Plans University? Funding the entire cancer center would draw a lot of scrutiny. Such scrutiny would threaten exposure of the shadow study with EJ 181, along with your role as principal investigator." Henry shook his head. "The risk is just too great. No, I think we get me better and I'll continue to hold the jackals at bay."

"Okay, Henry, I get the picture, but I have major concerns about what I may do to you."

Henry clasped Lars's arm. "I won't blame you, whatever the outcome. Let's just get on with it."

"I still want anesthesiology here. Somitra tinkers with the immune system. Even a test dose could result in anaphylaxis. We've both seen it happen with penicillin—and peanuts, for that matter."

"Did you take that precaution with Kate?"

Lars looked sheepish. "No, and that's just another reason not to have your doctor emotionally involved with you."

Henry looked at his watch. "Getting anesthesia here should be no problem. Surgery's over for the day. I'll get an anesthesiologist up here ASAP."

As the two waited, Lars produced a modified e-vaporizer.

"I was wondering what you had in the bag."

Lars grinned. "I got this contraption at the Vaping America store. I almost put on sunglasses and a fake mustache. I was afraid I'd be spotted. Can you imagine the rumors if the cancer center director was seen buying an e-vaporizer?"

"Don't make me laugh. It will start me coughing again."

Shortly thereafter, precautions were in place. Henry took a deep breath of Somitra. He tried to hold it in his lungs as long as possible. His face turned a scary, deep red as he attempted to suppress a cough. Henry waved off the anesthesiologist who came to his rescue. Lars anxiously inquired, "Can you breathe? Talk to us!"

Henry croaked, "I'm okay," as he let loose with a paroxysm of coughing.

"Jesus, Henry," the anesthesiologist grumbled, "you scared the shit out of us."

Lars collapsed in a chair. "I'll second that. However, it looks like you passed your test dose. Coughing after inhaling Somitra is to be expected. We can go forward with treatment next week, but we'll make sure you don't cough. Oh, and remind me to wear Pampers."

* * *

One week later, Henry, Lars, the anesthesiologist, and an intensivist assembled in the ICU. After initial protests, Henry consented to be intubated. All three of his doctors were adamant about controlling his airway and suppressing his cough reflex. Lars jury-rigged the e-vaporizer to fit the endotracheal tube. All were apprehensive, save Henry, who was heavily sedated for the occasion.

Lars delivered the Somitra, and oxygen was pumped into Henry's lungs to evenly distribute the drug. Lars breathed a sigh of relief, but the anesthesiologist looked concerned. "As I bagged him, I began to feel growing resistance. I think we've stirred up a hornet's nest in there."

Lars backed away as the anesthesiologist and intensivist conferred. They drew up medications from the nearby crash cart and delivered them intravenously. The three then waited anxiously as the ventilator adjusted to meet the increasing resistance in Henry's airway—and to the progressive drop in Henry's blood oxygen level.

The intensivist looked at Lars, who was ghostly pale and silent. He offered comfort: "At least Henry's problem appears confined to his lungs."

"Yeah, but you lose them, you lose the ball game," Lars said. He turned his attention to Henry. "Come on, Henry, we all know you like to be the center of attention, but you're carrying this to the extreme."

A tense two hours later, the ventilator began to adjust pressure and oxygen concentrations downward. The anesthesiologist gave a sigh of relief. "I think we're turning the corner. Just for the record, I doubled the dose of the steroid you suggested, Lars, and added epinephrine as well." He pointed to Henry's chest. "I think something else is going on down there to improve his airway resistance and oxygenation."

"Maybe Henry's yielding the floor to Somitra?"

The intensivist smiled. "Whatever, I'm just glad he's getting better."

Lars cursed under his breath. Damn! I forgot these guys don't know about prions and the Somitra story. I'll just let it drop. Hopefully, they'll forget Somitra and just focus on Henry's lungs.

He walked out to an empty ICU waiting room, took out his cell phone, and called the dean's office. "Yes, this is Dr. Sorenson. Dr. Mitchell had an urgent call from London. There's a high-level symposium ongoing, and the plenary session speaker has become ill. The dean has been asked to replace him. He's on his way to London even as we speak. He'll get back to you as soon as he can. Meanwhile, I'd recommend you clear his calendar for the next week."

He turned off the cell and shook his head. Chalk up another half-truth. Okay, let's begin again: chalk up another lie in the service of ElijahCo.

Lars returned to the IC. The intensivist was hovering over Henry. "His lungs sound better, and he's needing less supplemental oxygen and less force getting it into his lungs. If he continues to improve at this rate, I'm hoping we can get him off the ventilator and extubated tomorrow. Whatever the hell you gave him sure raised a stink in his lungs."

Lars chose his words carefully. "The drug is an immune modulator, with one of its side effects being an inflammatory reaction. Aerosolizing it can cause a brief but intense reaction—which, by the way, we've suppressed with steroids and epinephrine."

The intensivist seemed to accept his explanation, so Lars went no further.

The intensivist went back to his hovering but then paused. "Lars, will you inform his family? Security will clear them to enter the clinic so they can see Henry. I'm sure they're worried."

"That's kind of you to be concerned, but Henry is married to his work. There will be no visitors tonight," Lars said.

Lars glanced at his watch. Damn! I'm late for dinner again!

Lars arrived home exhausted. Kate met him at the door with a stiff scotch and joined him on the sofa with her glass of wine. "How's Henry doing?"

"Thank God we had him on a ventilator. The mouse prions didn't like the therapeutic dose of Somitra. He had a mini Kate reaction, but confined to his lungs. It was nip and tuck for a while; that's why I'm running late. But he's fine now. I'm going to stop the vaping and see what progress we've made."

"You look like you've been through a wringer."

He sipped his scotch. "The stress of treating that man is making me old before my time."

"I understand. I've been there."

Both laughed.

"So you have, love of my life," Lars said. He stroked her face and slowly worked his hand down her neck and onto her breast.

"Playing possum, were you?" Kate placed her hand on his knee and slowly worked her way up his thigh. "Whoops, I've encountered a stick."

"I prefer to think of it as a tree trunk."

"You never did have an eye for size."

"That's your opinion. I think we can resolve the issue. The tape measure is in the bedroom."

"I know a better way to measure."

"How's that?"

"We could plumb the depth."

And so they did.

*   *   *

They cuddled together in postcoital bliss. Kate ran her fingers through his hair. "You're my stud muffin."

Lars rolled over on his back. "I've been thinking."

"That's scary, particularly after sex. Did I do something wrong?"

Lars rolled back on his side, giving her a kiss. "No, no, it's not that. You were wonderful. It's just when you had your prion problem, you talked about releasing me from my vow of fidelity when the time came. Well, the prion is now on the other membrane."

"You were a stallion tonight."

"Thanks, but amortality lasts a long, long time."

"Isn't it premature to release me from my vows?"

"Oh, yeah, it's way premature, but you know me, I think ahead."

"And?"

"Well, I'm not sure I can do that—release you from your vows."

"Why don't you join me in youth? Somitra is gender neutral."

"I'm not sure I can do that either. Amortality is not for everyone. Fred taught me that."

"So what are you going to do, chain me to the bed in a chastity belt?"

"That's a thought."

Kate threw a pillow at him. "You're still the perv."

"I love it when you say sweet things about me. I've an idea: let's do it again before time runs out."

Kate pouted. "No, I've had enough for one night. Let's have dinner instead."

"Maybe we can have dessert first."

"You are totally hopeless. Now let me get dinner out of the Crock-Pot. Meanwhile, you'll find a fancy envelope on your desk. It's from ElijahCo. I snuck a peek inside. Yeah, yeah, I know you don't like me opening your mail, but my curiosity was aroused and I couldn't resist. And don't give me that look, or you can totally forget dessert."

"No use me wasting energy looking at my mail. What did it say?"

"We've been invited to a party."

"Party? What party?"

"It's an intimate gathering of the ElijahCo elite."

"When is it and what the hell is it about?"

"It's not for another six weeks. The invitation said, 'Details to follow,' but we're asked to reserve the date."

Lars thought for a moment. "I hope it won't turn into a memorial for Henry."

"I thought you said he was weathering the storm."

"He is, but if we're only seeing a steroid effect, and aren't chasing the prions away, I don't give him another month."

"Whoops! Maybe I better hold off getting your Brioni suit pressed."

Lars grinned. "I love your gallows humor. I also think you're being practical."

Early the next morning, Lars stopped by the clinic to see Henry and found him sitting at the side of his bed getting a nebulizer treatment for his breathing. He gave Lars a thumbs-up and in a raspy voice said, "The endotracheal tube tickled my vocal cords, but I'm breathing better than

I did before the Somitra."

"I reviewed last night's events on my home computer before coming in here," Lars said. "I'm amazed at how well you're doing."

"Thanks to you and Somitra. Oh, Lars, about my office—"

Lars held up his hand. "Don't try to talk now. I have you covered with them. I hope you're enjoying your stay in London. I'm sure the speech you give at the plenary session will be well received, particularly with you filling in at the last moment."

Henry gave a sigh of relief and continued his breathing treatment. Lars took out his stethoscope and listened to his chest. He chuckled. "I can hear the little prions running for the back door. I must say, you sound better. Incidentally, Kate and I received an invitation to attend an ElijahCo gathering. What's that about?"

Henry croaked, "It's on a need-to-know basis, and right now, you don't need to know." The comment was followed by a benevolent grin.

Lars shrugged. "At least your place at the table won't be empty."

Henry motioned for his high five. A reluctant Lars complied. As he left the ICU to get into his car, he texted Kate. "Get the Brioni pressed, baby doll. I'll bring home the Windex for your glass slippers. We're going to the ball!"

10

LARS SPIT-POLISHED his shoes and began donning his navy-blue, two-piece Brioni suit. He resisted wearing his brown wingtips. He wasn't Italian.

"I'm not privy to the agenda at tonight's dinner. You just never know with ElijahCo. The more I think about it, the more it bothers me, Kate. I'm as nervous as a whore in church."

"Well, I look like the whore in church."

"You're being silly. You're just not accustomed to wearing anything more revealing than a burka."

"You're right about that. I'm sick of trying to look older. But I'm not thrilled about being on exhibit either."

"It's okay. You'll be with the few people who know the truth and want to celebrate your youth."

"Maybe I can bring Henry's chest x-ray so they can gawk at his boyish lungs and not at me." She gave him a shy smile. "I have to admit it—I'm excited about the evening. How often are we invited to a private dinner in the Presidential Suite at the Ritz?"

"Stick with me, baby, and you'll be farting through silk."

"You are so gross."

He kissed her on the cheek. "You know you love it, my little tart."

Kate gave him a friendly smack on the butt. "Why don't you go through the guest list again? I know you've got a problem remembering names."

Lars held his cell phone up to his mouth like a microphone. "Okay, little lady, meet the inner circle of ElijahCo: Theodore Everett, CEO and host of the festivities, will be at the head of the table. He comes to us from Mount Olympus via Silicon Valley. Shoot a lightning bolt out your ass, Teddy, so we can all ooh and ah at your mighty powers.

"On Teddy's right, we have Henry Mitchell, our beloved dean and executive vice president. Give us a few laps around the table, Hank, so we know you can outrun the prions and catch the jackals. Yes, folks, look at him go."

Lars continued with a flourish. "Sitting on the left hand of power is . . . What's his name?"

"Jefferson Peterson," Kate inserted.

"Ah, yes, the little lady is correct. J. P. is vice president for security and comes to us on Teddy's leash. Shoot a few rounds at our feet, big guy, and we'll dance the ElijahCo two-step.

"I can't ignore Jenna McDaniel, the little girl sitting under the skylight. She's stepdaughter and niece of ElijahCo. Stand up and give us a cute curtsy; be careful not to hit your head on the skylight."

Lars bowed, and Kate feigned applause. "I hope our bedroom isn't bugged, or you'll be the janitor in charge of toilets."

"Are you ready for the ball, my dear?"

"I wouldn't miss it."

The Sorensons were greeted by Jenna, who was Miss Marzipan personified this evening. J. P. served drinks under the paranoid eye of Lars. All waited for Ted and Henry, who emerged from the library adjacent to the spacious dining area. The dean introduced Lars and Kate to Teddy. He then gave Jenna a family hug, as did her stepfather. Lars noted that her back stiffened with the hugs. He anxiously watched their host, who could make the evening pleasant or miserable. He proved to be a charmer. Lars relaxed and joined in the conversation. Drinks lubricated the conversation, but all present nursed them in anticipation of important events later.

Soon they were called to dinner, and everyone stood at their assigned places. Ted proposed a toast. "I want to raise my glass in proud salute to those assembled here for your contributions to the growing success of ElijahCo. First and foremost, I raise my glass to you, Henry, my dear friend and cofounder. You are the intellectual engine that drives us forward. I'm so pleased that your health is returning."

"And to you, J. P., we are so grateful to you for guarding our gates against the tyranny of the barbarians." He turned to Jenna. "I drink to you, daughter and niece of ElijahCo."

He turned away from her, missing the frown crossing her face.

"Dr. Sorenson . . . Lars, I offer you a special toast to your wisdom and courage in the conduct of your translational research. Your daring rescues of Henry and your beloved Kate hurtled the conventional bound-aries of research while advancing the science of human amortality. You represent the new and vibrant blood coursing through ElijahCo's veins."

He slowly turned to Kate, smiling. "I've saved you for last, Dr. Mrs. Sorenson, because you are why we are here tonight. Here's to your cour-age and your suffering, which have given us proof of principle that aging can be conquered. This is spurring us to go forward with our studies of Somitra."

All joined in the toast, but not all were enthusiastic.

The rustle of chairs drowned out Kate's whispered comment to Lars: "That bit of grandstand was both revealing and not. Keep smiling, but keep up your guard as well. I don't trust any of them."

They sat down to a sumptuous feast, with light banter as additional spice. Dessert was served, with Lars whispering under his breath, "I like yours better." He dropped his hand to her knee and was greeted with a sharp pain in his shin. Kate gave him a frown, followed by a sly grin.

At the conclusion of dinner, Henry and Ted asked Lars and Kate to join them in the library. Jenna looked pained as she and J. P. were left out of the inner circle.

Henry tried to put Kate and Lars at ease. "Please sit down and relax. This isn't an inquisition," he said. "Ever since the day you gave me the insufflation of Somitra, I've been soul-searching. I realize I've been my-opic. Prions and Somitra have far outgrown my research laboratory. That growth demands a re-examination of ElijahCo's goals and the methods by which we reach those goals." Henry coughed and took a sip of water. He cleared his throat and explained, "I'm happy to say I'm getting better, but I've still got a ways to go. Teddy, would you please take over from here?"

Teddy eagerly stepped in. "Sure, Henry, I'd be glad to. The goals of ElijahCo have been to understand why we age and to interfere in that process. We have had a measure of success in achieving both goals. We now understand that membrane prions play a major role in the aging process. We know that Somitra can eradicate membrane prions. Kate and Henry have given us at least a peek at the power of Somitra to reverse the process of aging. We have used the method of rigorous scientific research, carried out in absolute secrecy. I think we can all agree that prions and Somitra on cable news would be an absolute disaster. The recent events in High Plains and in Bangkok have taught us that absolute secrecy is no longer a viable option."

Lars had a question. "How do you manage to open up Pandora's box to a wired world without ensuing chaos?"

"I know that Pandora's box has been a powerful metaphor for us," Teddy replied. "It has kept us focused on protecting our findings. Now that metaphor needs to be replaced because it's not applicable going forward. Henry and I believe the gradual introduction of our findings at the highest levels will be the best method to achieve ElijahCo's goals—"

Kate interrupted: "What does that mean?"

"The whole is greater than the sum of its parts. Think of each ElijahCo prion study as a pixel in a computer-generated image. You won't know what the image represents until you have all the pixels and they're assembled in proper order. Continuing the analogy, we will give the scientific community one prion study—pixel—at a time, and out of temporal order. We'll start by releasing a case report of Henry's acquired mouse prion disease—"

Henry interrupted: "Lars, you scared the bejesus out of me when you told me I might be patient alpha of a prion pandemic. If this possibility would frighten me, it would certainly grab the attention of epidemiologists at the CDC and elsewhere. The case report will include details of my illness but leave out the cure. This will generate research to prevent my disease from going global. It will also justify further prion studies undertaken by ElijahCo. Please note that we will not mention aging, amortality, or Somitra."

"Why not release your successful treatment instead of another Elijah-Co half-truth?" Kate interjected.

"That would open wide the box. What Lars did was unethical and illegal. Our PI could be jailed, and our research efforts derailed by moral outrage. We would no longer be able to control the agenda. We're scientific ecdysiasts: we take off one veil at a time, leaving our audience excited by what they see and wanting to see more."

Lars emerged from deep thought. "The bottom line is that sooner or later all the pixels will be assembled. Amortality will be released on the world."

Ted regained the floor, replacing Henry, who had another fit of coughing. "You're right, and we believe it will be sooner rather than later. Research activity in prions and aging will grow exponentially with each new publication from ElijahCo. The more that is learned, the more ethical issues will be raised to curb further research. We have to be prepared to control the conversation. The growing community of researchers in amortality will give ElijahCo support and cover as we forge ahead. However, the public has a growing distrust of scientists. Just consider for a moment the reluctance to accept global warming despite the overwhelming support of scientists worldwide. So the controlled release of information is only one component of our new strategy. The other is to gain support of key thought leaders. We need to win over the naysayers."

Lars was getting hot. "How the hell are you going to do that?"

"Enter the good Doctors Sorenson."

Kate put her face in her hands. "Do I really want to hear this?"

"It's not bad, Kate," Ted continued. "You and Lars become ElijahCo's ambassadors."

"Is 'ambassador' a euphemism for 'prostitute'?"

"Of course it isn't! We have pictures of you before treatment with Somitra. Dr. Aak has your pretreatment biopsies. Discreet pictures of you now and post-treatment biopsies will impress our targeted thought leaders. These scientific exhibits will be reinforced by your lovely, youthful presence. Lars will be there to deliver unlabeled Somitra."

Lars almost came out of his chair. "Come on, Ted! Do you really think any real thought leader will buy into this snake-oil sideshow?"

"You underestimate the power of emotion over intellect, Lars. Many of these leaders are arranging for their bodies to be frozen at the time of death and to be thawed when the miracle drug comes along. Others are preserving DNA or using other means in a desperate attempt to attain amortality. These billionaires and political leaders have nothing left to conquer except death. They will do anything to achieve that victory, just as they've spared nothing to get where they are now."

Lars smirked. "So in exchange for amortality, ElijahCo gets their support as the data on prions and Somitra slowly trickles out. They control the debate, and ElijahCo controls them."

"I think they'll find the offer hard to resist," Henry added.

Kate spoke up: "What if one of these thought leaders refuses the offer or threatens to blow the whistle?"

"All of these upstanding citizens have done things they regret," Ted replied. "J. P.'s job is to find out what those things are and, if necessary, remind them of their sins. Remember my toast. His job is to meet the barbarians at the gate." He looked directly at Kate and then Lars. "I do mean meet all of the barbarians at the gate."

You could hear a pin drop as the four were lost in thought. Henry broke the silence, smiling as he spoke: "Both of you have a lot to think about. ElijahCo needs your help on a desperate operation to save the world from chaos. We will reward your efforts with continued access to Somitra. We all want Kate's continued good health."

Ted realized he'd gone too far with his implied threat and wanted to end the evening on a high note. "I will personally guarantee that Kate will get Somitra regardless of your willingness to be ElijahCo ambassadors. You have no need to fear ElijahCo."

Lars leaned forward, finger pointing at Ted. "You can't threaten us with J. P. and the goon squad one moment, and the next tell us we have no need to fear ElijahCo. Did you give the same reassurance to Dean Hanley before his apparent accident?"

"Jim's death has been an undeserved albatross around my neck," Henry said. "Let me tell you what really happened that night."

"Henry, don't bother," Ted said. "Lars won't believe you anyway."

"He needs to know, Teddy." Henry took a sip of water and continued, "The three of us met that night—Jim, Ted, and I. We were trying to work out a way for Jim to have his cancer center and for ElijahCo to be able to pursue amortality in secret. Things heated up, and, well, Jim threatened to take EJ 181 and the prion research public."

Henry started coughing again, and Ted took over. "Jim and Henry were dear friends, but I couldn't let Jim bully him. At my request, J. P. had gone dumpster diving into Hanley's past and found an affair between him and Norma Latchfield. It was brief but torrid. More importantly, it occurred just prior to Norma's appointment as chairman of the Pathology Department. Let's just say I offered that information as a counterthreat. Jim was outraged—I mean absolutely apoplectic—and stormed out of the room in a blind rage. That's why no seat belt and the reckless driving."

"My friend died alone in his shattered vehicle," Henry whispered.

Kate shook her head. "Why haven't you spoken up? Why let the circumstances around Jim's death remain a mystery? No seat belt and the reckless driving denigrate Jim's legacy."

Henry looked away and said nothing. Ted spoke for him. "We could find no way to tell the truth without revealing the content of our conversation with Jim, including his affair with Norma Latchfield. Of course, it was also our desire to maintain silence around 181 and the prions."

Kate continued pressing them. "What about the others—Steiner, Cooper, and especially Latchfield?"

Henry nodded to Teddy, who responded, "All were existential threats to ElijahCo and its mission to find amortality. What to do with them? Well, to our amazement, we watched them do it to themselves. J. P.'s boys planted fear based on the rumors surrounding Jim's death. 'Snitch on ElijahCo at your peril'—"

Kate broke in: "We felt fear but haven't died . . . at least, not yet."

"Ah, but we found that fear is only one ingredient in the recipe that sealed their fates. Each one had done something in their lives they wanted to keep hidden. So our security team suggested they were vulnerable to exposure. The desire to snitch on ElijahCo, coupled with the twin fears of reprisal and exposure, fueled a growing hatred of ElijahCo. J. P. and his team had unwittingly created an escalating dilemma. Blow the whistle on ElijahCo and pay the awful consequences, or continue to live in fear and hatred. As emotions intensified, self-awareness was lost, setting each one up for the fatal or near-fatal event of their own doing. ElijahCo was merely an observer."

Kate was aghast. "And you have repeated this scenario after seeing it unfold the first time? Are there more poor souls that we don't know about?"

"There may be, but we're not at liberty to divulge that information."

"What a disgusting strategy—"

Lars broke in: "Norma was in the midst of her death spiral the night she called me into her office. Aak must have been aware of her sleuthing and told J. P. Jesus! Norma must have felt so alone and vulnerable. She reached out to me, and I failed her miserably."

Kate came to his rescue. "Don't blame yourself too much. J. P. was in your head as well."

"You make ElijahCo sound like a den of villains," Henry complained. "None of us wanted harm to come to anyone. We just wanted to keep what we considered proprietary secrets. Those we turned on were trying to do us harm. J. P. was doing his job by protecting us from the barbarians."

Kate was skeptical. "If that story helps you sleep at night, stick to it. However, now that you know what can happen when you threaten to expose a person's past, isn't it time to shelve it? Ted said earlier that the strategy going forward included threatening the thought leaders if they didn't cooperate with ElijahCo. I see no difference between this so-called new strategy and what you've done in the past."

Ted nodded. "You have a point, but we believe there are critical differences. First, we'll be initiating the engagement by offering the thought leaders something precious in exchange for their help. Second, these people are in a different league than the Steiners of the world. They're tough, accomplished people who have vast resources at their disposal, which they could potentially turn against us. In fact, we expressed our concern to J. P. that he could face possible violence. He had no qualms. But he will be instructed not to use the threat of revealing a past transgression unless ElijahCo's mission is directly threatened. Under such circumstances, we cannot unilaterally disarm. On the other hand, if our offer is simply refused, our first tack will be to quietly leave the field and engage another thought leader."

Ted paused, and Henry smiled and said, "Honestly, I think we're making a big to-do about nothing. We're talking about a doomsday strategy I don't think we'll ever have to use. The commodity we offer is just too good to turn down."

Kate sniggered. "How come I don't feel any safer now than I did with Ted's implied threat?"

Henry continued smiling. "Gaining your trust will take time. ElijahCo is changing for the good. Please give us a chance to prove our sincerity."

Kate said nothing, and Henry proceeded, "I'll take your silence as a definite maybe."

Nervous laughter followed.

"Seriously, Kate, ElijahCo is evolving. In witness to that change, I would propose we drop the analogy of Pandora's box, and instead adopt that of a pressure cooker. We're trying to release the pressure slowly to prevent disastrous results. What could be wrong with that?"

Kate spoke slowly and deliberately: "If you don't understand why that's wrong, nothing I can say will enlighten you."

Another painful silence followed, which Kate refused to lighten with humor. She glanced at her watch. "It's been a long evening, Ted. Thank you for your hospitality. You are the perfect host. Speaking for Lars, I can assure you the Sorensons want to safely introduce Somitra to the world."

"I appreciate that, Kate. ElijahCo will try to limit the number of thought leaders you'll need to visit. Choosing one, or perhaps two, of the most important people may be sufficient for our needs. This will ease your burden and reduce the risk of, how shall I put it, an unfortunate confrontation."

Ted now turned to Lars. "We're proud of your achievements and want you to continue your role as principal investigator. The trip or trips you make with Kate should do little to interfere with your translational research."

All shook hands, even Henry, who avoided his usual high five.

Kate couldn't resist a parting shot. "By the way, we are not barbarians. Please convey that to J. P."

Ted forced a smile. "But of course. Thank you for your cooperation. Jenna will be in contact with you shortly. She'll be point person for Operation Thought Leaders."

Kate and Lars were about to leave the hotel when Jenna appeared. "Can I buy the two of you a drink?" she asked. "They have a quiet bar off the lobby."

Lars looked to Kate before responding. "Yes, of course, but let us buy you the drink, and perhaps toast your new position as point person for Operation Thought Leaders."

Jenna groaned. "Please spare me. I bugged the library up there and heard everything."

"What about J. P.?"

"He went out for a smoke."

Lars walked over to the bar as the ladies sat down.

Jenna delivered a peace offering. "Kate, you impressed me in there. You gave the two of them a badly needed reality check."

Lars returned with a waitress in tow and sat down between the two women. They gave the server their order, and then Jenna spoke: "I want you to know I'm not responsible for tonight's fiasco."

"If by 'fiasco,' you mean the strategy of gradually releasing Somitra into the world and manipulating the public into thinking it's no big deal, I think the three of us can agree," Lars said. "I'd also add that bribing thought leaders to spread ElijahCo's gospel of amortality is just wrong—"

"And parading my body before them is theater of the absurd," Kate interjected.

By now, the waitress had delivered their drinks. Lars took a sip of scotch and waited for Jenna's response.

"Look, I'm a trained molecular biologist. I've done credible prion research, which the world has yet to see. Henry and Ted rejected publication of my results, fearing they would expose the secrets of ElijahCo. I'll send both of you copies of those never-published papers, and you can judge for yourselves. Oh, and Aak's prion assay—that's my work as well."

Lars frowned. "You mean Aak's taking credit for your work?"

"Did Eli Whitney invent the cotton gin?"

"So you fancy yourself a slave?"

Jenna smirked. "If ElijahCo thought they could get away with it, I would be. Of course, Ted and Henry would claim they were enslaving me for my own good. In defense of Aak, Henry forced him to do so. Poor Aak was a puppet dancing on the string of his green card. I invented the assay in the new lab, which was technically in the Department of Pathology. It was subject to the scrutiny of the department chairman. Henry thought it too dangerous for me to take credit. Aak encrypted my data from the notes he took for me and locked them in his desk. Of course, Norma found them, and that's where you came into the picture, Lars. After Norma's death, Ted and Henry forced Aak to leave the country ASAP, taking the notes, encrypted data, and everything else tied to

Somitra with him."

Lars was confused. "You seemed to support Aak's claim on the assay and subsequent hasty departure to Bangkok."

"I frequently put on my game face for you. I personally thought Teddy and Henry way overreacted, but my opinion matters little when the two of them take charge of reality."

Kate reached out to Jenna. "I can only imagine your personal and professional frustration."

"I'm a scientist who has been lowered by my dear family to the level of a shill. I can't see any recourse for me. On the other hand, the two of you can abandon this fool's errand. I think the trial of EJ 445 is going far too well for ElijahCo to discipline you. That would draw the kind of scrutiny that is anathema to ElijahCo. Teddy assured you a continuing supply of Somitra, Kate. I won't let him weasel out of that. I still have influence through my mother. So the door is open if you want to leave."

Lars and Kate studied each other in silence. Jenna took a generous mouthful of white wine and sighed.

Kate squeezed Lars's arm and he nodded. She turned to Jenna. "We won't abandon the world to the Ted and Henry fiasco. There has to be more than one adult in the room."

Jenna smiled. "Thank you both. I'll accept my new role as point person for Operation Thought Leaders. We'll be going God-knows-where to influence some thought leader." She turned to Kate. "I'll try not to feel like a pimp, if you stop feeling like a prostitute."

Lars scratched his chin. "Maybe we should surreptitiously scuttle the operation. We could then point out to Ted and Henry just how flawed this plan is."

Jenna shook her head. "That won't be necessary; I think it will implode without our help."

"Okay, we play it straight. I'm concerned that J. P. will be left with a potentially explosive situation when we do fail to lure our thought leader into cooperating with ElijahCo."

Jenna smirked. "What goes around comes around."

Kate remained silent.

"Okay, ladies, what's plan B? If plan A is a bust, we don't want to give Ted and Henry time to cook up another cockamamie scheme."

Jenna was ready. "I've always favored Dean Hanley's plan: Be open about it. Show the world prions, Somitra, and amortality. Society will digest the information just as it has with every other scientific breakthrough. Besides, we all need a little recognition for our efforts."

Lars paled. "We'd be ripe for prosecution for the conduct of our human research studies and my unorthodox treatment of Kate and Henry."

"By being open, I don't mean the whole, unvarnished truth. We'd leave a few things out." She paused and then continued, "We certainly don't have to decide anything now. Executing plan A will be enough to keep us busy."

Lars and Kate were lost in thought. Jenna finished her wine and stood up. "I'm meeting J. P. first thing tomorrow morning. He's getting his instructions now. I suggest you air out your luggage and dust off your passports. I see travel in our future." She left with a quick hug for both of them.

Kate and Lars left the bar in silence. Lars gave his ticket to the valet service. While waiting for the car, Kate put her arm around her husband. "It seems that whenever we encounter ElijahCo, there's never a real choice. We're always forced down the darker path of more half-truths and lies. Even Jenna's plan B had to be a varnished truth."

Their car arrived, and they began the ride home. "You're quiet, Lars. I hope I didn't upset you."

"No, no. I was thinking about what you said. ElijahCo was built on lies and half-truths. It's in its genes. It will never change. The sad reality is that we've forfeited the moral high ground and have become part of it."

"It doesn't have to be that way. The unvarnished truth has to be an option open to us."

Lars waited until they were home before responding. "Exercising that option without opening the proverbial box and getting me prosecuted will be nearly impossible."

She kissed him on the cheek. "Against all odds, you got your cancer center and stopped me from dying of old age. Keeping you out of jail shouldn't be that difficult. Besides, you wouldn't look good in a jumpsuit."

"What about the box?"

"Come on, Lars. We both know that opening it again is inevitable."

* * *

Lars tossed and turned the night away, the what-ifs devilishly denying sleep. He greeted the sunrise with a fresh pot of coffee. He was surprised by Kate, who found him giving Bart a tummy rub on the kitchen table.

"Aha, I caught you two again. Bart, you know better than to coax a tickle on the kitchen table. I wish I could say the same for the tickler. Lars, you just never learn."

"My defense is that petting a cat lowers blood pressure and releases a relaxation hormone," Lars said.

"So you didn't sleep well either. I would have slept soundly except a large person next to me kept rocking the boat."

"From my frequent observations, it's my opinion you slept the night away."

"Whatever. Tell me, what kept you awake?"

"How about the events of the whole damned ElijahCo party? But thanks to you, it ended with a ray of hope."

"And that was?"

"Your faith that we could shake loose from the lies without me in a jumpsuit."

"Before you tell me more, would you please stop with Bart's tummy rub on the table?"

"Okay, but my hypertensive crisis will be on your head."

"I'll take that chance. Now, off with you, Bartholomeow."

The cat complied, but not before chastising her with a whiny meow.

"So, hon, my first thought was to fly off to Indonesia. They don't have an extradition treaty with the US," Lars said.

"That sounds like a really bad idea," Kate replied.

"I agree. I'd forfeit the cancer center and Somitra. Judging from the look in your eye, I'd be sitting alone on a very long flight."

"If that was your first idea, I hope the next one is better."

"Idea number two is simply that I can't go forward with the truth until I have revealed my past lies."

Kate poured herself a cup of coffee and sat down next to her husband. "How do you propose doing that?"

"The 'you' has to become 'we,' my youthful wife. Your dog in the fight is as big as mine. So I need buy-in from you on whatever I do going forward."

"So exposing past lies starts where?"

"I think it has to be the EJ 181 shadow study. I have to throw myself on the mercy of the university's scientific and human trials committees."

Kate put a hand on his shoulder. "That will leave you totally vulnerable. The jackals will tear you apart."

"I'll have to take that risk. Anything else will be another half-truth, allowing the jackals to expose the other half. That would make things even worse." Lars thought for a moment. "Do you remember the night I met with Norma in her office?"

"Do you mean when she told you she was going to accuse Aak of a shadow study? Oh, yeah, I remember. You were sure he'd put the blame on you. As I remember, you laid out to me two options should that happen. One was to tell the whole truth, and the other was to tell a series of half-truths. Fortunately, that choice was taken out of your hands."

"Yes, but the scenario of half-truths I laid out added up to the whole truth—at least at the time we initiated the shadow study. You had a mysterious disease that we thought was incurable; Aak had discovered the excess membrane prions in your tissue biopsy. No one knew the significance of those prions in humans. I only used remnants of tissue samples, which would otherwise have been destroyed. Finally, I was desperate because I was losing you. In retrospect, by either scenario I was denied the opportunity to tell the truth, which may have saved a whole lot of heartache."

Kate got up from the table for another cup of coffee. "Can I warm yours up?"

"No, no, hon. Another cup and I'll be wired for a week."

Kate sat down across from him. "If it soothes your conscience to remember the past that way, fine, but we are here and now. The issues that matter most are what you did, not why you did them. You did wrong by conducting the shadow study. You're admitting to that. You also acted on the results of that study. If you're going to tell the whole truth, you have to tell my story and Henry's."

"I can't tell Henry's story," Lars said. "That would violate patient confidentiality. But I will have to tell them about you."

"Wow! You'll blow the lid off the box!"

Lars got up and began to pace. "Maybe I will. But you said last night that opening it is inevitable, so maybe it's best we do it. I pledge not to distort what's in there."

Kate thought for a moment. "On the other hand, I'm amazed at how unwilling people are to accept new ideas that don't fit into their world view. I have a friend who once speculated that the Second Coming of Jesus Christ occurred during the last Super Bowl and no one noticed. My story may be totally ignored. Whatever the outcome, I will support you telling the truth."

"Thank you for that. Above all, I need you by my side. I will do everything I can to protect you. Aside from worrying about you, I spent most of the night deciding what impact my confession would have on the others and how they would react to it."

"And what did you conclude?"

"I don't feel a need to point fingers at ElijahCo or the university. I think Henry will pay lip service to those who will be out to tar and feather me. In the end, he'll have to support me. Too much is riding on the EJ 445 study and the randomized trials in Bangkok. He also has a personal stake in this. He'll need to vape more Somitra."

"What about Jenna?"

Lars kept nervously pacing. "All of the human research at High Plains came with my signature as principal investigator. She needs to take no responsibility. Anyway, she's employed by ElijahCo and subject to their discipline, not the university's." A smile tripped across his lips. "She may actually benefit from the confession. She told us last night she was itching to publish her own studies and renew her credibility as a research scientist. I'll open the door for her."

"You are really wired, Lars. Why don't you sit down and continue petting Bart—just not on the kitchen table."

He sat down but remained tense. Bart had gone into hiding.

He moved on to J. P. and Ted. "I remain concerned about the goon squad. Unless we heard lies, they're Machiavellian but nonviolent. I'm giving up my darkest secrets voluntarily. So what could they possibly expose? Besides, they're tethered to Ted's leash. He can't risk turning them loose. Ted's entrepreneurial. Sooner or later, he'll want to take ElijahCo public, so he'll want to avoid adverse publicity."

"He promised not to withhold Somitra from me," Kate said. "I believe

Jenna will keep her word and hold him to his." She stood up and began to massage Lars's neck. "You are one tense dude."

"Ahh, that feels soooo good."

"So where do we go from here?"

"Well, you might want to move your hands to the ventral side of my body and move them sensuously downward."

"You are such a pervert. Nothing seems to blunt your sexual drive."

"Our time may be limited. I'm not sure they allow conjugal visits in the hoosegow."

"Who says you're going to prison?"

"Why take the chance?"

"You're avoiding my question. Where do we go from here?"

"I need a Father Confessor."

"How about a Mother Confessor?"

"Are you thinking about the ethicist on the human trials committee?"

"Not really, Lars. I favor the new pathology department chairman, Jasmine Washington. She's a tough cookie but fair-handed."

"Good thought. I love the way she outfoxed Henry to get her position. Aak's appointment, followed by his abrupt departure, crippled Henry's credibility. He had no other option but to name her the new department chairman, despite his desire to name someone he could easily manipulate."

"She's also one of a dwindling number of female pathologists in this county, and we've grown closer since Norma's death. Oddly enough, she inquired about my makeup the last time we met. I think she suspects something's afoot."

"That may be helpful. She won't be totally blindsided when I approach her. She's the wild card in the game. I don't know how she'll react to my confession. She has a lot of credibility among the academics. Many will take her lead in determining what punishment will be appropriate for me. That's another reason to go to her first. It's best she hears my confession before it's contaminated by the opinion of others."

Kate finished kneading his neck. "You're much less tense than when I started. I'd like to think I helped, even though I didn't gratify you sexually."

"Oh, you did help! You helped me devise a viable plan. The neck massage helped as well. I'll set up a meeting with Jasmine when I get to the office Monday morning."

"Then let's treasure the weekend," Kate said cheerily. "We'll lock the doors and torch the phones. Maybe after breakfast I'll resume my massage. If you're a really good boy, I'll let you get beyond first base."

"Speaking of boys and girls, did you get your friend?"

"Yup, and I didn't get a migraine this time."

"I've been so busy lately, I forgot about the headache. I was really inquiring about possible pregnancy."

"Oh, no, the rabbit is alive and well. Changchang put me on the pill. She said it would curb the migraines. I'd say she was spot-on." Kate paused for a moment. "I welcomed the pill as much for contraception as for migraine prevention. I'm concerned about what might happen if we conceive a baby. I don't know if my biological clock has continued its backward ticking. If it has, it's slowed."

Lars interrupted with attempted humor: "So you don't want to play dolls or jump rope. How about a sippy cup?"

"I'd rather have my bottle come with a cork."

The two went silent for a moment. Lars sensed her distress and got serious. "So pregnancy frightens you?"

"I have so many unanswered questions. Will our baby have my prion disease? Will Somitra cross the placenta and affect the baby's maturation? Will I be able to carry the baby to term? I mean, will my biological clock continue its backward bent and deprive the fetus of necessary hormones?" She began to choke on her words and stopped.

Lars stroked her cheek. "I wish I could reassure you that everything will be fine, but that would be whistling in the dark."

Kate felt herself slipping back into depression and fought back. "I think it's best we postpone the decision to have children. We need more time to monitor my biological clock. And you, my dear husband, should not have to add that to your problem list. It's long enough."

"But we also have to keep practicing. I mean, what if we decide to have children and have forgotten how to make them?"

"That's highly unlikely."

"I, for one, don't want to take any chances."

"I'm absolutely positive we'll remember how until after breakfast. I'm starved."

* * *

First thing Monday morning, Lars set up a meeting with Jasmine, asking her secretary to give him a full hour. As he was doing this, he got a call that went to voice mail. Oh, crap! It's Jenna.

"Hi, Lars. Meet me in the lab at eleven. It will only take a few minutes. If you can't make it, call me. Otherwise, see you then."

He put in a couple of hours doing paperwork. The new ODOM would have his scalp if he didn't do it. Fortunately, Patty was running errands before coming to the office, so he could appease her and still sneak out in time to meet Jenna. He kept running through scenarios of what might happen when he met with her. As time neared, he sighed and told himself, No shenanigans, Lars. Keep reminding yourself that the truth is our new friend.

"Thank you for meeting me here on such short notice, Lars. I know you're busy, so I'll get straight to the point. Ted and Henry want us to initiate Operation Thought Leader by taking a trip to Knowakistan."

"Where in the hell is that?"

"It's an Asian province adjacent to Kurdistan. We'll be trying to meet with a major thought leader by the name of Yuri Patrova. He's a Russian oligarch who has set up a remarkable computer-hacking center. Since most people receive their news through cable TV and social media, that news is subject to manipulation—witness the 2016 elections. Patrova's wealth and political influence shield a small army of geeky misfits who manipulate the news to order. How it's manipulated is the choice of the highest bidder. ElijahCo has the highest-possible bid—the promise of amortality for Yuri Patrova."

"I see, Jenna. So as information on prions and Somitra is released through scientific journals, ElijahCo will control the interpretation of the data, and the implications for amortality. The lies and half-truths can be fine-tuned to blunt the social impact. Very clever. Silly me. When I heard 'thought leaders,' I thought we'd get to meet the Pope or the Dalai Lama. The world has changed, and, I'm afraid, not for the better. It's ironic that thought leaders have given way to thought manipulators."

Jenna shrugged. "It is what it is, and we have to take advantage of it."

"Meaning we visit the oligarch in his lair, so Kate and I put on our snake-oil show."

"That's a harsh way to view Operation Thought Leader, but you get the picture."

Lars shook his head. "Kate and I aren't going. I'm meeting with Jasmine Washington to tell her about the Somitra shadow study."

"You're going to do what?" Jenna was appalled. "Here, let me get you a gun so you can shoot yourself in the head. It'll be faster and a lot less painful."

"We just can't go on with the lies and half-truths. It has to end somewhere. It might as well be now. Look, Jenna, I'm only going to tattle on myself. I'll expose only my role in the Somitra story, not yours, not Henry's, and not ElijahCo's."

Thoughts bounced through Jenna's head like ping-pong balls. She sat down and exclaimed in a dazed voice, "That will bring everything out into the open!"

"Maybe, but if it does, I'll make certain only the truth comes out. Look, you said you wanted to publish your own prion research. My confession will make those publications more valuable and relevant."

Jenna shook her head in disbelief. "Are you absolutely certain you know what you're getting into?"

"I do. I'm High Plains University's principal investigator. The human trials of Somitra have been tainted, and I'm ultimately responsible. I can't and won't dodge that responsibility or point fingers of blame at any of my colleagues."

"ElijahCo will fight you in court. You're divulging proprietary information. You're violating your nondisclosure agreement. Ted and Henry won't let you get away with it."

"Are you sure about that? If they openly challenge me, attention will focus on ElijahCo. Skeletons in the closet will be exposed by the tabloids. I can see a headline now: 'ElijahCo Hides the Elixir of Life. Public Denied Amortality.' I doubt even our media-manipulating oligarch will be able to put a positive spin on that."

Jenna looked thoughtful. "Maybe you're right. I need time to get my head around this whole thing."

"You told Kate and me that you favored Jim Hanley's approach. You felt, however, that you needed to varnish the truth."

"Yes, I favor an open approach and letting history judge our work. I wanted to varnish the truth only to protect your hide from prosecution. Do you think I want to see you humiliated because of your courageous and unorthodox approach to researching this wildly exciting and terribly frightening concept called amortality? You . . . you have the nerve to pronounce all of us guilty of tainted research. Then you threaten to nail yourself to the cross to redeem yourself and protect the rest of us from judgment. This deluded act of penance threatens to destroy all the work we've done by consigning it to the judgment of a ravenous media, or worse, a bloated bureaucracy."

Lars sat down, dumfounded. "I had no idea—"

"Of what? The potential harm you could bring with your admission of guilt? Jesus, Lars, go back to Kate and rethink what you're going to do. Then if you're dead set on throwing yourself on the mercy of Jasmine Washington and the university committees, so be it. No one will stop you."

"Will you despise me, Jenna?"

She paused for a moment and then shook her head. "No, I won't despise you. A woman's first love also stays with her forever."

epilogue

DR. DENTON BRADLEY, a pulmonologist, practiced what he preached and would often preach about what he practiced: "God gave you two sets of teeth. So you get a second chance with them. Not so with your lungs; you get one pair and one pair only. Treat your lungs like you would your best friend. That means exercise regularly and absolutely no smoking, vaping, or snorting. Your lungs have to last a lifetime."

Every day, rain or shine, Dr. Dent would jog on the track of the High Plains Family Y. Well, almost every day; on rare mornings, the wind would shift to the south, bringing God's pure air over the thousand-cattle feedlot before passing over the track. Today was such a day, so Dr. Dent drove over to the High Plains University campus to exercise his "best friends" in the gardens there.

He was doing his ritualistic stretching when his mouth dropped open. "Lord in heaven, I'm seeing a ghost." He waved down the man. "Is that you, Henry Mitchell? No, it can't be. Sorry I bothered you, sir."

The sweating jogger came to a halt. "Yes, it's me, Denton. What brings you here today? As I recall, you run at the Y."

Dent stuttered, "I do, but the feedlot and the wind . . ."

"That certainly can foul the air."

"You seem so nonchalant, Henry. The last time I saw you was after the bronchoscopy. Your lungs looked like that of a centenarian, and now you're running like a racehorse."

"I remember you saying they looked like the lungs of an eighty-year-old, but I guess you were trying to make me feel better."

"You stopped seeing me after that. I felt like a failure. I mean, I couldn't give you a diagnosis beyond 'old lungs,' much less help you breathe better. What did you do—see another pulmonologist? Not that I would blame you. Did you get a definitive diagnosis? How in the world did you get better?"

"Whoa, slow down, man! One question at a time! No, I didn't get a second opinion. The politics at High Plains University wouldn't allow the dean of the School of Medicine to show weakness. The lung docs there are not my allies. They'd jump at the chance to declare me unfit to continue my academic responsibilities. Your independent practice, as well as your competence, was what brought me to you in the first place. No, I didn't go elsewhere."

"So you didn't get another opinion?"

"No, your diagnosis of old lungs was adequate for my needs."

Denton was perplexed. "Then how did you get better?"

Henry paused for a moment. "Dent, you are both a physician and a lay preacher. You know very well that medicine has its limitations. You might say my cure was the result of divine intervention."

"You want me to believe you're here jogging because of some miracle? That's against God's natural order. We age. Our bodies get older, not younger."

"Believe what you want, Dent. I need to finish my run. I have a meeting in an hour. It was good seeing you again."

A flummoxed Denton Bradley watched as Dean Mitchell jogged off.